URBAN STRIKE

ALSO BY J.T. SMITH

A Sucker for Love

URBAN STRIKE

A NOVEL

J.T. SMITH

To my dad, Joseph L. Smith,
and his black leather belt named "Joe."

"Not engaging in ignorance is wisdom."
BODHIDHARMA

ONE
FATIMA

The alarm clock jolted Fatima Richardson awake much too soon. It had taken her almost three hours before she was finally able to settle down into a somewhat peaceful slumber due to all the noise outside her bedroom window. Now it was Monday morning and she had to go to her damn job. The diminutive, well-shaped twenty-five-year-old slowly dragged herself across the bed and angrily slammed her palm on the alarm. Shuffling down the hall, she made her way into the small kitchen and placed some coffee in her tiny coffeemaker. She then fired up a cigarette on the stove and trudged back to the bathroom.

Fatima gazed wearily at her tired reflection in the mirror before sitting down on the toilet. She used to be self-conscience about her dark chocolate skin when she was younger, but that angst went away when she realized how gracefully her mother was aging. Pamela Richardson was pushing fifty hard and her dark skin had yet to show any wrinkles. Fatima yawned as she ran a hand through her locks and made a mental note to get her hair re-twisted soon.

Forty minutes later she was out the door of her apartment. Walking out of the building she had to step over rain-soaked trash piled up on the sidewalk. People always celebrated making it to another weekend in New York City, and the folks in West Harlem seemed to celebrate twice as hard. On more than one occasion, she'd thought about moving out of her overpriced, undersized residence, but the hassle of trying to find another decent, reasonably safe and affordable place to call home always deterred her.

The cost to live in Harlem had become ridiculous. The Caucasian invasion that crept above 110th Street fueled higher rents. Older buildings were rehabbed, rundown properties were being restored, and more condos were being built. Most of the people who could afford the new rents and mortgages for these places had little skin pigmentation. Quality shops, food stores, and eateries were opening up as well to address the needs of Harlem's newer, moneyed residents.

Walking along West 156th Street to catch the subway, Fatima hugged her trench coat tightly as she stared up at the cloudy February sky. No sun would shine today.

The main reason she dreaded going to work on Mondays was because shit always jumped off over the weekends in NYC, and the nature of her profession required that she and her coworkers address some of the dramatic fallout. When she got off the train in downtown Brooklyn the first thing Fatima saw when she turned the corner onto Flatbush Avenue, where her job was located, was a line of people snaking down the block.

The queue was composed mainly of young mothers with baby strollers or small toddlers in tow. There were quite a few of the elderly as well. There were also several Methadonians, the name some called the former addicts who now partook daily of the government-designed narcotic, methadone. Fatima spied a couple of people who were doing their best to obscure their identities. They were clearly down on their luck and uncomfortable with needing public assistance.

Sighing deeply, Fatima lit a cigarette and took a few long pulls on it before extinguishing it on the sidewalk under her black leather boot. She removed her employee identification card from her bag and used it to gain access from a side entrance of the Human Resources building. Instead of waiting for the elevator she took the steps to the fourth floor, where the Income Maintenance unit was located. She didn't want to risk being late again.

Fatima maneuvered her way through a maze of cubicles until she got to her own. The phone was ringing before she had a chance to sit down at her desk. She ignored the call and hoped that her voice mail wasn't already full.

"Well, look who's here on time on a Monday!"

"Don't start, Inez," Fatima said to her coworker sitting in the cubicle across the aisle.

.   .   .

Inez Tyler was a twenty-nine-year veteran with the Department of Human Resources. People at the agency referred to women like her as "Silver Backs." There wasn't much that happened in the office that Inez didn't know about first. The still attractive, divorced sixty-year-old grandmother was counting down the months to when she could retire and spend more time playing her numbers and visiting casinos.

"Grouchy today, huh? Andre wasn't over last night?"

"Leave me alone old woman."

"I might be old, but I still got it going on," Inez grinned.

"It's going all right… straight downhill."

Inez couldn't help but chuckle at Fatima's remark.

"Shit… you *hope* to reach my age and look this good if you do."

Before Fatima could respond, her phone rang again. This time she answered it. A few seconds later, she slammed the receiver down.

"I gotta go downstairs already!"

"I'm making coffee. You want a cup?" Inez asked.

"Please?" Fatima answered as she searched her cluttered desk for a pen.

Mounds of paperwork occupied the majority of the surface. On the walls of her cubicle were photos of her mother Pamela and her baby sister, Nikki. On a small shelf, next to a dying cactus, was a recent photo of Fatima hugging her boyfriend Andre Ellison.

They'd met three years ago at a Mary J. Blige concert out on Long Island. Andre had been generous enough to let Fatima and her girlfriend, Marisol, cut in front of him as they waited in line. Fatima figured that the least she could do was talk to the guy until she got inside to see the show. It turned out that Andre's rap was smoother than Fatima had anticipated. She'd been impressed by his good looks, polite mannerism, and the fact that he didn't have his jeans hanging off his ass. She wound up giving him the digits. Not too long after they became an item.

.   .   .

After rummaging through stacks of papers, Fatima found the forms she was looking for and headed to the elevators. The reception area downstairs was crowded with the people she'd seen standing outside. Most of the chairs in the room had people in them, busy filling out applications. Dozens of others stood against the cream-colored walls of the room, obscuring posters detailing information about Food Stamps, Medicaid, and prenatal care programs.

Fatima greeted her coworkers in the receptionist booth and then went over to one of the available microphones on the counter.

"Lisa Johnson?" She said as she scanned the reception area. "Lisa Johnson?" she repeated over the intercom system.

Fatima was about to call Ms. Johnson's name for the third and final time when she spied her client maneuvering a baby stroller through the crowd with one hand, while she held a cell phone pressed against her ear with the other.

The twenty-nine-year-old woman was short and stocky with a well-built frame. Fatima pressed the buzzer that allowed Ms. Johnson to open the door to the interviewing area. It took Fatima only a few seconds to find an empty cubicle to conduct her interview in since she was one of the first caseworkers to come downstairs that morning.

"Please, have a seat, Ms. Johnson."

Fatima was thankful that the toddler was asleep. Crying children were a distraction during interviews. She tried hard to ignore the new leather jacket her client was draped in. She tried equally hard to ignore the three gold rings that adorned her fingers.

"How can I help you today, Ms. Johnson?"

Lisa Johnson reached into her pocketbook and retrieved a letter, which she handed Fatima.

"What's this?"

"My pregnancy verification," she answered.

Fatima scanned the letter from the neighborhood health center and learned that her client had another child due on the twenty-second of September. She picked up her pen.

"Do you have information on the father, for the Child Support Unit?"

"No."

"Excuse me?" Fatima said.

"I don't have no information on the father."

"Why not?"

"Don't know who he is," she said nonchalantly. "I met him at a party," she added with a shrug.

Fatima bit down on her lip. She did this whenever she needed to keep her mouth from getting her in trouble. It was at this moment that Ms. Johnson's cell phone began chirping a rap tune. She quickly put her phone to her ear.

"Girl, let me call you back. I'm taking care of some business right now. What? No she didn't!"

Fatima cleared her throat.

"I'll call you back in a minute," she said and ended the call.

"How many children do you have, Ms. Johnson?" Fatima asked politely.

"Four. Why?" she asked defensively.

Fatima ignored the question. "If I recall correctly, you don't know the father of *any* of your children?"

"Yeah… and?"

Instinct again told Fatima to bite her lip but she chose to ignore it this time.

"Don't you think it wise to find out who you're dealing with before you sleep with them?"

"Bitch! Who you talking to? It's my damn business how I do, or who I do!"

Fatima remained calm.

"Use profanity again and I'll be forced to terminate this interview."

"Whatever!" Ms. Johnson shot back.

"I strongly recommend you talk to someone else who was at that party, and try to get information about your unborn's father. The agency needs it for child support enforcement."

"Motherfucker! I told you, I don't know who he is!"

"That's it, this interview is now terminated. Come back when you can control your foul language."

"I oughta kick your ass!"

"Whatever," Fatima said as she stood up and gathered her paperwork. As soon as she was distracted, Lisa swung at her. Fortunately for Fatima, growing up in public housing had taught her a few self-defense skills. She saw the punch coming as soon as it was thrown. Fatima dropped the items in her hand and grabbed Ms. Johnson's arm, surprising her.

"Bitch, let go of me!"

Fatima knew better than to let go. Enraged, Lisa ducked her head and charged. The two women tussled out into the aisle. Due to the volatile situations their profession regularly placed them in, none of the other coworkers in the interviewing area were shocked to see a scuffle taking place.

Thankfully, one of the Department of Human Resources employees had the foresight to press the panic button installed under each table in the interviewing booths when she heard Lisa threaten Fatima. A policeman was on the scene in a matter of seconds. By then, Fatima had Lisa pinned up against a wall.

"I'ma beat your ass!"

"Not in here, lady," the cop said as he pulled Fatima away from her client.

Undeterred, Lisa sneered and lunged at Fatima, but the officer stepped in front of the angry woman.

"You really feel like going to jail this morning?" he asked.

"I ain't scared a no cop!" she yelled. This woke up her dozing baby who started to bawl.

"I want you to leave the building. If not, you and me are going for a ride," the officer said sternly.

Lisa was mad, but she wasn't stupid. She walked back into the booth and retrieved her crying child.

"This shit ain't over!" she yelled as she pushed her stroller to the exit.

"I get off exactly at five," Fatima informed her.

.   .   .

Inez offered Fatima a cup of French Vanilla coffee before she could even sit down in her cubicle. Her clothes were still disheveled.

"Here you go champ, drink this," she said.

Fatima looked at Inez in surprise.

"Somebody already told you?"

"You know how the grapevine is in here. Who were you down there throwing hands with?"

"Lisa Johnson," Fatima answered with a sigh.

"Lisa, 'don't know the baby daddy,' Johnson?"

"With the same ole shit."

"Pregnant again?"

"Yep."

"That's a damn shame."

Feeling winded, Fatima took a few slow deep breaths.

"You okay?"

"I'm fine."

Their conversation was interrupted when a tall black woman with streaks of gray in her hair walked up.

"I need to see you in my office, Ms. Richardson."

"Yes, Mrs. Baker."

Fatima was silent as she stood up and trailed behind her supervisor.

.   .   .

Roselyn Baker listened intently as Fatima explained exactly what happened. She then had Fatima write down in detail what transpired in case a complaint from Ms. Johnson went up to the Commissioner's Office. It was common for clients to file false grievances in a malicious effort to get a worker fired.

After working eighteen months for the agency, Fatima quickly became disillusioned about the whole welfare system. Doing social work was a thankless job as far as she was concerned. As long as you gave folks what they wanted, you were the greatest thing since sliced bread. But as soon as you denied a client's request, or informed them of an agency requirement that they didn't agree with, they cussed you out and called you everything but a child of God.

The plethora of other people's problems Fatima had to deal with on a daily basis was wearing her out. She was amazed at the number of people in New York City who got evicted or had utilities disconnected for nonpayment. Her own personal issues seemed petty compared to clients who were living with HIV or fighting other serious medical conditions. Fatima was definitely quitting Social Services as soon as she completed her Master's degree in International Studies at City College.

TWO
THE DARK TOWERS

Saturday morning, Andre was positioned firmly between Fatima's thighs as they rocked passionately to the slow grove of the jazz group Incognito's "Deep Waters." Fatima's man had plenty of business and knew how to handle all of it. His thrusts were helping her temporarily suspend the past week's troubles. And his deep loving gave Fatima hope for a brighter tomorrow.

The sweet scented oils that Andre always wore drove her mad when she inhaled the scent of his hot brown skin. As far as Fatima was concerned, there was nothing better than having a good-looking, good-smelling, good-screwing lover to make you twist and shout first thing in the morning.

She'd had other lovers. Living in public housing guaranteed that. It took Fatima a while to sadly realize that the few boys she had chosen to sex only wanted what was between her legs. By the time she'd enrolled in college she was hip to the game. The guys on campus who stepped to her never got the time of day. That was because Fatima kept a battery-operated lover in her lower sock drawer to help take the edge off when needed. Back in the day, she and Bobby the Bullet spent many intimate nights together in her dorm room. Her mechanized relationship lasted several years. Then she met Andre.

He was all she desired. Tall, dark, handsome, and educated. Andre Ellison had his Master's degree from NYU in real estate development and was a rising star with a black-owned firm located in Lower Manhattan making near six figures.

Erotically content, Fatima lay across Andre's chest like a baby. And she would have stayed there all Saturday morning if his stomach hadn't growled.

"You feel like waffles, sweetie?"

"Sure," Andre said.

"Coming right up," Fatima said reluctantly crawling off the bed. She hunted down her black satin panties and matching bra, and slipped them on. She then grabbed a cigarette off her nightstand.

"Aren't we supposed to be cutting back?" Andre asked.

"We supposed to be cutting back on boning, too. Don't hear you stressing me about that," Fatima replied as she searched in her cluttered nightstand drawer for a lighter. She found one hiding under a box of condoms.

Andre smiled and nonchalantly picked up a magazine. He began to peruse the publication.

"That's what I thought," Fatima chuckled. She lit her cigarette as she left the room. She loved teasing her boyfriend. She also hated when Andre admonished her about smoking. She'd had to deal with that shit from her mother and sister when she still lived with them. That was one of the motivations for getting her own place.

It started back in the day as peer pressure from the clique Fatima roamed Harlem's streets with, and the hurry to be an adult. She knew smoking wasn't healthy. But nothing, besides good sex, calmed her as much as a rush of nicotine. She did plan to quit. One day.

In an effort to stifle further harassment about her cigarettes, Fatima cooked omelets along with the waffles, which she topped with strawberries and a little whipped cream. (She saved some of the dairy product in case Andre was still frisky after breakfast.)

"Damn!" Andre said when he saw the meal presented before him. "I might not be able to go to the gym after eating this."

"I know a better way you can burn off some calories," Fatima said coyly.

Andre smiled.

•   •   •

In the beginning it was hard for him to believe how much Fatima loved to sex. The main reason Andre was attracted to Fatima was because she had a good head on her shoulders and was always trying to learn new things. He'd met countless fine sisters in New York City who only had what was packed tight in a pair of pants or stuffed in their bras going for them. And back then he didn't care. Over time though, he wanted more.

Fatima was the first sister Andre met who not only read, but also understood Shakespeare's dramatic works. That shit was all Greek to him. The girl was well read, had very good culinary skills… and she had excellent credit.

If only she wouldn't smoke so damn much. How anyone could bear to walk around smelling like an ashtray all day was beyond his comprehension. He knew working as a caseworker for Human Resources was stressful, but it was still no excuse for Fatima to jeopardize her health. Andre wanted to ensure that the woman he loved would be around a long time in case he decided to ask for her hand in marriage.

"How was work this week?" Andre asked as he loaded his plate with food.

Fatima knew better than to bring up Monday's altercation at the job. Andre had been pressing her to quit and do something less hectic.

"I'd rather talk about something else."

"How's school?"

"I aced that group project," Fatima said as she piled food on her plate.

"That calls for a celebration. Want to go see a movie?"

"Sure, but I have to visit my Mom's first."

"No problem. How's Nikki?" Andre asked.

"Taking care of business," Fatima answered matter-of-factly. "Still making good grades. Scored high on her SATs. And still at her part-time job."

"She choose a college yet?"

"Last I heard, she was leaning toward Howard."

"Good choice."

"To be honest, I don't care where she goes, Andre. Just as long as her butt goes somewhere."

Fatima was proud of her little sister, but it was hard for folks to know it from the way she stayed on the girl's case. She scolded Nikki more severely than their mother did whenever she used to bring home a bad grade. Fatima always found time to help Nikki with a school subject she had difficulty with. She tutored her about boys too. Especially on the mind games they played. New suckers were born every minute in New York; Fatima made it her mission to ensure her baby sister did not become one.

·　　　　　·　　　　　·

It took only ten minutes for Fatima to walk down 155th Street to the four tall buildings that composed the public housing development known as The Dark Towers. The name was appropriate because of its unusual height compared to other public housing buildings. The brick and mortar monstrosities were actually built with good intentions. During that turbulent decade known as the sixties, both the state and federal governments were willing to use any means necessary to cool off the hot tempers of riotous and rebellious minorities. This included crowding people, who had grown disillusioned with being treated as second-class citizens atop each other and charging them a cheap monthly rent.

Fatima was raised in The Dark Towers and was well accustomed to the cacophony of ghetto life that assaulted her ears as she neared the buildings. The obscene lyrics from hip-hop music, the canned laughter from television sitcoms, the young cries of infants and the older shouts of adults all fought to be heard at the same time. Fatima was even nonplused when she saw the cemented paw prints of a rat that had obviously trudged across a section of recently poured pavement.

Standing in front of the building Fatima grew up in was a thin, scraggly looking man clutching a large, well-worn, winter coat around him. He smiled at Fatima, revealing the few stained teeth he had remaining.

"Hey, girl."

"What up, Birdman?"

"You got a dollar so I can get me something to eat?"

"Birdman, I don't have money for you to smoke up."

"I'm really hungry, Fatima."

"Come upstairs and I'll fix you something to eat at my mom's."

"That probably won't work. I'm vegan now," Birdman said pulling down his Yankee's cap when another icy breeze blew in from the Harlem River.

"I gotta go, Birdman. It's too cold out here."

"Can't I have a couple of dollars, Fatima?"

"Later, Birdman."

"How about a cigarette?"

Fatima sighed as she opened her purse and handed him a cigarette.

She was in the sixth grade when Gregory Sease and his family moved into The Dark Towers. Gregory was two grades ahead of her in school and smart as a whip. The skinny, pigeon-toed, teenager with a high-pitched voice tried hard to make friends but was for the most part, unsuccessful. Boys laughed at him in his face, girls giggled about him behind his back.

To compensate for his physical shortcomings, Gregory began to dress sharply. This turned out to be a bad move. The bigger boys in the projects used to beat him mercilessly and rob him of whatever brand-name item of clothing his mother bought for him. It didn't matter whether the attire fit the assailants or not. Things got so bad that Gregory finally began shopping at the Salvation Army for secondhand clothes. The ass whippings abated. Just when things started to get better, Gregory came outside shirtless one hot day to shoot some hoops. Seeing his skinny torso and ribs sticking out some little kids in the projects laughed and called him "Birdman." The name stuck.

Fatima was one of the first friends Birdman made at The Dark Towers. She'd felt sorry for him when others joked about his skeletal appearance. They'd even walked to school together on occasion. Fatima had been impolite to him only once after Birdman misconstrued the parameters of their friendship and made an unwanted sexual advance. The swelling around his left eye from Fatima's right hook went down a week later.

It was during his last year of high school that Birdman foolishly took his first hit of crystal meth. The drug commandeered his brain and then proceeded to rob him of everything—his money, his friends, his family, his future.

Fatima felt pity for Birdman but not enough to finance his habit.

The lobby of her mother's building smelled of piss and chlorine. Fatima walked to the elevator and pressed the button. After the usual long wait, the graffiti-tagged door creaked open to reveal a baby stroller and a teenaged mother inside. Fatima stepped aside as the young woman pushed the stroller into the lobby.

"Tamika?"

"Hi, Fatima."

"Whose cute little girl is this?"

"Mine," Tamika said proudly.

"How old is she?"

"Lexus will be seven months next week."

"Lexus? Like the car?" Fatima asked.

"Exactly," Tamika said with a smile. "I haven't seen you around. Didn't you go get married or something?"

"No. Just working and going to school. And you? What grade are you in now?"

Tamika lowered her eyes.

"I dropped out last semester."

"Why?" Fatima was unable to hide her disappointment.

"Couldn't find anybody I trusted to take care of my baby."

Fatima was silent.

"But I'm going back," the teen added for good measure.

"Make sure you do that soon, Tamika."

"I will."

The two looked at each other awkwardly for a few seconds before Fatima stepped into the elevator. The malodorous stench of piss was far stronger inside.

"Take care," Fatima said as she took a last gasp of semi fresh air and then held her breath as she pushed the button for her floor.

Pamela Richardson was dumping the last ingredients for a peach cobbler into a mixing bowl when she heard her daughter walk into her two-bedroom apartment.

Fatima dropped her winter coat on the sofa in the living room and continued across the tiled floor to the kitchen.

"Hey, Mama."

"You're late."

"I got sidetracked with Andre."

"I bet you did."

At forty-six, Pamela Richardson looked ten years younger than her actual age. And she was quick to remind others of this. Originally from Birmingham, she'd moved to New York City after two years of college at the University of Alabama. Pamela had fallen in love with James Allen, a classmate two years her senior, and became pregnant with his child after a long, passionate homecoming weekend.

Pamela followed James back to his native Brooklyn after he graduated school and then presented her with an engagement ring. But things soon fell apart. Pamela grew tired of being home alone with little Fatima while James partied with his friends. She finally decided to move out their cramped Bedford Avenue apartment.

Too embarrassed to return to Alabama as an unwedded mother, Pamela took up residence in The Dark Towers. The fact that she had fallen in love with New York City also influenced her decision to stay up North. Pamela loved hanging out in Central Park with Fatima in the summertime and people watch. And there were always museum exhibits happening in the city for them to visit. And then there was the shopping. Pamela actually got a rush from taking the subway down to Lower Manhattan to bargain hunt on Canal Street.

Raising a child by herself occupied so much of her time that she almost forgot the heartache the baby's father had caused. James Allen quickly moved on and married an old girlfriend from Hollis, Queens after Pamela gave up on him. He came by every now and then to see his child, and to hand her mother some money, but eventually he disappeared altogether.

Pamela became disillusioned with the opposite sex. However, she did allow a few gentlemen callers to address her womanly urges when they overwhelmed her. She would often declare to herself—and anyone who would listen—that she was through with love; until she met Charles.

Charles Gilmore was a U.S. soldier Pamela met one Friday night at a fish fry in The Dark Towers. Sergeant Gilmore was a cousin of the host of the event. He had traveled to NYC after recently being transferred up to Fort Drum, New York. By this time Pamela was already working at her current job as an office assistant at a law firm. She'd stopped by the gathering on the way home from work to grab a plate for her daughter. Before Pamela knew what hit her, Charles Gilmore had her hemmed up in a corner of the kitchen laughing her ass off.

The man was a natural comedian. He made wisecracks about every person in the apartment, including his own kinfolk frying the fish. Charles had a wide pearly-white grin and eyes the color of jade that most sisters could not resist. Pamela was no exception. Sergeant Gilmore ordered her not to go back to her own apartment until she gave up her phone number.

Six months of wining and dining followed. Pamela could not believe her good fortune. Charles not only spent money on her, but on her daughter as well. He usually brought toys for Fatima to play with whenever he took her mother shopping.

Not wanting to be the same fool twice, Pamela delayed offering her nectar to Charles for almost seven months. When he surprised her with a full-length fur coat for Christmas, she surrendered her love. She was not disappointed. Sergeant Gilmore knew how to wage war between the sheets and Pamela found herself marking the calendar until the day Charles was due to drive down and pay her another visit.

It was during one of their sexual skirmishes, on a rainy Sunday morning, that Nicole Adrianne Richardson was conceived. Pamela was sure Charles would be elated when she informed him of his impending fatherhood. He disappeared instead.

All of her phone calls and letters went unreturned. Humiliated, and with no other alternative, Pamela had to ask Charles' cousin to intercede. She nearly had a nervous breakdown when he sympathetically informed her that Charles already had a wife and kids in Savannah, Georgia. It was only after a blood test confirmed Charles was indeed Nikki's father that the child support payments began to come in, courtesy of the U.S. Army.

.   .   .

"What do you want me to help you with?" Fatima asked.

"You smell like a ashtray."

"You need any help with the food?" Fatima said, ignoring her mother's comment.

"Wash your hands and peel me some sweet potatoes. I promised Reverend Yizar I'd make a few pies for his pastor's anniversary."

"You still chasing that clown?"

"I'm not chasing anyone."

"You and every other single female at church always cooking for him. I don't trust that man any further than I could throw him."

"Go wash your damn hands!"

Fatima did as her mother ordered. On the way down the hall, she passed her sister's room. Fatima tapped on the door. She was careful not to damage the huge poster of some tattooed, barely clad rapper that hung on it.

When Nikki didn't answer Fatima pushed the door open. Her sister was in bed reading a textbook. The earplugs she wore kept her from hearing Fatima's knock. She was briefly startled, then quickly pissed.

"What's your problem? Barging in here, like you the police?" Nikki closed her book, jerked her earplugs out, and sat up.

"I knocked," Fatima said.

"Did I tell you to enter?"

"No."

"So you can leave now…"

Fatima fought the urge to jack-slap her little sister as she backed out of the room, though she left the door open behind her. She then washed her hands in the bathroom and returned to the kitchen. Her mother was busy rolling out pie dough.

"What's your daughter's malfunction?" Fatima asked as she grabbed two sweet potatoes.

"What you two fussing about now?" Pamela asked with a sigh.

"I went into her room to say hello, and she wanted to bite my head off."

"I think she's anxious about getting into a good college."

"That's still no excuse for acting like she's on the rag."

"Watch that mouth, Fatima."

"Sorry. What's up with that nappy-headed boy she's so in love with?"

"Freddie?"

"Yeah."

"She still calls him down at that naval base in Norfolk. He calls her too."

"Isn't that cute?" Fatima said. She rinsed the vegetables off in the sink and then started removing the skins with a paring knife.

"I give Freddie credit for trying to make something out of himself after graduating, instead of hanging around here, waiting to become another statistic," Pamela said.

"Nikki's too young to have an older boyfriend," Fatima said.

"You did the same thing when you were sixteen."

"But I was more mature, Mama."

"As long as he's down in Virginia and she's up here, I'm fine with it."

"Who you two talking about?" Nikki asked at the kitchen door.

"We were discussing you and Freddie," Fatima answered.

"Need to discuss why you so dang nosy," her sister replied as she opened the refrigerator and grabbed a bottle of water.

"Don't start, Nikki!"

"Just telling the truth, Mama."

Fatima was silent as Nikki walked out of the room. *Hope that bitch ain't on drugs?* she thought, and then resumed peeling sweet potatoes.

THREE

I'M NOBODY'S ROLE MODEL

Marisol Aquino was one of the finest educators who ever walked the halls of Harlem's W.E.B. Dubois High. She was tall for her gender and looked younger than her twenty-seven years. Marisol's curvaceous body made many a horny student watch her like a one-eyed cat peeping in a seafood store.

A standout basketball player at Evander Childs High School up in the Bronx, she'd played on the college level at SUNY Cortland while pursuing a degree in Physical Education. Marisol enjoyed her job as a PE teacher and constantly pushed people to go all out during physical training. This was the one attribute Fatima hated about her best friend.

"Girl, if you don't slow your ass down! I'm out of breath!" Fatima said as she strained to keep up with Marisol. The two women were jogging south along a thin paved path that ran parallel to Manhattan's Westside Highway. Due to climate change it was an unusually warm Saturday morning so Fatima consented to Marisol's badgering to go for a run. The promise of a free meal for Fatima had sealed the deal, and her doom.

The game plan was to jog down to Riverside Park and then walk back up to their starting point, 158th Street. Fatima had known that idea was iffy from the start. Now her sides felt like they were being kicked in with steel-toed boots. Her heart felt like it was about to explode, her lungs were burning, and her feet ached. She had been jogging for exactly nine minutes.

"Maybe you should give up smoking. Then you'd have some breath."

"Maybe I should just stop this bullshit," Fatima said. She found a patch of grass without litter on it and collapsed.

"I can't believe you!" Marisol said in disbelief standing over her. "We're just getting started."

"You go on ahead. I'm going back to bed."

"What about that prime rib I promised you for lunch?"

"I'm worrying about my own damn ribs right now."

"Fatima, you are so sad."

"Fuck you, Marisol!"

"And that nasty mouth of yours! So unladylike."

"Wanna hear more cussin'? Keep popping shit."

•   •   •

They'd met at a beauty shop in Washington Heights some years ago while they were getting their nails done. When one of the customers near them started a discussion about the abundance of trifling men in New York, they both joined in the conversation and a friendship was born.

Fatima and Marisol exchanged cell numbers and began hanging out. They went to concerts around the city, hung out at the latest clubs that were jumping, and of course shopped at major clearance sales. The primary activity they enjoyed together however, was eating. They visited every chic restaurant that opened in Manhattan.

"You gonna stay down there in your new jogging suit, Fatima?"

"Only until you leave."

"How about a compromise?"

"You wanna split a cab?" Fatima asked hopefully.

"No, we'll walk, instead of run."

"I like the cab idea better."

"Get your lazy behind up!"

Fatima grunted loudly and slowly stood up. Her heart had yet to slow down from its frantic pace, yet she matched Marisol's steps as the two hiked in the direction of Lower Manhattan.

"This jogging stuff is almost as hard as trying to convince some of my young clients to get a job."

"Doesn't Jersey look pretty?" Marisol asked as she gazed across the Hudson River at the Garden State's shoreline. Her attempt to change the subject proved futile.

"You should hear some of the excuses they give for not being able to work."

"We still bowling Friday?" Marisol asked. It was another effort to alter the conversation.

"Some folks get addicted to welfare like it's a drug."

"Raphael wants us to meet you and Andre around seven."

"Did I tell you one of our client's got caught breaking into our office? How damn trifling is that?"

Marisol stopped suddenly and turned around.

"Let's call a truce, Fatima. Quit complaining about your damn job, and we'll quit exercising and go grab a bite at Mike's."

"Deal!" Fatima said with a sly grin.

·   ·   ·

Amsterdam Avenue, where Mike's Coffee Shop was located, was already bustling with Harlemites. The street was filled with young mothers maneuvering baby strollers, young men scoping out the young mothers, street hustlers looking to generate income, and unsupervised children enjoying their freedom. As Fatima and Marisol approached the popular eatery, they saw that it was already crowded.

"You wanna go inside and see if you can get a booth, Marisol? I'll be back."

"Where you going?"

"To grab some cigarettes."

"You can't be serious," Marisol said in disbelief.

"Watch me."

Fatima had no problem finding a bodega to buy a pack. After lighting and smoking a cigarette for a few minutes, she joined Marisol at the back of Mike's near the kitchen. The clatter of dishes and silverware resonated around them as they talked between bites of chocolate éclairs and sips of cappuccino.

"Girl, this sugar rush is almost as good as sex," Marisol said as she devoured the rest of her pastry.

"You must be crazy. Nothing beats the Big O."

"While we're on the subject, I was wondering if you could do me a favor?"

"What is it?" Fatima asked as she reached into her jogging pants and retrieved her vibrating cell phone.

"My school's having a youth conference in a couple of weeks. I'd like you to be one of our speakers."

Fatima laughed.

"What's so funny?" Marisol asked defensively.

"Andre just sent me a kinky text message. What were you saying?"

"I want you to speak to my students about the importance of staying in school and getting an education. So they can avoid needing public assistance."

Fatima looked at her friend skeptically.

"You don't have to commit today," Marisol added. "I can give you a few days to think it over."

"I can answer right now."

"Really?" Marisol said hopefully.

"I don't do speeches, Marisol. The answer is no."

"But—"

"But, my ass," Fatima said dryly. "You have my answer."

"Don't you understand you're a perfect role model for my students? You grew up here in the projects, you finished high school and you graduated from college. You have a good career, where you see daily what happens to young people who don't make the same choices you did."

Fatima took a sip of her cappuccino as she gave Marisol a hard stare.

"I'm nobody's role model."

"Please, Fatima?"

"No dice. I suggest we change the subject."

Marisol sighed… and complied. "How did Nikki do on her SAT test?"

"Scored higher on it than I did when I took it."

"Really?"

"Yes. Isn't it funny how somebody can be book smart and still ignorant at the same time?"

"She decided on a school yet?"

"She's thinking about Howard."

"So she can be close to Freddie."

"Norfolk Naval Base is about four hours away."

"Isn't that romantic," Marisol said as she finished the rest of her coffee.

"It won't be romantic if Nikki screws up her grades running behind that Negro. I'll break my foot off in her ass. His too."

Marisol wasn't surprised to hear her friend talk like that. She knew how concerned Fatima was for her baby sister's welfare.

"Calm down, Fatima. You worry too much."

"It's from all that running I did. I need another cigarette," Fatima said as she stood up.

"You serious?" Marisol asked in disbelief.

"Watch me," Fatima said and pulled out her lighter. "Order me another éclair when our waiter passes by? Thanks, sweetie."

With that, Fatima once again headed outdoors.

FOUR
CHELSEA, NIKKI, & MELODY

Chelsea Rivers noticed that the bulb in her room needed to be changed. She often picked an object to focus on when she was screwing a brother she didn't dig. And though Perry Brown was doing his best to ensure Chelsea received gratification, she wasn't feeling him. The high school senior endeared himself to her even less when he began humming along with the R. Kelly song playing on her mini-stereo.

It was almost 10:30 PM, and if Chelsea hurried this Negro up, she could make it to Manhattan Live and get in free. They didn't charge women admission on Fridays until midnight. She loved that nightclub because she never spent her own money. Guys always tried to get Chelsea drunk to try to get her in the sack. She always obliged them with a thirsty smile.

Passing for an adult was not a problem for Chelsea. Her fake identification card was well made. And her sixteen-year-old body was well advanced. She'd initially felt like a misfit when she'd started filling out in the fourth grade. Then boys started hanging around her. All the time. Some of her own male cousins used to cop a feel on her when they played tag in the playground area of The Dark Towers. Soon Chelsea developed an apple-shaped bottom that made men stop, look, and lust as she strolled by.

Her moist body smelled like fresh melon, a scent Chelsea knew boys loved. The aroma drove Perry Brown mad. Because he couldn't kiss her on the mouth like he yearned to, (she had warned him against that) Perry decided to lick her insides instead.

His tongue action surprised Chelsea, and she stifled an impulse to moan. She didn't want the fool to assume too much. She also didn't want to wake her little brother in the next bedroom. Nine-year-old Tyrell Rivers was always snitching on Chelsea unless she bribed him.

She also had an old brother Rahiem, who also used to rat Chelsea out to their mother until he botched an armed robbery and earned a six-year vacation to beautiful Chemung County, New York. The location of Elmira Correctional Facility.

Chelsea's mother, Billie, was waitressing at a diner in the Bronx and wouldn't return home until morning. Billie Rivers hated leaving her children home alone on Friday and Saturday nights, but she needed the extra income to make ends meet. Welfare only gave her so much help. Working off the books as a waitress was one of the few jobs Chelsea's mother could do without having her income reported to the IRS... and to HRA.

Billie initially assuaged concern for her kids' well-being by calling them two or three times a night from work. But her daughter was so cognizant of her worries that Chelsea soon began to call Billie at the diner first, to assure her that things at home were fine. Chelsea's mom considered herself blessed to have such a responsible teenager.

Perry, the young man between Chelsea's thighs, had been possessed with the craving to explore every inch of her high-yellow skin with his fingers. That was the first thought that had crossed his mind when she sat down on the subway seat next to him three months earlier. It had taken the poor boy a pair of new shoes, the latest pre-paid cell phone, and two pairs of low cut designer jeans to convince Chelsea to sex him. Now Perry was so excited by the fact he was actually making love to the girl that he finished sooner than planned. Embarrassed, but happy nonetheless, he grunted atop of her.

"Did you come?" Chelsea asked softly.

"Yes," Perry sighed as he collapsed beside her on the bed.

"Good. Now you can go."

"Go?"

"Hell yeah."

"Can't we cuddle?"

"Hell no! My moms gonna be home any minute."

Chelsea got up, slipped her pants on and headed for the door.

"Where you going?" Perry whispered.

"To get you a wash rag."

Twenty minutes later he was dressed and hesitant to leave.

"Uh… Perry?" Chelsea asked as the boy reluctantly opened her bedroom door.

"Yeah?" There was hope in his voice.

"You got something for me?"

"What!"

"Why you so loud?"

"Didn't I already hit you off with fresh gear, and that phone, Chelsea?"

"Yeah, but I need to get my nails done. You do want me to look good for you?"

"I'm not sure," Perry confessed. "How much this gonna cost?"

"I can get me some French tips for sixty dollars downtown."

"Sixty!"

"You trying to wake up my brother, fool?"

"Isn't that kind of expensive?" Perry asked in a lower tone.

"Actually, that's a good price."

Not wanting to appear cheap, Perry grudgingly fished the money from his wallet and handed it over. He'd have to put in more hours at the auto parts store to make up for the unexpected expenditure.

"Thanks, boo," Chelsea said as she gave him a hug. Perry was surprised by the gesture and instinctively bent to kiss her.

"What I say about kissing?"

Chelsea turned her head and Perry settled for a peck on the cheek before she led him out the apartment. As soon as Chelsea fastened the lock on her front door she pulled out her phone.

"Lorraine, can you come downstairs in thirty minutes? I gotta take a quick shower and get dressed. All I have is twenty dollars for you to watch Tyrell. That's cool? Thanks, girl. See you in a little while."

•   •   •

Birds were chirping at the arrival of another dawn when Chelsea dragged herself back into The Dark Towers. She'd had a great time and met three prospects she deemed worthy enough to give her cell number. As soon as

Chelsea woke Lorraine up and paid her for services rendered, she went into her room and passed out on her bed. That was the reason she was late for her date with Nikki to the movies that afternoon.

"You gonna make us miss the movie with your slow ass!" Nikki said as she pushed Chelsea toward her bedroom closet. Chelsea was still sluggish from clubbing.

"Pick out something to wear so we can leave?" Nikki added.

"Don't rush me. I've got to coordinate," Chelsea said as she opened her closet and eyed her vast wardrobe. Men were very benevolent to Chelsea. They gave her a lot of nice shit in exchange for her spending time with them. (Her naive mother believed she ran a lucrative babysitting service in the projects.)

"If you don't hurry, I'm gonna coordinate my foot in your behind."

"Bitch, please… you ain't that crazy," Chelsea said.

The teenagers had known each other since they were third grade classmates at Public School 46. Their friendship blossomed after Chelsea began bribing Nikki with snack cakes and cookies in exchange for the exclusive right to copy her homework. It was not exactly a win-win situation. As Chelsea gained praise from her teachers, Nikki gained weight.

"How does this pink cashmere joint look?" Chelsea asked as she retrieved the sweater from its hanger.

"Nice. Put it on so we can bounce."

"Douglas got this for me," Chelsea said.

"When does he get out of jail?"

"Good question," Chelsea said as she slipped the sweater over her head. "I'll ask his mother next time I see her."

Chelsea retrieved a pair of designer jeans and pulled them on. She then returned to her closet to survey her cache of winter boots.

"Open my pocketbook drawer, Nikki."

Nikki walked across the room to the giant oak armoire and did as instructed.

"It makes no sense to have all these bags!"

"Quit hating and let me get that black argyle joint on the left."

"Want me to find you a matching pair of argyle socks while I'm over here?" Nikki asked sarcastically.

"Okay, look in the third drawer."

"You know I hate to stand in line at the movies," Nikki grumbled as she opened Chelsea's sock drawer.

"I'll get us a cab," Chelsea said. She then walked over to Nikki and eyed her with concern.

"Something bothering you, Nikki?"

"Why you asking that?"

"You been awfully bitchy lately."

"I'm fine."

"Could you please act like it, then?"

Nikki was silent as she placed the pocketbook and socks on Chelsea's bed. She then pulled out her cell.

"Who you calling?"

"Melody."

"Why?"

"To tell her we're taking a cab instead of the bus."

"I'm not paying for that thang to ride with us!"

"Don't start, Chelsea."

"I'm not paying for her. I'm serious, Nikki."

"Why you always treat her so bad?"

"I'm not treating her bad, I'm just not paying that heifer's cab fare. I don't see why she has to tag along anyway."

"Melody's always nice to you, Chelsea."

"It don't matter. The bitch looks like a dude."

"You need to stop."

"And you need to quit hanging with her so much. Unless you want a bad rep, too," Chelsea said. She then walked to the jewelry box on her nightstand and fished out a pair of platinum encrusted hoop earrings.

"Douglas gave me these too."

"How cute. Let's go," Nikki said.

"How's your sister?" Chelsea asked as she attached the bling to her ears.

"She's fine. Where's your coat?"

Ignoring the question, Chelsea said, "I plan on moving out this shithole as soon as I can… exactly like Fatima did. Fuck hanging around, dropping babies and getting fat, like most of the older girls around here did. I'm on a mission."

Nikki sighed deeply and plopped down onto Chelsea's bed.

"What's up, Nikki?"

"Melody's voice mail came on. We'll stop by her apartment on the way out."

"You didn't answer my question."

"What you talking about?"

"I know your ass well enough to tell when you're stressed. You and Freddie have a spat?"

"Freddie and I are good."

"Ugly ass Henry Johnson still begging you for some ass?"

"Please, don't talk him up!"

"Those girls from Queens trying to fight you again? If so, we can ride on over there and—"

"Ain't nobody threatening me," Nikki said, cutting Chelsea off.

"Don't wanna talk about it? Cool. Let's go get Ms. Thang," Chelsea said as she pulled a new goose down jacket from her closet.

. . .

Melody Knight was not considered pretty by anyone. Even her own mother found her uneasy on the eyes. It seems that during her conception, the decision for her to have another X chromosome was made at the last possible second and she begrudgingly became female. Melody still had the facial features of a male however. Her wide flat nose made her look like she'd caught a straight right jab in the face as a baby.

What Melody lacked in looks, she made up in sexual aptitude. Her tactical feats while giving "brain" (oral sex) were legendary. Little Melody had been coerced into blowing some older boys in her building when she was a six grader. Word quickly spread that she had a mean head game.

Local boys began to devote just enough interest in Melody to get her to drop to her knees. The girl was so attention-starved and desperate to find love that she complied over and over again. She was soon referred to as "The Kneeling Knight" by many of the boys in Harlem.

Melody and Nikki became acquainted several years earlier when they'd been assigned the tedious task of washing their family's clothes in the grimy basement of The Dark Towers. Nikki had gone down first that morning, after returning to retrieve her clothes from the ancient dryers she found they were still damp.

With no extra quarters on her, Nikki had to return upstairs for more. Melody arrived a few seconds later to move her wash to the dryers. The only units available had clothes inside that someone had been too lazy to come down and remove. They were still damp, but that wasn't her problem. She didn't intend to spend all morning doing damn laundry.

Melody had just fed the machines the required amount of coins to dry her clothes and started them up when Nikki returned and found her family's damp clothes piled on one of the broken-down tables in the laundry room. She was past pissed.

"Motherfucker! What you doing!?"

Melody had seen Nikki around the projects plenty of times. However, that still didn't give the bitch license to cuss at her.

"Motherfucker! What it look like?" she replied.

"I was still using those dryers!"

"Your ass shoulda been back down here sooner!"

"I had to go get more damn quarters!"

"Did you leave a fucking note saying that?"

Nikki was about to give another nasty retort, but she thought about the question.

"No… I didn't."

"Okay, then," Melody said. She was caught off guard by Nikki's reply. Her fists were already balled up, in case the confrontation escalated.

"Sorry for swearing at you," Nikki said. She then began to place her wet clothes into a laundry cart.

"I apologize, too. You going over to the building next door?"

"Yeah," Nikki answered. "Gotta finish this shit so I can go catch that new Idris Elba movie."

"That joint looks good. I plan on seeing it too," Melody said. "You got enough quarters to dry your clothes?"

"Yeah, I'm straight."

"I'm Melody."

"I'm Nikki."

The two girls shook hands and parted ways. After the laundry room episode, Melody and Nikki began to speak to each other in passing. Soon, they started to hang out together.

.   .   .

"Melody's Mama sure named her correctly, cause' I hear that thang has a knack for humming on niggas' balls."

"Chelsea, if you gonna act up, I'm going back home."

"I'll behave, Nikki."

They were in the hall outside Melody's eighth floor apartment. When Melody opened her door and stepped out, she was dressed in a white New York Rangers hoodie, baggy jeans, and rubber boots. A matching cap with the hockey team's logo covered her braided head.

"What's good?" she asked them.

"Hey," Nikki replied.

"Hi, Melody," Chelsea said.

Melody patted her hands over her jeans pockets in search of an object she could not find.

"Forgot my keys," she said and disappeared back into her apartment.

"You see what she's wearing? That chick's confused!"

"I'm warning you, Chelsea."

"I'm just saying—"

Melody reappeared before Chelsea could finish dissing her.

"Okay, we can bounce," Melody said locking the apartment door.

The teenagers walked down the hallway to the elevators.

"Melody what's that perfume you wearing?" Nikki asked as they waited for the lift downstairs.

"It's called Temerity. You like it?"

"Kinda strong," Nikki replied.

"They shoulda named it, Severity," Chelsea mumbled as an elevator dinged its arrival. The mixture of Melody's fragrance and the odor of piss in the elevator car was too much for Nikki's nostrils. She felt queasy and began to gag.

"You okay?" Chelsea asked.

It was sheer luck that Melody wore rubber boots that day. The bile Nikki spewed on them could easily be wiped off.

"What's wrong with you?" Melody asked as she jumped from the path of puke.

Nikki wiped her mouth with one hand as she braced herself against the elevator wall with the other. She sighed deeply.

"Can you guys keep a secret?" Nikki asked softly. She then began to cry.

"Of course," Chelsea answered. "Aren't we all friends?"

FIVE
JAMAAL

Human Resources was abuzz with activity as usual when Fatima eased into her cubicle chair Friday morning. She was late. There were a dozen case re-certifications due to her supervisor before she went home for the day and her office phone was already ringing. Fatima needed caffeine.

"You colored folks tickle me with your lack of punctuality."

A round of laughter came from the vicinity of Inez's cubicle. She was holding court there with Drew Morgan, a thirty-nine-year-old assistant supervisor, and Jackie Cooke, a forty-three-year-old office assistant.

"Morning, folks. We in a pleasant mood today, Inez?" Fatima asked.

"Yeah, girl. Got my sinuses opened up good this morning before I got out of bed. Never knew Brooklyn smelled so fresh."

"That's way too much information," Drew said.

"If my building superintendent wasn't married, he'd be my next ex-husband," Inez added.

"You don't have any scruples, do you?" Jackie asked her.

"Lost them years ago… along with my virginity," Inez laughed.

"You guys hear about that shooting last night?" Fatima asked in an attempt to change the conversation.

"Which one?" Drew asked.

"In Red Hook," Fatima answered.

"That boy bled to death in the street because nobody called an ambulance," Jackie said.

"Police need to arrest everyone who was out there on the block when it happened," Drew added.

"These New York niggas done lost their minds. That's why I'm moving back to Mississippi."

"Inez, you've been moving back to Mississippi for the last ten years."

"I'm still packing, okay? Mind your business, Drew."

"The generation coming up now is gonna have black folks out there picking cotton again if they don't get it together," Jackie said.

"You sure about that? Some of these young folks today too lazy to work in a pie factory," Drew said.

Drew's eighteen-year-old son, Avery, was born with Down syndrome. Even though he was mildly retarded, his mother made sure he learned enough basic skills to get hired as a bag-boy at a local grocery store. Able-bodied young adults who applied for welfare daily at the agency was a touchy subject for Drew.

"Look, you ladies can sit around here all day gossiping if you want, but I've got work to do," Inez announced loudly. She then whispered, "Roselyn's coming."

The group dispersed before the supervisor reached Fatima's cubicle.

"Good morning, Fatima."

"Morning, Mrs. Baker."

"Latisha Fuller left a complaint on my voice mail. You denied her request for a furniture allowance?"

"We just moved her last month."

"So what exactly did we pay the moving company to move for Ms. Fuller?"

"That's what I asked her."

"And?"

"She told me to kiss her ass, and then she hung up."

"See if we have an itemized breakdown of the moving bill so I can review it before I call her back?"

"I will."

"Thank you."

Mrs. Baker then turned to Inez.

"Inez… are you losing weight? You look different."

"I lost about two pounds working out this morning, Roselyn."

"Keep it up. You look good."

"Thanks, I will."

Fatima kept her mouth shut until her supervisor was out of earshot.

"That Latisha Fuller asks for everything but a damn job!"

"I don't blame her," Inez said. "If I thought I could get some extra money from this place, I'd ask your ass for it too."

"I can't wait to finish school and find me a better job."

"They're hiring down in Mississippi. Wanna come with me?"

"I got your damn Mississippi, Inez."

Even though she was still angry, Fatima chuckled at her coworker's silliness. Her cell phone interrupted her.

"Hello, Mama…" Fatima paused. "Say what?" she said. Her voice revealed her astonishment. "I'll be there shortly." She ended her call and stood up. Fury was all over her face.

"Fatima, what's wrong?"

"Shit done hit the fan, Inez," was all she said.

•   •   •

A straight razor could not have carved the tension that hung over the Richardson household. Nikki sat at the kitchen table with her head lowered. Her eyes were bloodshot from crying. Ms. Richardson sat across from her. Lines of worry wrinkled her brow. Fatima leaned against the stove with her arms folded tightly to prevent her from slapping the shit out of her sister. A forsaken breakfast of cheese grits, sausage, and eggs sat on the burners behind her.

"Does Freddie know?"

Fatima's question conjured up more tears from her sister. Nikki lowered her head even further.

"Freddie hasn't been home since Thanksgiving," Ms. Richardson said softly.

"You knocked up by some other nigga!?"

"Watch your mouth, Fatima!"

"Sorry, Mama."

This new piece of information was too much for Fatima. She pulled out the cigarettes and lighter she had in her pocket. She was just about to spark up when her mother intervened.

"Have you lost your damn mind? You know not to smoke in here!"

"Can't I go in the bathroom?"

"No!"

Fatima sighed and returned her cigarettes to her pocket.

"Who's the father, Nikki?"

"What?"

"Don't act stupid! You didn't do this by your damn self!"

"I'm not going to tell you again about your mouth, Fatima."

"Jamaal," Nikki said weakly.

"Jamaal Jackson?! That sorry motherfucker?"

"Fatima!"

Nikki's silence confirmed the answer.

"I gotta go outside!" Fatima announced as she went into the living room and retrieved her jacket.

The remains of a recent snow coated the naked branches of the few trees that surrounded The Dark Towers. With warm smoke flowing from her nostrils, Fatima's anger at her sister's stupidity burned hotter. Her eyes misted up as she leaned against the side of the building and pulled once again on her menthol cigarette.

"Yo? You okay?"

Fatima was so deep in thought that she had failed to notice her surroundings.

"What's up, Birdman?"

"I was walking around the building and saw you here looking all stressed. What's wrong?"

"My sister's knocked up by Jamaal Jackson."

"That motherfucker made another baby?"

"Yeah," Fatima sighed. "I warned Nikki that life was hard, and even harder when you're stupid. She's about to find out what I meant."

"Yo, sorry to hear that. Got another cigarette?"

"Yeah," Fatima said as she supplied Birdman with a smoke and lighter.

"Nikki decide what she's gonna do?" Birdman asked after lighting up.

"I have no clue. Wait 'til I see that nigga."

"He usually deals along Manhattan Avenue."

"You sure?"

"Certain. He usually works those blocks with his boy, Po-Dog."

"Thanks, Birdman."

"No doubt."

"I gotta get back inside."

After taking a few more drags on her cigarette, Fatima dropped it and mashed it out.

"Yo, Fatima?"

"Yeah?"

"You got a couple of dollars to help a brother get something to eat?"

"Here," Fatima said as she reached into her pocket and handed him a five-dollar bill.

"Good looking out."

"Better not go smoke up my damn money, Birdman. I'm serious."

"Ain't nothing like that. I'm going to grab me a cheeseburger."

"You still a vegan?"

"No doubt. Tell Nikki I said to stay strong."

Fatima lowered her head as she reentered her mother's building.

●   ●   ●

"How'd you find out she was pregnant?" Fatima asked her mother while she helped put away the remains of breakfast.

"My friend Janet overheard some girls talking about it in the laundry room last night and called me early this morning. I asked Nikki point blank if it was true. She broke down crying."

"What do you think she should do?"

"I'm not sure. But I know she needs to go see Reverend Yizar."

"She'd be better off seeing an obstetrician."

"Don't get smart, Fatima."

Nikki was in her bedroom when Fatima returned to the apartment. The door was closed so Fatima knocked. Hearing no response, she knocked once more. Silence greeted her again, so she tried the knob and found it unlocked.

"Nikki?"

Nikki was on the bed with her arms folded under her head, staring up at the ceiling. Still crying.

"Yeah?"

Fatima's heart softened on hearing the despair in her sister's voice.

"You alright?" Fatima asked as she walked in the room and sat at Nikki's computer desk.

"No."

"Sorry how I spoke to you earlier."

"Forget it."

"What do you plan on doing?"

"I don't know."

"You sure it's Jamaal's baby?"

"He's the only guy I've been with. Besides one time with Freddie."

"Word is, Jamaal has three or four kids already."

"I heard."

"Why didn't you at least use a condom?"

"We did... the first time."

Fatima turned away from her sister in an effort to hide her disgust. She then turned back.

"You know you have to get tested?"

"For what? Nikki asked, concern in her voice as she sat up on her bed.

"For everything. Ain't no telling who else, or *what* else Jamaal done fucked."

"Okay."

Fatima sighed and headed toward the bedroom door. She then stopped.

"One last question?"

"I was waiting..."

"What in the world made you wanna fuck that hood rat, Nikki? Freddie's a decent guy. With a legal occupation."

"I don't know. I guess I liked all the attention Jamaal showed me."

Her dumb ass answer made Fatima's blood boil.

"That's it?"

Nikki was silent.

"You tell Freddie about your situation?"

"I don't know how," Nikki said weakly.

"Well, you're all grown now, you'll figure it out," Fatima mumbled as she left the room.

•   •   •

Manhattan Avenue was teeming with midday traffic. Fatima cursed herself again for not taking the subway. She had gotten her used Volkswagen Beetle as a gift from her mother, while completing her degree in African American Studies at the University of Buffalo. Slowly easing through the streets of Harlem was costing her about a dollar a minute in fuel consumption. New York City's high gasoline prices and its ludicrous traffic fines were the main reasons that Fatima rarely drove. (It had taken her almost seven hundred dollars in parking fines to finally grasp the concept of alternate side of the street parking rules.)

Fatima kept her eyes peeled for a silver Lincoln Navigator. She was soon rewarded for her efforts after she drove across 110th Street. The glare from Jamaal's chrome, twenty-two inch rims could be seen a block away. Following the required search for legal parking, Fatima began to hunt for the fool on foot.

•   •   •

Twenty-two-year-old Jamaal Jackson stood on the corner of 105th Street and Columbus Avenue. A laced Dutch Master dangled from the corner of his mouth smoldering as he talked on his cell phone. The brother was clad in standard urban attire: a hooded sweatshirt, large goose down jacket, sagging blue jeans, and unlaced work boots. He had a black bandana wrapped around his head that was partially obscured by his Jets cap.

Many folks mistakenly assumed that Jamaal was younger than he looked due to his small stature. His slight build came from from his diminutive father who suffered with sickle cell. People also assumed that Jamaal suffered from sleep deprivation due to his barely opened, bloodshot eyes. This was the result of his daily intake of marijuana.

Jamaal had dropped out of high school after failing his second attempt at passing tenth grade. He then chose to pursue the illegal American dream of dealing drugs. An older cousin had shown Jamaal how to get his hustle on and had even fronted his young trainee a startup supply of crack cocaine. Before Jamaal could prove how skillful he was at rock slinging, his cousin Richie was shot dead early one morning at a Lower East Side nightclub. Richie's drunken killer had meant to shoot the bouncers who had thrown him out of the club, but the bullets he fired had been unaware of his intentions.

Jamaal took over most of his cousin's customers and made new ones. Having lots of disposable income and flexible working hours enabled him to become a ruthless chicken hawk. Jamaal swooped down on as many young, unsuspecting females in the community as he could. The thrill of the hunt for new chicken-heads was what Jamaal craved. Busting a nut in a fresh piece of ass brought him unspeakable joy.

Jamaal's conversation was temporarily interrupted by the eardrum-piercing wail of an ambulance on its way to aid another New Yorker in distress.

"I'm back, Tawanna. What were you saying?"

"Jamaal Jackson!"

Jamaal spun around to see who the hell was calling his name like they'd lost their damn mind. Nikki's sister approaching him with a snarl on her face was not a pretty sight. Jamaal had a strong distaste for Fatima ever since they were kids growing up in The Dark Towers. To him, she was stuck up.

"Shit!" Jamaal sighed. "Let me hit you back, Tawanna? I got something I needs to handle."

Jamaal put away his cell phone just as Fatima rolled up on him. She was mad that it had taken her almost thirty minutes of walking around to finally locate his sorry ass. There had been a lot of brothers in the area idling on street corners.

"What you doing having sex with my little sister?"

"Huh?"

"You heard what the hell I said!"

"Yo," Jamaal said as he grabbed his manhood. "Nikki wanted it, and I wanted her to have it," he sneered.

Fatima promptly looked along the ground for a brick or some other hard object to bash Jamaal's fucking brains in. Luckily for him, the corner they were standing on was surprisingly litter free.

"You're going to take care of that baby! If she keeps it!"

"Baby?"

"Did I stutter, nigga?"

"Everybody wanna pin a damn baby on me, 'cause I got paper! How you know it's mine? Ain't no telling who all Nikki's done gave the pussy to!"

"You piece of shit!"

Fatima was livid as she lunged for Jamaal. Before she could punch him she was restrained from behind. Fatima spun around and found his minion, Po-Dawg, holding her right arm.

Marion Byrd aka Po-Dawg, didn't grow up in The Dark Towers, but he hung out there so often many people thought he lived there. He was thin, tall, and very un-cute, hence his alias. In a lame attempt to stand apart from other brothers in the hood, Jamaal's underling sported an antiquated high-top fade. The twenty-one-year-old dropped out of high school several years ago to make easy money selling drugs.

Po-Dawg never strayed too far from Jamaal. He had been across the street en route to pick up a few slices of pizza, when he heard some female yelling out his homeboy's name. Po-Dawg had obediently hurried back across the street to see what the static was about.

"Take your hands off me, fool!" Fatima yelled as she struggled in Po-Dawg's grip.

"Let her go, Dawg. Fatima can fuck around and get her chips cashed in if she wanna."

Po-Dawg obeyed and shoved Jamaal's attacker away. Fatima recognized a risky situation when she saw one. She would have to confront Jamaal another time.

"Don't think your ass getting off easy!" Fatima yelled as she stalked off. "This shit ain't over, Jamaal!"

"Bitch, be gone!" Jamaal hissed.

The two men shared a laugh as they watched Fatima disappear down the street.

"Good looking out, bro."

"No worries," Po-Dawg said. "You might wanna watch your back though."

"Nigga please, Fatima's all mouth, just like the rest of these hos."

SIX

NO SHE DIDN'T!

The Harlem Bowl was one of the community's most popular hangouts. The bowling alley occupied two floors of a large commercial building and was always packed. There were several large, flat-screen, televisions around to keep people entertained while they waited for their chance to bowl.

There was a huge game room to keep youngsters occupied while parents enjoyed a break from their asses. The bar served excellent mixed drinks and beer that was always fresh and cold. However, it was the fact that The Harlem Bowl's kitchen dished out some of the tastiest buffalo wings to be found in Manhattan that Fatima and Marisol patronized the place regularly with their boyfriends.

The two couples were engaged in a heated contest. The losing team had to spring for all bowling expenses. Fatima was still upset about her earlier encounter that day with Jamaal and the bowling pins were paying for it. She glared hard at her victims before she side stepped to the right and then rapidly approached the lane with her twelve-pound ball. Fatima slung the graphite sphere with all her might. It angrily rolled in a straight path and collided with the lead pin.

"Baby, you need to be pissed off more often when we bowl!" Andre said after watching his girl throw yet another strike. It was her fifth of the match.

"I'm more annoyed having to carry your butt in this game," Fatima said as she waited for her ball to return. She had just bowled her tenth frame and had another coming.

"Show those pins a little mercy?" Marisol's boyfriend, Raphael, said.

Marisol met her beau at The Sports Expertise store on Bleeker Street during a sale on all exercise apparel. She was holding a pair of loose fit capris to her abdomen for Fatima's appraisal when a handsome Latino brother walked between them and gave his endorsement for the clothing item in Fatima's stead. Marisol was impressed with how bold and cute Raphael Oliveira was. The two exchanged numbers.

Their romance began with a thorny start. For a first date, Raphael had invited Marisol to dine with him one morning at a local café. The breakfast had been good and the conversation had been pleasant. Then the bill arrived. Checking his pockets, Raphael discovered he'd left his wallet home. He reluctantly informed his date. Marisol was about to pay for her share of the meal and cuss Raphael's sorry ass out, when he dialed his brother and plumbing business partner, Zachary, on his cell phone. Raphael explained his situation and pleaded with his brother to bring some cash.

Embarrassed, Raphael ordered more coffee as he waited for his brother to arrive. Chatting to kill time, they found that they were born three days apart. Marisol interpreted their mutual horoscope as a good omen (and the fact that he had figured out a way to pay for their meal) and decided to keep dating him.

Raphael was growing uncomfortable as he mentally added up the evening's possible expenditures. This was only the first game and the group usually bowled at least four matches. Fatima's angry ass was going to break him.

"I can't believe Nikki fucked that hood rat!" Fatima grumbled as she picked up her ball from the return belt. She assaulted her pins again. It was another strike.

"We need more beer!" Andre said with a smirk.

"We'll win the next game, Raphael," Marisol said softly.

"I hope so," Raphael answered as he pulled out his wallet and made his way to the snack bar.

Marisol's turn was next. She promptly threw two gutter balls to end the match and then sat down next to Fatima.

"That was some game, girl."

"Thanks," Fatima sighed. She was in no mood to celebrate the highest score she'd ever bowled.

"Still upset?"

"Nikki knew better. I told her a long time ago to use condoms if she became sexually active."

"Imagine the number of girls here who never got advice on birth control at all."

"No thanks, I'm already depressed."

"That's why I need you to speak at this youth conference, Fatima. I can still get you on the program."

"You want Fatima to speak, in front of a crowd?" Andre chuckled. "Good luck with that one."

"I'll do it," Fatima said softly.

Andre was stunned into silence.

"You *will*?" Marisol asked.

"Yeah, I'll do it..."

•   •   •

The ancient auditorium of W.E.B. Dubois High School seated twelve hundred students on its wooden bleachers. The place was over halfway full with teenagers who had ventured out on a cold Saturday morning for a special assembly. At the front of the auditorium, over the stage, a huge colorful banner read: First Annual Harlem Youth Conference. The majority of the audience, which was comprised mostly of Black and Latino girls, had turned up due to the promise of extra credit for attending the school sponsored event. There were also many students present who had shown up to get information about the numerous pitfalls adolescents face growing up in New York City and how to avoid them.

The din of talking, shouting, and laughing reverberated throughout the building. The five invited speakers who made up the panel, and the symposium's lone moderator, Marisol Aquino, sat onstage. They were seated behind a set of folding tables draped in the school's colors of red, black, and green. Fatima's nervousness was mounting as she sat and faced the crowd. It was a week ago that she had agreed to participate in the event. Now she wished to high heaven she could opt out of it.

The first guest to lecture was one of New York City's finest, Detective Alfred Crawley. A bald, short, spectacled fifty-three-year-old white man with a thick neck, barrel-chest, and muscular arms. Fatima wondered if the mustached lawman used illegal substances to enhance his physique. Detective Crawley got things cracking when he walked up to the lectern and told a lame joke about criminalizing all high school cafeteria food. Not one person laughed.

The cop wisely proceeded to discuss the problem of gang activity in New York City. Crawley sounded like a robot with his monotonous croaky voice. A wave of restlessness soon swept through the auditorium. Individual conversations started up as the detective warned that gangs were now recruiting younger men and women to join their violent, criminal enterprises. Fatima's mind wandered as well, and she contemplated what type of vegetable to make for dinner that evening.

The detective's speech dragged on for thirty agonizing minutes. Crawley wrapped up his tedious talk by warning students not to adhere to that asinine "Don't Snitch" code of the streets. He assured them that there was nothing wrong with people informing the police of criminal activity. After giving out a toll-free number for reporting suspected gang activity, Detective Crawley wished his audience well and sat down next to Marisol. (The officer had no clue the majority of applause that came from the audience was for him shutting the fuck up.)

Fatima was next at bat. She nervously shuffled the note cards she held while Marisol gave her a warm introduction. The last thing she wanted to do was give a damn speech. The second to last thing she wanted to do was give a boring ass speech like the one Crawley delivered.

Fatima scanned the navy blue pantsuit she wore for a fifth time since walking into the auditorium. Everything was still impeccable. She then glanced at the black pair of pumps she'd purchased while surfing online one sleepless night. They still went perfectly with her outfit.

"And now, ladies and gentleman, I'd like to introduce to you, my dear friend, Ms. Fatima Richardson!" Marisol announced. "Let's give her a big welcome to W.E.B. Dubois!"

The students obediently offered a decent reception. Fatima stood up and slowly approached the lectern.

"Kick some ass," Marisol whispered as she passed Fatima and returned to her seat. Fatima cleared her throat and gazed at the back of the building as she had been trained to do in her Speech 101 class in college. (She'd barely passed the course.)

"Good morning, folks."

Fatima received a half-hearted response from the audience. She knew then that her speech was not going to be a cakewalk. She sighed once before looking at her note cards and beginning her spiel.

"Working at the Department of Human Resources, I frequently encounter the problems many young people face today. This is because—"

Detective Crawley suddenly sneezed loudly behind her. Fatima stopped in her tracks. She quietly tucked her note cards away in the pocket of her blazer.

"To uh, be perfectly honest with you guys, I originally declined to speak at this event. But a current crisis involving a teenager close to me led me to change my mind."

Some of the students in the audience perked up when they heard Fatima mention teen drama.

"A young lady I know, who's planning to go to college next year, told me recently that she's pregnant."

At this point, all cell phones were put away and all idle chatter ceased. The audience was all ears.

"So now, this young lady's future is in jeopardy. And the really sad part of it all is that the father of her unborn child is nothing more than a chain-snatching, drug-dealing, hood rat."

Fatima heard giggles from the crowd. She was not amused.

"This ain't funny! Not in the least! A smart, promising, teenager made a stupid decision and got herself knocked-up by some wanna-be thug!"

The laughter died down. This inspired Fatima.

"I especially want to talk to you young ladies here this morning, because you're the ones who get the short end of the stick if an unplanned pregnancy occurs. To the young men here today, I hope you guys accept my apologies should I offend you with what I'm about to say. But, if the shoe fits you, wear it."

Something miraculous then transpired. The majority of young people inside that auditorium actually wanted to hear what the short, dreadlocked lady onstage had to say.

"What's going on with you young ladies today is absolute madness. Instead of dealing with a young man who has a good head on his shoulders and is trying to do something positive with his life, many of you'd rather have a thug! You want someone who hangs out on the corner all day with one hand around his genitals, and the other around a malt liquor bottle!"

A murmur swept through the girls in the crowd. The boys in the audience remained silent.

"These are the knuckleheads you girls are having babies for! You're dropping out of school! You're throwing away your future! And… while you're shoving a baby stroller around, worrying about finding money to buy infant formula, Pookie is laying up with his side chick!"

Another murmur swept through the girls in the crowd. The boys still remained silent.

"Can any of you young ladies here tell me what's so attractive about a young man walking around with his pants hanging down off his butt?"

The crowd's laughter at Fatima's question emboldened her. She stepped from behind the lectern and imitated waddling across the stage pulling up imaginary trousers. The females went berserk.

"You girls laugh now, but evidently you all must think prison fashion is cool."

The laughter in the audience died down.

"Yeah, that stupidness comes from prison, where you're not allowed to wear belts. While we're on that subject, any of you out there notice all the guys coming back from prison with their hair in cornrows? Now, I don't know exactly how they do it upstate, but here in Harlem, most people get their hair in cornrows by sitting between someone else's thighs."

Whispers of agreement swept through the girls in the audience. The boys in attendance were not feeling Fatima at all.

"And these are the same guys some of you are having unprotected sex with!"

Marisol was amazed as she watched her friend step from the lectern again and walk to the edge of the stage.

"Any of you ladies here think I'm lying about all this?"

"No!" a lone female voice yelled.

"That's funny," Fatima continued. "I could have sworn I only heard one person answer! You girls think I'm making this stuff up?"

"No!"

"Am I right about it?!"

"Yeah!"

The roaring responses further energized Fatima. Her adrenaline surged as she was finally able to express in public, some of the anger she felt, watching her people piss their lives away because of poor choices. Fatima cleared her throat and then a faint smile grew across her face.

"You girls wanna know how we can stop this madness?"

"Yeah!"

"You girls wanna know how we can end this lunacy?"

"Yeah!"

"It's easy! Just say no! If your little boyfriend, or whoever he's supposed to be, wants to have sex… don't do it!"

The girls in the audience were hysterical. The boys in the audience began to grumble.

"However ladies, if you are gonna sleep with someone… and I know some of you are doing it already, use protection! You guys can get condoms for free!"

Onstage, behind Fatima, other members of the panel squirmed in alarm at her suggestion. Even Marisol grew uneasy. Teachers seated in the audience were worried as well.

"AIDS and HIV are real, ladies! An unplanned pregnancy can ruin your future! I don't care how much your boyfriend says he wants to feel the real you? Make him use protection! Listen, if he won't get it? He don't hit it!"

Pandemonium ensued. Over two hundred female students jumped to their feet with loud applause and laughter. Back onstage, Marisol choked on the bottle of water she was sipping. Meanwhile, Fatima Richardson was in the zone.

"And it wouldn't hurt you girls to deal with a guy who has a future, okay? If he love you so much, make him prove it by getting a job! Make him prove it by going to school! Better yet, tell him to do both!"

The girls' laughter reverberated throughout the crowd. The sounds of deep voices booing were also heard.

"What can a broke, dumb, man do for you?"

"Nothing!" Dozens of girls answered.

Fatima cupped her right hand behind her ear in dramatic fashion.

"My hearing's bad! What was that answer?"

"Nothing!"

"Exactly! Ladies, if he ain't doing nothing with his life... fuck him!"

All who attended the Harlem Youth Conference that day would remember the giant gasp that came from the audience.

"No, she didn't!" one of the girls said.

"Yes, she did!" a girl sitting beside her answered.

Fatima panicked at her blunder.

"I meant, don't fuck him!"

Once more, the audience gasped. The only sound heard after that was some kid's Lil Wayne ring tone.

Fatima stood paralyzed before the students and faculty. She knew she'd fucked up. She had gotten caught up in her own emotions. Behind her, Marisol sat motionless too, frantically wondering what to do.

Before either woman could decide, seventeen-year-old Shaconda Miller, stood up and began clapping fiercely. Other female students joined her. Within a minute, every young lady inside W.E.B. Dubois High School's auditorium stood and applauded.

"I apologize for the foul language, folks," Fatima said and quickly sat her ass back down.

SEVEN
QUINN

The sheet of ice on the sidewalk was deadly. It had snowed for five hours before the sleet began. Frozen water was everywhere. Fatima deliberately stepped with care so she wouldn't bust her ass on the cold hard ground. She was burdened with four bags of provisions from the local Super Pathway.

When inclement weather threatened New York, its inhabitants scrambled to food stores to hoard bread, water, and milk. Fatima had gotten there just in time to grab the last loaf of pumpernickel and a crumpled carton of skim milk. She hated the taste of the stuff, but the shit was better than a bowl of dry cereal.

Her fifteen block trek home had been further delayed by the new Super Pathway trainee in the checkout line. While other customers sighed in exasperation, or cussed under their breath because of the slow movement of the line, Fatima remained silent. She was proud that the young sister had chosen to seek legal employment.

When Fatima neared the front of her building she slipped on a patch of ice.

Bags went one way and she went the other.

"Hey! You alright?"

Fatima heard a car door slam as she tried to get up. The embarrassment of falling in public outweighed concern with the stabbing pain coming from her left wrist. She tried to stand and felt herself sliding again when a strong arm steadied her.

"Fatima?"

"Quinn! When did you get back?"

The muscular, bald-headed brother smiled at Fatima, revealing his set of straight white teeth.

"Been home almost six months. Driving taxi for the last three."

Quinn (nee Quentin) Cumberbatch was another partially educated, young black man in New York City with a criminal record. His father was unknown to him and his teenaged mother, Bartina, had no problem bedding older men in order to pay her share of The Dark Tower's rent.

Quinn got caught up in the game quick once his mother started doing drugs. He became fascinated with the pretty shiny things the dope boys who pleasured themselves with his moms wore. After flunking the eleventh grade, Quinn started hustling full time. Bartina didn't care what her son did for a living as long as he handed her money to get high with.

Things went well for Quinn. He soon amassed pretty and shiny things of his own. He had beautiful women, plenty of bling, and two SUVs he paid for with cash. And then one day Quinn sold cocaine to an undercover NYPD officer. He'd had a negative vibe about the guy and had asked him three times if he was a cop. The dreadlocked officer had laughed each time before he assured Quinn that he was definitely not a patrolman. (He later informed him that he was a detective.) Quinn served five years in Attica before the correctional system even thought about paroling him.

"You've gotten bigger."

"I had plenty of time to work out."

"So I see."

"You gonna get yourself killed," Quinn said.

"What are you talking about?" Fatima asked as she cautiously retrieved the skim milk.

"Trying to look cute out here in flat bottomed boots."

"I don't have to try, Quinn."

"So I see."

Before Quinn became a dope boy, he played sax in his high school band. He was good. After band practice, he would sit near the playground area of The Dark Towers and blow what little Kenny G tunes he could master. Fatima's bedroom window just happened to be nearby. And she just happened to be a sucker for a major chord. Quinn noticed her often looking out of her window as he practiced.

Once he got her name and number, it didn't take long to convince fifteen-year old Fatima to sneak out her apartment one night and meet him on the roof of her building for a personal performance.

Noise from the city below them muffled shrieks of pain and pleasure as Quinn deflowered her. Fatima fell in love instantly and Quinn screwed her every chance he got. Until one night she caught him banging her neighbor's teenaged daughter in the building's stairwell. Fatima never forgave him.

"I got this," Quinn said as he picked up her scattered groceries. "Where do you live? I'll take you home in my cab."

"I live right here."

Ten minutes later, Fatima was cooling her swelling wrist with ice as Quinn put her food away.

"You lucky I drove by when I did."

"Yeah right? So, what else you do besides drive a taxi, Quinn?"

"I finished my high school education upstate. I'm starting at City College next semester. Saving money for tuition now. Yo, paying for college ain't no joke."

"Forget tuition, buying textbooks is gonna break your ass."

"For real?" Quinn asked.

"It's a big hustle. You gonna pay out the ass for a book you'll only use once, and then be lucky if you can sell it back to the bookstore for half the price you paid."

"Why is college so expensive?"

"Because being an ignorant motherfucker will cost you more."

"I really missed your refined vocabulary, Fatima."

"Fuck you, Quinn."

After putting her groceries away, Quinn scanned Fatima's apartment for traces of a male occupant. He saw none. The only item he deemed questionable was the overloaded ashtray on her kitchen table.

"Damn, you smoking like a chimney with all of these cigarette butts."

"I get enough flak from my boyfriend about smoking, Quinn. Change the subject."

"Who's the lucky fellow?" Quinn asked, after silently swearing. (Years of being out of touch with Fatima had done little to quell his affection for her. And her ass had grown juicier since the last time he'd seen it.)

"His name is Andre."

"Hope he's treating you right."

"And then some. How's the kids?"

"Can I hit you up for a smoke, first?"

Fatima furnished him a lit cigarette. Quinn inhaled the menthol deep into his lungs as he sat at the kitchen table. Fatima lit herself one.

"Georgina's driving me crazy about goddamn child support."

"Those kids didn't ask to be here, Quinn."

"I know that."

Eight-year-old Quentin Jr. and six-year-old Keshawn were Quinn's inspiration for getting his act together once paroled. He did everything for them when he was hustling in the streets and making money. Their mother, Georgina Hammonds, had to apply for welfare when he was sent away. Quinn was thus shocked to learn he owed the State of New York back child support after his release from prison.

In order to keep his driver's license and continue to drive a cab, he had to fork over every extra dime he could get to the local child support collection office. And though he paid the monthly amount the State of New York asked of him, Georgina needed more.

"Georgina don't understand how hard it is to make it out here."

"And raising two kids by herself is supposed to be easy?"

"I'm not saying that."

"Then make it plain for me."

"They got things set up for the Black Man to fail, so they can keep him locked up."

"I'm sorry, Quinn. Who are they?"

Quinn took two long drags on his cigarette and then tilted back in the chair. (Dropping science was always easier when he was relaxed.)

"*They,* is the White Man. Haven't you heard of the Prison Industrial Complex? You can't sling a dead cat here in Harlem, without hitting a motherfucker that's out on parole. Locking up niggas is a business! It's the new Jim Crow!"

Fatima sucked on her cigarette before she composed a rebuttal.

"Funny, Quinn, but I don't recall ever hearing a white man tell young brothers not to take their education seriously, and to drop out of school. And I've yet to see one white man hold a gun on a young brother and make him sell drugs, or steal what don't belong to him."

"Hold up, Fatima—"

"Don't interrupt, Quinn. Now, based on my observations, if brothers wish to avoid being caught up in the Prison Industrial Complex cycle, they need to obey the law. A good education would also help."

"That's easier said than done, Fatima. Especially with the program the White Man has in place to keep us oppressed."

"What program is this?"

"Fatima, how is it you can go to any 'urban area' in this country and find the same shit? Unhealthy fast food joints? Predatory financial institutions like pawnshops and check cashing places? Overcrowded schools? Underfunded hospitals? An aggressive police force that's quick to lock your Black Ass up, if they don't shoot it up first?" Quinn took another hit from his cigarette before he continued. "Oh yeah, and there's always a Martin Luther King Jr. Blvd running down the middle of those damn places!"

Fatima giggled at his last statement.

"That ain't funny. And it's not coincidental. That shit is designed to keep a foot on a brother's neck… nonstop."

"Because you're born in a bad environment doesn't mean you have to remain there, Quinn. A diploma, instead of a rap sheet, will get you out a hell of a lot quicker."

Quinn shook his head in disagreement and took another pull on his cigarette.

"Can we talk about something else, Fatima?"

Before Fatima could respond, her cell phone rang.

"Marisol?"

"Hey, Fatima. What are you doing?"

"Entertaining company."

"Tell Andre I said hello."

"I will next time I see him."

"Who's over there?"

"None of yours."

"You right, it's none of my business. Anyway, I've got great news!"

"What's that?" Fatima asked.

"Do you have any idea what you've started?"

"Give me the short version, Marisol?"

"That speech you gave at the youth conference last week? It worked!"

"That's nice."

"Some of my girls want to start a group!" Marisol said excitedly.

"A group of what?"

"An organization of girls who are not going to be pressured into having sex. They want to spread your message to as many other young ladies as possible."

"That is good! Glad I could be of service," Fatima said proudly.

"I'm happy to hear that, because my girls want you to lead them."

"Are you shitting me?"

"I'm serious, Fatima. We need you to do more speaking engagements."

"Marisol, the only reason I gave that talk was because I was upset about Nikki's situation. I have enough on my plate with my job and grad school. No dice."

"Please… Fatima?"

"I've gotta run. I have company."

"You know I don't give up easily, Fatima?"

"Bye, Marisol."

Fatima ended her call and looked over to find Quinn eyeing her. He smiled.

"Quinn, my man's coming through in a little bit. So, uh…"

Awkward silence and cigarette smoke mixed in the air of Fatima's apartment for a few seconds. Quinn knew a hint when he heard one.

"Yeah… I need to get back to work anyway. Listen," Quinn said as he stood up. "I'm playing down at The Razzle Dazzle with some guys for the next couple of weekends. We call ourselves 'Quality Control.' I'd love for you to come check us out."

"I'd be glad to."

"Okay, bet. Nice running into you again, Fatima."

"Same here."

Quinn knew hugging Fatima goodbye would only awaken erotic memories. He smiled, kissed her right hand, then turned and walked out of her apartment.

.　　　　.　　　　.

The mood in the office the following morning was unusually upbeat. It was payday. Inez was holding court at her cubicle once more with Jackie, Drew, and Fatima in attendance.

"I heard on the news yesterday that Oprah paid off the mortgage for this single mother in Houston," Jackie informed the group.

"She should've just gone and bought them a brand new house," Drew said.

"Yeah, right?" Fatima agreed.

"I'll sure be glad when you all quit spending Oprah's money for her," Inez mumbled as she scraped another New York Lottery scratch-off game with her lucky nickel. As usual, she didn't win a dime.

"Guess who's transferring back here from Food Stamps?" Inez asked as she threw the scratch-off game in the trash.

"Who?" Jackie asked.

"Ella Watkins."

"Oh no!" Drew said.

"What's wrong with this, Ella Watkins? She a lazy worker?" Fatima asked.

"Ella's a damn good worker. Right, Drew?"

"She knows her stuff back and forth. Just don't let her borrow anything."

"You'll never see your shit again," Jackie said. "Pens, staplers, umbrellas…"

"And especially money," Inez added.

"You guys need to stop," Fatima laughed.

"Don't say we didn't warn you," Drew said.

Fatima's desk phone rang.

She grabbed her receiver before the call switched to voice mail.

"Human Resources, Ms. Richardson speaking. Tell her I'll be right down, Consuela." Fatima then hung up and hurried to meet her next client.

.　　　　.　　　　.

Kareema Brown was a fragile looking mother who had already aged far beyond her twenty-one years. The tiny newborn she cradled in her skinny arms mewed every now and then as she and her caseworker talked. Fatima was doing her best to remain stoic as she listened to her client.

"Ms. Richardson, I need to change health plans as soon as possible. The one I have now won't pay for the new medication my doctor wants me to try."

"Why not?"

"The lady on the phone said the medication I asked for hasn't proved effective at fighting HIV yet."

At this moment, little Melvin Brown expressed discomfort again at being born two months premature. His mother kissed him on the forehead in an effort to shush him. It was too much for Fatima.

"Let me get the phone number you need to call to change plans, Ms. Brown. Be right back."

Fatima hurried out of the interviewing booth. She didn't want Kareema to notice her eyes filling with tears.

EIGHT
THE GOOD REVEREND

"So, I'll help you guys until you all find someone who can devote the proper amount of time to this endeavor. Okay?"

Fatima barely made the meeting she was speaking at on time. One of her clients came in at the last minute with a utility shut-off.

She observed the young women she stood in front of for a reaction to her statement. Marisol had assembled the group in the school chorus room two days after being informed of Fatima's change of heart. Guilt had eaten at Fatima's conscience since. The nature of her job made her well aware of the type of problems people in her community faced. She knew that there wasn't much one person could do to address these problems, many of which had been happening in Harlem for decades. The Kareema Brown episode already had her thinking about volunteering when another incident helped her to decide once and for all.

Fatima had been browsing the aisles of a black-owned bookstore on Lenox Avenue when she spied a faded poster of Eldridge Cleaver hanging on the wall behind the cash register. A caption below the picture caught her eye:

If you are not a part of the solution, you are a part of the problem.

Fatima took the words to heart. What little time she could donate to the girl's cause would be better than none.

Many of the girls sitting before Fatima did little to hide their disappointment. Especially Shaconda Miller. It was she who had approached

Ms. Aquino with the idea of having Fatima mentor their fledgling group. Shaconda was a cornrowed, lanky teenager who had just enough assets on her to keep boys interested in what she held between her legs.

Shaconda was lucky to have a good head on her shoulders and even more blessed to have both parents in the Miller household. Her mother, Janelle, and father, Robert, constantly reminded Shaconda that her body was a temple and that she should not defile it with harmful chemicals nor foreign male objects.

The teenager had seen plenty of girls fall victim to peer pressure, bring a newborn into the world sooner than planned, and begin a life of struggle.

Needless to say, it didn't take much coaxing for Shaconda to heed her parents' advice.

"But we want you," Shaconda protested.

A dozen other girls nodded in agreement.

"Sweetheart, my schedule is hectic," Fatima said. "Matter of fact, I have to go home and work on a school project when I leave here."

It really was hard for Fatima to ignore the sad faces before her. But she knew better than to commit more time than she had to give them.

"Look, I'll make sure whoever Ms. Aquino gets to help you guys will be well qualified."

"Will they give speeches as good as you?" a teenaged girl with two huge afro puffs asked.

"Probably not," Fatima teased. No one laughed.

A short heavyset teenager then stood up. "The only reason I came this evening is because the flyer said *you* was going to be in charge. If that's not the case, I'm out."

Marisol had heard enough. She spoke from her seat next to her friend.

"People, we need to be more understanding. Ms. Richardson said she'd help as much as possible. We should be thankful. She didn't have to come here at all."

The chorus room fell silent. Being the subject of debate made Fatima uneasy.

"Didn't we meet here today to discuss a plan of action?" she asked.

"Yes, we did," Marisol said.

"So, does anybody have an idea where we should begin?" Fatima asked.

"You should give a speech to all the boys around here, and cuss them out good!" a redheaded girl yelled. Everyone in the room, including Fatima, giggled.

"That's not exactly what we had in mind," Marisol said.

"Guys, what happened that day was an accident," Fatima said uneasily. "It won't happen again," she added.

.   .   .

Anyone who has ever lived in the projects will agree that there is no heat like public housing heat. All windows in the Richardson living room were pulled half way up and Fatima was still sweating in the new blouse Nikki bought her for Christmas. The family was gathered on a Saturday afternoon watching a bootleg DVD of the latest superhero action film playing in theaters.

"You heard from Jamaal lately?" Fatima asked her sister as they watched a city block in Cleveland get demolished by a pissed off space alien.

"No," Nikki answered weakly.

"And you probably won't," Fatima continued.

"I know."

"Then why in the world would you want to have his child?"

"I know you're not asking your sister to have an abortion?" Pamela said tersely.

"I'm just saying, Mama."

"You ain't saying shit! Don't start no foolishness!"

Pamela remembered a familiar discussion with her family during her first pregnancy. Things turned so sour that she and her mother had stopped talking until after Fatima's birth.

"You still plan on going to college next year?" Fatima asked.

"I want to," Nikki sighed.

"And you will," Pamela said. "Now, everybody hush and watch the damn movie."

A second later the door buzzer sounded. Fatima got up.

"Who is it?" she asked over the ancient intercom system.

"Reverend Yizar."

"What's he here for?" Fatima asked her mother after taking her hand off the intercom button.

"I asked him to come over and counsel Nikki."

"Why'd you do that?"

"Because I'm the head of this here family. Now let him in before you require medical attention."

Fatima had painfully learned years ago that Pamela never issued empty threats. Reverend Yizar was promptly buzzed into the building.

.　　　　.　　　　.

Lonnie Yizar was a fetching, silver-tongued clergyman in his mid-forties. The preacher shunned expensive suits. Jeans, dress shirts, loud ties, blazers, and comfortable leather shoes were his clothing of choice. He rarely wore jewelry, except for a small gold cross. Reverend Yizar did not believe in the idiocy of wearing shiny, costly objects around others and thus invite the risk of becoming a crime statistic.

However, he did maintain the black preacher's symbiotic relationship with General Motors. He pushed a shiny, midnight blue Cadillac Escalade that had all the trimmings. His congregation (mostly women) felt he was entitled to drive a nice whip, so Reverend Yizar didn't argue one bit when he received the keys and a gas card from his faithful flock last Christmas.

"Hello, Fatima," Reverend Yizar said cordially when she opened the door and allowed him to enter.

"Hi, Reverend," Fatima replied nonchalantly.

"How come I haven't seen you at service lately?"

(Fatima had joined the ever-growing flock of St. Mattress Baptist, but it was none of the pastor's business if she chose to sleep late on Sunday mornings.)

"I've... been busy with work, and school."

"You too busy for the Lord?"

"He knows my heart," Fatima answered.

"That's still no excuse," Reverend Yizar continued.

"Tell you what, Rev," Fatima began—

"You know better than to speak like that!" Pamela interrupted.

"It's alright, Sister Richardson," Reverend Yizar said. He smiled at Fatima again and walked over to the couch.

"How are you feeling, Nikki?"

"I'm okay, sir."

"And you, Sister Richardson?" Reverend Yizar asked this as he sat in Fatima's former spot, next to her mother.

"I'm well, Pastor. Thanks for coming."

"Don't mention it. I'm supposed to keep watch over my congregation."

"Can I get you anything to snack on, Reverend?" Fatima's mother asked.

"Sure, if you don't mind?"

"I have a sweet potato pie in the fridge."

"That's fine, Sister Richardson."

After her mother stood and went into the kitchen, Fatima took a seat next to the pastor.

"So, Reverend, you still haven't found yourself another spouse?"

"I'm afraid not, Fatima. I'm still looking."

"I hear there's some good prospects in the women's choir."

(Rumor had it that the pastor had run through that group like a buzz saw.)

"Any gossip you hear about me and the women's choir of Greater Harlem Baptist is a lie," Reverend Yizar replied.

Nikki sensed her sister was up to no good.

"I have to go check on something," she announced to no one in particular and quickly left the room. Fatima went back on offense.

"I'm not one to gossip, but I've heard since organist Denise Greene's husband's been locked up, she's doing solos for somebody else."

(Rumor also had it that Reverend Yizar had been running through Denise way before he started in on the women's choir.)

"Sister Greene is a saint! The devil's always busy," Reverend Yizar said uneasily.

"Yeah, right?" Fatima concurred.

"What are you two talking about?" Pamela asked as she walked in with a slice of pie for Reverend Yizar.

"Mrs. Greene's organ," Fatima said.

Pamela glared at her daughter as she handed the pastor the plate. She'd also heard gossip about that tramp and sensed what Fatima was up to.

"Thanks, this looks good, Sister Richardson."

"I made the crust from scratch, Reverend."

"Just the way I like it," Reverend Yizar mumbled after shoving pie into his mouth. "You want me to counsel Nikki?" he asked a few seconds later as he handed Pamela his empty plate.

"Would you?"

"Sure."

"Nikki!" Pamela yelled.

Nikki reluctantly returned to the living room.

"Yes?"

"Sit."

She did as her mother ordered. Reverend Yizar swallowed hard and then leaned forward in his seat.

"I was surprised when your mother told me of your situation, Nikki. You have always been one of our brightest Sunday school students."

Nikki sat quietly.

"If anything, I thought it would have been..." Reverend Yizar abruptly stopped.

"You thought it would have been, who?" Fatima snapped.

"Apologize," Pamela said through gritted teeth.

"Sorry," Fatima said as she glared at the pastor.

"Apology accepted," Reverend Yizar said and smiled at Fatima. "What I was going to say, Nikki, was that if anything, I thought it would have been easy for you to come to your mother, or me, to help you avoid temptation of the flesh."

"I should have," Nikki said softly.

"Well, we all fall short of the glory. Have you asked the Lord for forgiveness?"

"Yes, sir."

"Good. Have you informed your partner in sin of his pending child?"

Fatima felt herself grow nauseous.

"Reverend Yizar?" she said pleasantly.

The pastor ignored her.

"Does your boyfriend know he's going to be a father?" he repeated to Nikki.

"Pastor?" Fatima said and then stood up.

"Yes?"

"How long you've been a minister?"

"Almost twenty years," Reverend Yizar said defensively.

"You quote scripture?" Fatima asked as she retrieved her coat from the closet.

"Infallibly."

"You remember what Christ said in St. Luke, Chapter Twelve, verse one?"

"I do," Reverend Yizar answered with a smug look. "Beware ye of the leaven of the Pharisees, which is hypocrisy."

Pamela was too pissed to yell at her eldest daughter without cussing.

"See you guys later," Fatima said and quickly exited the apartment.

·　　　　·　　　　·

Nikki was forced to sit through an hour long, monotonous lecture on the perils of sexual urges. When Reverend Yizar finally ran out of shit to say, Pamela granted her permission to leave. Nikki put her winter coat on and went straight to Melody's apartment and banged on the door. Melody opened it seconds later. She was dressed in a large T-shirt, a pair of jeans and flip-flops.

"What happened to you, Nikki?"

"My moms had our pastor come over and warn me to stop fucking."

"Really?"

"Really."

"You look stressed."

"I am. Wanna go see a movie?"

"I'll go change… have a seat."

Nikki did as instructed and plopped down on the couch. She then looked around the room. The same pictures of Melody in her formative years were displayed on a shabby bookcase that held more photos and plants than novels. The same dusty basketball trophies Melody was awarded in middle school sat on the same dusty corner shelf. The same old photo of Melody's mother, Alfreda, in the arms of the man Nikki presumed to be Melody's father, hung in a corner above a cheap flat screen television. The gruesome couple wasn't much to look at.

Even though Nikki had seen the photo countless times, she never bothered to confirm that the man with Melody's mom was indeed

Melody's dad. His jacked-up mug and wide, smashed nose betrayed the lineage. As Nikki looked at the picture, it dawned on her that Melody had never mentioned anything about her father.

Most of Nikki's friends lived in single-parent households and they usually commented on their absent parent during special occasions, such as birthdays or holidays. Either they bragged about something the missing parent gave or did for them, or they cussed the missing parent out for not being worth shit. Melody had done neither.

She returned to the room a few minutes later wearing the same T-shirt and jeans. Only now she wore a pair of beige chukka boots and her hair was covered with a Yankees cap. Nikki pointed up at the photograph.

"Is that your dad?"

Melody didn't bother to look at the picture. She headed straight to the closet and opened the door.

"Yeah," she said as she grabbed a coat.

"He here in New York?"

"You ready to bounce?" Melody asked. She closed the closet and then opened the front door. Nikki took the hint and quietly followed her out the apartment.

.   .   .

The cold weather did nothing to slow the city's hidden economy. Vendors, hawking everything from women's underwear to classic soul CDs, operated along 125th Street. The girls chatted as they ambled down the street and dodged native pedestrians and European tourists.

"You confront Chelsea about putting your business out in the street?"

"No."

"What you waiting for?"

Before Nikki could respond, three sharp beeps from a double parked Jeep caught their attention. They watched the window roll down a little.

"Melody!"

"Who's that?" Nikki asked.

"Not sure," Melody answered with a puzzled expression.

"Sounds like he knows you."

The Jeep's horn beeped again and the window rolled halfway down.

"Melody! Let me holler at you!"

Glad for the attention, Melody strutted over to the Jeep. As she approached the vehicle, she recognized Ishmael Paxton behind the wheel.

The two had met three years earlier at a house party in Washington Heights. Melody was there with a few of her schoolmates. Ishmael was there because he was friends with the young lady hired to deejay the event. At the time, he was an eighteen-year-old line cook at a popular buffet restaurant in Harlem.

Already tipsy and horny that night, Ishmael didn't have the time nor desire to play games with the fine girls in attendance. He had to work the next morning and needed to let off some steam before clocking back in at the job. The son of an Army veteran, he had been schooled by his father on the secret to picking up women at social events. It was an old military maxim: *Start ugly early... and avoid the rush.*

Ishmael's father had astutely drilled into him the lunacy of wasting breath, time, and money, buying drinks, and food for the cutest girls at clubs, bars, and similar venues. When all your begging and pleading was done, you were usually out of luck. And money. It was far better to find an unattractive female to pick up and take home from the jump and avoid having to compete with other guys trying to "snatch and grab" leftover girls at the end of the night.

When Ishmael spied Melody standing against a wall by herself, watching her friends grooving on the cramped dance floor, he glided over with a megawatt smile and struck up a conversation. Ishmael showed interest in everything Melody mentioned about herself. Her pleasant-sounding name. The subpar school she attended. Her affection for cat videos.

Melody took Ishmael's apparent interest in her as genuine and fell for him quicker than the price of chocolate bunnies after Easter. She was desperate for a boyfriend so she sought to please whatever guy she could to obtain that objective. It was not hard for Ishmael to convince her to leave the party with him. It also was not that difficult to get Melody to give him some head later that night behind his apartment building.

The two kept in touch mostly via text message after that. When they did meet face to face, Ishmael was always pressed for time. He was also always trying to press Melody's shoulders down toward the floor and make her kneel. Whenever he tired of that, he would throw her ankles around his neck instead. Melody finally realized Ismael wasn't about shit and moved on. But now he was behind the wheel of a new whip.

"This you?" she asked.

"Got it a few weeks ago," Ishmael said. "After I started working maintenance for the New York City Housing Authority."

"Congratulations."

In full pimp mode, Ishmael leaned back and coolly pulled down on his skull cap, covering more of his braided hair.

"Take a ride with me."

Melody smiled and leaned into the warm Jeep. It had that new car smell she loved.

"Where to?" she asked.

"I was thinking we get a bite to eat somewhere and then cruise to the South Bronx. Maybe chill around Hunt's Point for a little…"

"Sounds good, but I'm going to the movies with my girl."

"Ditch her. I haven't seen you in a minute. We should spend some time together."

"Can we eat at that diner on Southern Boulevard?"

"If it's not too crowded… sure."

"Give me a minute…"

Melody walked back over to Nikki with a grin on her face.

"Who's that cat?" Nikki asked.

"My friend, Ishmael."

"He looks kind of thuggish."

"He alright. He wants to take me to a restaurant," Melody said proudly. "Can I take a raincheck on the movie?"

"You sure this guy's okay, Melody?"

"I've hung out with him before."

Nikki knew then that her friend was going off to get screwed. She was in no condition to be judgmental, so she forced a smile and kept quiet. The Jeep's horn sounded once more.

"I'll call you later," Melody said as she glanced back to Ishmael and smiled.

"Melody?"

"Yeah?"

"Be safe."

"No doubt."

NINE

CAN I ASK YOU GIRLS A QUESTION?

The phone on her desk was ringing off the hook but Fatima paid it no mind. She had a mound of paperwork to get done and a stack of mail to read. She didn't believe in working late like some coworkers did. There was too much grad school work to do, and more importantly, she was not compensated for overtime.

"Who the hell's calling?" Fatima complained as she scrutinized documents of a new case she received.

"Answer the phone and find out," Inez mumbled.

Fatima didn't respond. She had long ago learned the art of ignoring folks in the workplace. The ringing stopped. And then started again.

"Dammit!" Fatima said as she angrily snatched the receiver off the hook. "Human Resources, how may I help you?" she asked pleasantly. "You're here? I'll be down in a few minutes."

"Who was it?" Inez asked.

"Yetta Middleton. She's here with some pay stubs."

"Somebody gave that evil thang a job again?"

"Hopefully, she can keep this one."

"Shit… you'll quit smoking first," Inez chuckled. Fatima ignored her coworker once more and went to see her client.

·   ·   ·

Yetta Middleton was an unhappy woman. The twenty-seven-year-old welfare recipient was angry at the hand life had dealt her. Back in the day when she was the hottest thing on Putnam Avenue between Bedford and Nostrand, all the rutting boys in her Brooklyn neighborhood used to sweat her from sun up to sun down. Yetta couldn't venture far from home without getting wolf-whistles, hard stares, or graphic sexual gestures.

It was too much for the voluptuous sixteen-year-old to handle. Regrettably, she allowed nineteen-year-old Calvin Crawford to whisper in her ear one time too many and Yetta fell in love. She started sexing him on the regular. A pregnancy followed. She became ashamed to walk the halls of her high school with a protruding belly and before long quit attending classes. Yetta didn't lament that decision much at the time, because it gave her an opportunity to be around Calvin more. She soon learned that the only time he didn't lie to her was when he was fast asleep.

Tim Bartley replaced Calvin Crawford. And Pernell Gary then replaced Tim Bartley. These men also fathered a child with Yetta, and soon her glory days were done. The ninety pounds she accumulated during her childbearing went to the wrong places on her once-banging body. Men no longer hungered for her as before and it became hard for Ms. Middleton to find a serious suitor once they found out she had three kids and was on public assistance.

With a subpar education, Yetta could only find low-paying jobs in the customer service field. These jobs never lasted long. It was hard to deal with nasty attitudes when yours was worse. Monday mornings were usually when Yetta got fired for cursing out customers.

Sitting across from Fatima with her youngest child, Troy, in her arms, Ms. Middleton wore a frown as she presented copies of her latest pay stubs.

"How often do you get paid?"

"Every two weeks."

"Who's doing your childcare?"

"My mom."

"Did she fill out a childcare provider form?"

"Got it right here," Yetta said as she placed little Troy on the seat next to her.

The child quickly slid out of his chair and made a crawl for freedom while his mother rummaged her pocketbook for paperwork.

"Get back here!" Yetta growled after finding what she was looking for. She handed the paper to Fatima. Meanwhile, her son sped across the floor.

"I'll do a budget and let you know what the changes in your benefits will be by tomorrow."

"You not gonna cut my food stamps that much, are you?"

"It depends on the amount of money you make, Ms. Middleton. You already know that."

"Me and my kids need to eat, Ms. Richardson."

"I understand."

"When will my moms get her check for babysitting?"

"I can let you know that tomorrow as well."

Troy reached the perimeter of the cubicle and made a sharp left.

"You might want to go after your son," Fatima said nonchalantly.

"Troy!" Yetta yelled as she jumped up and grabbed her belongings. She then went in pursuit of her child.

As Fatima collected her paperwork, a loud smack informed her that Troy had been apprehended. Crying ensued.

"Hush that noise, before I give your ass something to really cry about!" Yetta yelled. Fatima shook her head in dismay as she walked past mother and child on her way back upstairs.

·   ·   ·

"You young ladies need to be wise, because if you're not, you may regret it!"

It was raining cats and dogs outside the Adam Clayton Powell State Office Building. Fatima didn't think many people would turn up to hear her speak due to the inclement March weather, but a sizable crowd was assembled. Marisol and her group had done a good job advertising the event.

"When a guy's hormones are raging, his sole purpose at that moment is to tell you whatever it takes for you to slide your panties down."

Several members of the audience gasped.

"Am I being too real? Good! Let me break this scenario down to you ladies further, because I see it all the time at my job. You're walking around high school and you think you got it going on!"

Fatima's statement made the majority of the audience chuckle.

"Because that's what Kevon, Raheim, or whoever, have all been whispering in your ear."

The audience giggled again.

"Lo and behold, you slip up, have a baby, and gain a little weight. But then you get souped up by another guy buzzing the same crap in your ear, have a second child, and gain more weight. Now what happens?"

Fatima paused to let three late attendees shuffle to their seats.

"What happens is you don't get sweated that much now, because guys think you're a bit plump. Plus, you've got two mouths to feed in addition to your own. It's gonna be hard for you to find a guy who'll get serious with you. And why would he? He's gonna want what you've gave away free to everybody else."

Sporadic laughter echoed through the audience.

"That wasn't meant to be funny."

The laughter stopped.

"There's no humor in being the girl guys won't marry because she already comes with a family…"

Fatima's audience was silent.

"Can I ask you girls a question?"

"Yes," Shaconda answered. She was in the front row with two friends she had convinced to attend.

"Anyone here today hoping to have a hard life in their future? Let me see your hands?"

Fatima scanned the crowd and nodded in approval when no hands were raised.

"Then why are so many of you getting pregnant and dropping out of school?"

No one answered.

"Why are so many of you hooking up with the wrong type of young men?"

Still no responses.

"Maybe you don't know how to pick out a good man? Should I tell you all what to look for?"

"Yes," Shaconda said.

"A good man is safe. He won't have a problem with wearing a condom."

"Yes," Shaconda continued.

"A good man finishes school. He knows the importance of education."

"Yeah!" Shaconda hollered.

Her enthusiasm induced others near her to also yell. Fatima became inspired and her southern roots surfaced. She began to gesticulate like an old Baptist preacher as she whipped her flock into frenzy.

"A good man has a legal job! He's not out there hustling drugs!"

"Yeah!" more girls yelled.

"And a good man wears a belt! He knows it's ludicrous to walk down the street showing everybody his damn drawers!"

Pandemonium broke out as everyone cracked up with laughter.

"Should I tell you all about a no good man?"

"Please!" one of Shaconda's friends yelled.

"A no-good man will worry more about his pit bull than you."

"Yeah!"

"A no-good man would rather stand on a corner and do nothing, instead of stand in line to register for school, or apply for a job!"

"Yeah!"

"A no-good man won't think twice about referring to you as a female dog when he's mad.

If he ever does, tell him to go straight to hell!"

Even the reserved teens in the crowd gave high-fives and laughed along.

Standing in the back of the room, Marisol watched in awe. It was sinful for Fatima's ability to inspire others to remain hidden, she thought. The girl has a gift. And her message desperately needs to be heard. Marisol decided then and there that she would help Fatima spread the gospel.

.   .   .

That night Fatima and Marisol were sitting in a booth at the Pizza Shed on Broadway and West 155th Street. The cramped eatery was renowned for its thigh-fattening, delicious, brick-oven cooked pizza. A large, loaded pie sat before them.

"How do you know exactly what to say to reach people when you speak?" Marisol asked.

"I'm not sure. The right words just pop up inside my head. As well as a few wrong ones."

"We do have to work on your swearing problem, Fatima."

"Fuck you."

Fatima used her finger to flick olives off her slice while Marisol scraped chunks of unwanted pineapple from hers with a fork.

"You don't know how great you did tonight. You have so much potential."

"What I do know is that I have to get home and study for Professor Turner's class. Microeconomics ain't no joke. Why'd you order this big ass pie?"

"Because you always rave about how good the pizza here is."

"You're up to no good."

"What are you talking about?" Marisol asked innocently.

"Cut the bullshit," Fatima mumbled, her mouth full of pizza. She washed it down with a gulp of water. "You always feed me my favorite foods before begging me for something. If you were a guy, we'd have three kids by now."

"Very funny, Fatima—"

Before Marisol could finish, her cell phone chimed.

"Hey, Boo…"

Her greeting informed Fatima it was Raphael.

"You can't make it tonight?"

Fatima removed olives from another slice as Marisol continued her call.

"If he needs help, then go help," she sighed. "Call me later on." Marisol returned her phone to her purse.

"Raphael?"

"He has to help his brother install a stand-up shower in Jackson Heights."

"Can't be mad at a guy for putting in overtime."

"That's true."

"Now, back to us. What do you want, Marisol?"

"You need more exposure."

"I need a suntan?"

"Don't get smart! I'm talking about your message, Fatima."

"Did you *not* hear me mention how hard my microeconomics class is?"

"I heard, but—"

"But, my ass!" Fatima said. "I'm helping these young ladies as much as I can. However, I do need to pass these courses I'm paying for."

"You can do both."

"I'm flattered you have that much confidence in me."

"You have a gift."

"I have student loans," Fatima mumbled between bites of pizza.

"What if we get a little coverage for you in the press?"

"What if we get someone who has more time to devote to this endeavor?"

"You're being impossible."

"I'm being real. I've gotta finish my degree and find a better job. You think I wanna work at social services forever?"

"I know you hate your job."

"Then find somebody else to help you, Marisol."

Marisol sighed in defeat and then grabbed another slice of pizza.

TEN
HOW LONG HAVE YOU BEEN SMOKING?

Traffic along East Fourth Street was unusually hectic for a Thursday night.

"Is this it?" Andre asked sarcastically as he stopped his black Lexus in front of a path of purple carpet that guided patrons into a building.

"That's what the flashing sign on the roof says," Fatima said with a smile.

The Razzle Dazzle jazz club was aptly named. Besides the huge blinking sign on top of the ornate white structure, purple pulsating lights snaked around four columns that supported the long purple awning over the entrance.

Fatima was not in the mood for Andre's funky attitude. He'd been more than willing to drive her to see Quality Control's performance until she casually mentioned on the way there that she used to date the horn player. (Some things are indeed better left unsaid.)

"Hunting for a space to park is going to be fun," Andre muttered. He hated driving in Lower Manhattan. The whole area was bait for parking tickets. A honk from a car horn encouraged Andre to keep moving.

"You should get out, Fatima."

"No, I'll walk back with you."

They located a parking spot eight blocks away. As they approached the building, Fatima looked up and still saw traces of a scowl on her boyfriend's face.

"It was a long time ago, Andre."

"It wasn't *that* long ago."

"I'm only here to lend Quinn moral support."

"He know that?"

"Of course."

A cold breeze ripped through the streets and Fatima hugged her man as they entered the jazz club.

Chairs, tables, and patrons were crammed tight in order to maximize seating. And profits. The brick walls of the club were decorated with astonishing murals of jazz artists playing to admiring crowds.

Fatima noticed several patrons vaping on electronic cigarettes due to New York City's harsh smoking restrictions. She needed the real thing. She reached into her purse for her smokes. They weren't there. Neither was her lighter.

"Looking for these?" Andre asked. He revealed the coveted items in his palm.

"Don't ever go through my purse again, Mr. Ellison."

"I'm trying to get you to stop smoking, Fatima."

"Hand them over."

"I don't think so."

"Andre, you must be off your meds if you—"

Before Fatima could finish, The Razzle Dazzle's ancient hostess appeared. She'd had every cosmetic trick known to man down, in a futile attempt to camouflage her age. Her black, curly wig was slightly tilted to one side, exposing traces of gray naps in the opposite corner. The light foundation she wore on her face was applied thickly and haphazardly, ironically giving the woman a deathly pallor. The disheveled navy blue dress she wore was in need of a thorough dry-cleaning.

It was obvious to Andre the old woman was working because she had to, not because she wanted to.

"Table for two?" she asked with a stained smile.

"Yes," Andre answered.

The couple was led to the back of the club to a small table near the small bar.

"Here you go," the hostess said with a practiced grin.

"And here you go," Andre said as he tipped her a ten-dollar bill.

"Thank you, son."

Andre was treated to another smile before she headed off to seat more guests. It took a few seconds before the couple could maneuver their way into the tiny wicker back chairs. Once seated, Fatima scoped out the joint.

"Will you look at that mess there?"

"Where?"

Fatima indicated the direction with her pinky. Andre slowly turned his head. Sitting on one of the barstools near them was a healthy-sized young lady. She was donned in a red, satin dress that snuggly clung to her and her large breasts.

"Hope she don't sneeze in that tight shit."

"Why can't black women give each other compliments? I think she looks sexy."

Fatima watched the young lady empty her glass and then spin around on her stool with her legs open.

"Looks like Big Sexy don't wear no drawers," she said nonchalantly. "I wish you would," she hissed at Andre when he attempted to look back again.

He grinned and surveyed the stage instead.

"Which one up there is homeboy?"

"Quinn's playing the sax."

Up on stage, all four young members of Quality Control had the same objectives. That was to produce harmonious, crisp notes, give the audience their money's worth, and find female companionship after the gig.

Black Mack Mallory, the aptly named drummer, kept perfect time as he eyed a table of five lovely females located to his left. Keenan Evans, the piano player, was checking out the same cute quintet as he banged out chords. Tyrell Peterson, the rhythm guitarist, strummed gingerly on his instrument while also focused on the pretty young things.

Quinn, on the other hand, was scanning the place for Fatima as he blew smooth melodies through his horn. She had sent a text message earlier, saying she would be in attendance. Quinn had even worn his lucky blue blazer for the night's performance in the hopes of rekindling their romance. Carnal thoughts involving Fatima had occupied his mind ever since he'd run into her. Finally, Quinn spied Fatima sitting with some

Negro who had to be Andre. His heart sank as he glanced at the two making eyes at each other as they listened to *his* music.

"One more," he called loudly to his band mates as they enjoyed the energetic applause from the crowd after finishing their last song.

"That was the final song for this set!" Black Mack protested. "I gotta piss!"

"Same here," Keenan added.

"One more. It won't take long," Quinn promised. He then made sure the wireless microphone attached to the bell of his horn was secure. "Next round of drinks are on me."

"What song?" Black Mack asked.

"Just My Imagination…"

"Oh, hell! Where she at?" Keenan asked.

"Can't believe this motherfucker's in love again," Black Mack groaned.

"We playing, or what?" Quinn asked.

"Let's get this over with," Tyrell sighed. He then skillfully began plucking the intro to the song. Black Mack kept time along with him and Keenan fell in place on the piano. Then, it was up to Quinn to do his thing.

His sax soulfully wailed away the first notes of the song, generating a gleeful cry of recognition from the audience. Standing at the edge of the stage, Quinn began bending notes smoothly on his horn before doing some vibrato. (It had taken some time to master this technique while playing upstate in the prison band.) Quinn's performance elicited more delight from the crowd. He was killing it.

Then, to the disbelief of his band mates, Quinn hopped off the left side of the stage and slowly walked over to the table of five women. They began salivating over the notes he fed them. One of the women even grabbed the sleeve to Quinn's lucky blazer to try to prevent him from walking away, but Quinn was on a mission.

He walked toward a table where an older couple sat with their arms around each other. Quinn bent down in front of the couple and blew tones so lovely that tears of joy welled up in the woman's eyes. Her partner hugged her tighter. The man smiled at Quinn and shook his hand in appreciation. The saxophone player then moved on.

Back onstage, Black Mack and the rest of Quality Control began playing even more precisely as they watched Quinn. His performance was definitely ensuring them some ass for the night. The women at the table to their left were now staring at the band with hungry eyes. Quinn methodically worked his way through the crowd and stopped where Fatima and Andre sat. Quinn then emptied his diaphragm, as well as his heart, as he produced perfect notes from his horn.

Fatima was mesmerized as she watched her first lover play. Memories of the two of them up on the roof of The Dark Towers returned. A huge smile appeared on her face.

Andre was pissed. The urge to jump up and ram Quinn's instrument down his fucking throat grew stronger with each note the bastard played. Fatima was oblivious to her boyfriend's displeasure because her eyes were closed as she enjoyed the music.

With his mission accomplished, Quinn returned to the stage and the band wrapped their song up to a thunderous applause. He was thrilled to see Fatima standing with others and cheering loudly. Andre sat there looking glum.

"Thank you!" Quinn yelled. Still smiling, he blew into his horn and made the instrument "laugh." Andre knew that special effect was meant for him.

Black Mack and Keenan dashed to the facilities as Quinn walked to the back of the club to order his band their drinks. On the way he made a stop at Fatima's table.

"So, Fatima, what you think?"

"You guys are off the chain!"

"I've heard better in The Village," Andre countered.

"That's your opinion, brother."

"I'm not your brother."

"Would you two like a formal introduction?" Fatima asked sarcastically.

"I got this, baby." Andre said as he stood up. "I'm Andre Ellison, Fatima's boyfriend."

"Quinn Cumberbatch. I'm a *very* good friend of hers."

"Funny, I haven't heard Fatima mention anything about you until recently. Did you live elsewhere?"

Quinn smiled at Andre's thin reference to his incarceration. He resisted the urge to knock his ass out. The fool was not worth violating parole over.

"Enjoy the rest of the show, Fatima."

Quinn headed outside and lit a cigarette instead of getting his band's drinks. He needed to calm his nerves and stay focused on his gig.

"Can I get a pull?"

He turned around and found Fatima behind him.

"Sure," Quinn answered and held his cigarette to her.

"Andre confiscated my pack," Fatima said and promptly took a hit.

"How did you meet that clown?"

Fatima laughed as she exhaled smoke.

"What's funny?" Quinn asked with a smile.

"Andre asked the same question about you a minute ago," she said.

Quinn's smile faded. He watched Fatima place his cigarette between her lips again. It brought back pleasant memories.

"Yo, Fatima, why don't we get together sometime?"

"Save your breath, Quinn. Andre's good to me. I am not fucking that up."

"I didn't mean it like that."

"Well, I did," Fatima said as she handed him back his cigarette. "Thanks for the smoke," she said before walking back into The Razzle Dazzle. Quinn took a long pull from his cigarette and hung his head.

.   .   .

When Andre got Fatima butt naked in her bed later that night, he laid pipe like a master plumber. No mercy was shown as he slid in and out of her fast and furiously. Fatima, sopping wet, yet still on fire inside, greeted his penetrations with little resistance.

"Damn! You... should... be jealous more often!" Fatima grunted as she absorbed Andre's thrusts. She was about to grunt something else when her head slammed into the headboard.

This nigga's trying to kill me! Fatima thought as she ignored her aching skull. She held onto Andre's back for dear life. Joy and pain overloaded the synapses in her brain as he continued his loving assault. A rapturous moan escaped Fatima's lips as her insides began to sizzle from the heat

Andre's manhood was generating. She felt herself grow dizzier with every thrust he made.

"I can screw way better than that jailbird! Got that?" Andre growled.

"I'm getting it!" Fatima grunted.

"I'm the only motherfucker you want hitting this! Feel me?"

"I feel you!"

It was times like this when Fatima could *almost* understand how so many women unwisely became impregnated. The frenzy from the friction she received was driving her insane. All she cared about at that moment was the sweet release that was due. Hopefully the condom Andre wore didn't break. He continued his hard, steady rhythm for another twenty minutes and Fatima finally reached her boiling point. She was about to let loose steam when her cell phone interrupted her flow.

"Who's that?" Andre asked suspiciously.

"Damn… if I… know…"

Her cell phone continued to ring. It stopped for a few seconds and began ringing again.

"You want to answer?"

"Fuck… them."

The phone stopped ringing. A few seconds later it beeped to let Fatima know she had a message. Her landline rang next.

"Somebody's trying bad to reach you. Go ahead and answer," Andre said as he pulled out of Fatima.

She slowly crawled across her bed and picked up her cordless phone.

"Hello?"

"You in bed yet?"

"What is it, Marisol?"

Fatima shot Andre a glare that made him regret doubting her faithfulness.

"I just came up with a great idea, Fatima."

"You what?"

"We need to get you on television."

"I thought this was an emergency!"

"This is important."

"Marisol, if you ever call me this late again over some bullshit, I'm gonna block your number!" Fatima slammed the phone back in its cradle.

"What she want?" Andre asked gently. He hated to let a good erection go to waste and hoped Fatima would let him finish what he started.

"Nothing important," Fatima said as she maneuvered back underneath him.

"Sorry," Andre said.

"For what? Questioning my commitment to you?"

"Yeah," Andre answered weakly.

"Listen, as long as you don't fuck up, I'm in this for the long haul."

"That's all I needed to hear."

The two kissed briefly before Andre reentered Fatima and resumed their voyage to ecstasy.

.   .   .

Fatima was all smiles as she limped into the office the next day. She stopped by Inez's cubicle and found her in conversation with a woman she'd never seen before. The svelte, silver-haired lady leaned on a partition of Inez's workspace as the two talked. After cackling for a few seconds, Inez looked up and saw she had more company.

"Morning, Fatima."

"Morning, Inez."

"Introduce yourself to your new coworker, Ella Watkins."

"Hi, I'm Fatima Richardson."

"Nice to meet you, Fatima," Ella said as she turned around.

"So, you and Inez worked together in the past?"

"We go way back. That's why we're such good friends."

"Inez recently expressed her feelings about you to me," Fatima said with a grin.

"What she say?"

"Go on, tell her what you told me," Fatima urged Inez.

"I forgot," Inez said gruffly, hoping Fatima would shut the hell up.

"If I remember correctly, you said—"

"Ella, did I tell you Fatima's trying to quit smoking?" Inez said quickly.

"Great!" Ella exclaimed. Her face lit up. "I was a heavy smoker. Right, Inez?"

"Yep. And everybody here was so happy when you stopped buying them things."

"Gave it up almost two years ago. I'll be glad to help you quit, Fatima."

"Uh, okay…"

"How long have you been smoking?" Ella asked.

"Almost ten years," Inez said before Fatima could open her mouth.

"That's way too long. We need to start at once! I can show you some websites with tips for smoking cessation. When do you go to lunch?"

It was hard for Fatima to reply as she watched Inez silently laughing at her behind Ella's back.

"I usually go at noon, but I may have to run out to the bank."

"Try to get back in time for us to talk?" Ella asked.

"We'll see," Fatima said weakly.

"I've got to get back upstairs. See you later, Fatima. You too, Inez."

As soon as Ella was out of earshot, Inez continued…

"Hope she hits you up for every cent you got."

"I'm not speaking to you!"

Inez chuckled. "Don't you wanna quit smoking?"

Fatima started to walk away.

"Fatima, wait!"

"What?"

"You've got the glow," Inez observed.

"The glow?" Fatima asked.

"The 'good dick' glow. Did you and Andre do it last night?"

"Mind your business."

"I'd rather mind yours."

"Inez?"

"Yes?"

"Please seek professional help?"

ELEVEN
YOUR LOVE IS KING

Both sides of the intersection of Third Avenue and 116th Street were jammed with Saturday morning shoppers hunting for bargains. Banners in storefront windows and flyers littering sidewalks advertised the deals to be had. The vast selection of foreign-made merchandise for sale in Harlem seemed endless.

The hottest electronic gaming devices that kids craved, the latest prepaid cellular phones to hit the market, the most recent pairs of overpriced sneakers, and the newest collection of corporate-logo-ed clothing could all be had, even if you couldn't afford it. High-interest charge card applications awaited low-income customers near store cash registers.

Fatima and Nikki made slow progress against the throng of fellow shoppers. Fatima's impatience was rising. She was already pissed that she'd allowed her mother to cajole her into chauffeuring Nikki around town to buy household items when she needed to be home studying for an exam.

"Look at these damn clowns," Fatima hissed. Nikki looked up and saw four black teens horsing around in front of them. The sisters heard the word "nigga" uttered by the boys a half dozen times as they neared them.

"No respect for your own people!" Fatima mumbled loudly as she and Nikki walked around the group. One of the youngsters heard what she said and started to reply… until he saw the foul expression on Fatima's face. He chose to let the shit slide.

"It's a disgrace how the word "nigga" is used by everybody these days!"

"Fatima, you can leave if you want. I can catch a cab back when I'm done."

"Mama asked me to take you shopping, so that's what I'm doing."

"Can you do it without the social commentaries?"

"You trying to be funny?"

"In the last ten minutes, I've heard your negative remarks about those boys we just passed using the word 'nigga,' the irony of black people paying to have names tattooed on them after the era of slavery, and the vulgarity of the rap lyrics coming from that loud SUV that drove by us."

"And?" Fatima asked with an edge in her voice.

Nikki dropped the subject. She then stopped to examine a collection of fancy three-wheeled strollers with extra-wide tires chained together near the entrance of a store. The one with the adjustable sun canopy and Burberry pattern caught her eye.

"Isn't this nice?" she asked.

Fatima lit up a cigarette as she walked closer to inspect the stroller.

"What are those red things at the bottom, near the wheels?"

"Shock-absorbers," Nikki answered.

"How many miles to the gallon this thing gets?"

"You know it don't run on gas."

"It should, for the money they asking for this shit."

"The strollers I saw on the Internet cost way more."

"I'll get a stroller for your baby."

"Thanks, Fatima!"

"But it won't be one I have to finance."

"That's cool."

The sisters began to weave their way through the heavy pedestrian traffic.

"And while we're on the subject of your baby, you'd better not give that child one of those fucked up, ghetto names nobody can pronounce, Nikki."

"I won't."

"The black community has enough phonetically-challenged kids running around already."

Nikki didn't hear Fatima's last response. She was too busy looking at Chelsea approaching. She was holding a large shopping bag in one hand and her cell phone in the other. The girls had rarely spoken since word got out about the pregnancy. Nikki surmised that Chelsea had been dodging her out of guilt. The impulse to confront her about blabbing her damn mouth arose for a few seconds. Nikki ignored it.

Chelsea ended her call. A fake smile appeared as she hugged Nikki.

"Hey, girl!"

"Hi, Chelsea."

"Hello, Fatima."

"Hey, Chelsea."

"How you feeling, Nikki?"

"I'm fine."

"You look good," Chelsea said.

"Thanks."

"What you guys doing out here?"

"A little shopping," Nikki said. "You?"

"Same thing," Chelsea said. She then opened her shopping bag. "Check out these satin-lined hoodies I got from Sam Levy's!"

"Nice," Nikki said.

"I got a black one, and a gold one."

"They look expensive," Fatima said.

"These joints aren't cheap," Chelsea said matter of fact.

"Is that right?" Fatima asked.

"I'm on my way now to find some jeans to go with them."

"You got room in your closet for more stuff?" Nikki asked.

"No, but my little brother does," Chelsea chuckled. She then closed her shopping bag. "I'll call you later."

"Okay," Nikki answered.

"Take it easy, Fatima," Chelsea said as she walked off.

"You too," Fatima replied. She turned to her sister once Chelsea was gone. "She sounds like a shopaholic."

"She is."

"Where she work at?"

"Who said Chelsea had a job?"

"What you mean?"

"Boys give her money."

"For what?"

"What you think?"

Fatima puffed on her cigarette one last time and then tossed it. "Chelsea?"

"That's what's up…"

"Oh my God."

Fatima was about to further pry into Chelsea's business when her cell rang. It was Andre.

"Hey, babe. What you doing next Friday after work?" he asked.

"Finishing a paper on Women's Suffrage. Why?"

"I want us to go out to dinner."

"Can we do it another time? I need to hand in a tight paper to my professor, Andre."

"What if we go to dinner next Friday, and then Saturday I help you finish your paper?"

Fatima wasn't stupid. She knew her man was an intellectual.

"That'll work," she said as she stepped around a pile of dog poop. "What place did you have in mind?"

"The Chill Factory."

"It's a deal. I'll call you back when I finish shopping with Nikki."

"Give my regards to your sister."

.   .   .

The Chill Factory was located in the South Bronx on the bottom level of a three-story, red-bricked warehouse. Bright halogen lights lit up the outside of the entire structure to thwart late night criminal activity. The building was situated across from Harlem, on the other side of the Willis Avenue Bridge.

The popular hangout was laid out in an L-shaped design. The smaller wing was furnished with plush, dark-colored couches, and beer-stained coffee tables. All the brick walls were decorated with photos of people drinking alcohol during Prohibition. A sign posted near the front door by the FDNY warned that no more than two hundred people were supposed to occupy the lounge at one time. It was not uncommon to see three hundred patrons milling about The Chill Factory on Fridays.

Karaoke Night was the reason Fridays were so crowded. It's common knowledge that New York City is chock full of aspiring chanteuses, crooners and rappers. Inspiration from coworkers, friends, and alcohol generated an endless line of people willing to get up and embarrass themselves at The Chill Factory. And even though friends and loved ones constantly reminded Fatima that she couldn't sing worth a damn, that never deterred her from sipping a few drinks and proving them right.

Everyone close to Fatima knew that Mary J. Blige was her favorite recording artist. However, she was a bit partial to the soulful vocalist, Sade, when it came to love ballads. Perusing the list of songs recorded by the singer, Fatima selected her tune and gave it to the karaoke hostess.

"Can't believe you're getting up there again to make a fool of yourself," Marisol said when Fatima returned from signing up.

"Don't hate," Fatima replied and then sipped her margarita.

Marisol had called Fatima earlier in the day and asked what she was doing after work. When Fatima mentioned her date at The Chill Factory with Andre, Marisol volunteered to meet her there. She showed up with Raphael in tow.

It was two margaritas later when Fatima's name was called over the PA system to sing. She carefully strolled to the front of the establishment in her black heels, matching black jeans and pink ruffled blouse and took the mike from the karaoke hostess. When the intro to "Your Love Is King" pumped through the speakers, the crowd began to stir with anticipation. Fatima took a breath, closed her eyes, and sang.

Initially she did okay. She sounded decent as she pranced around the small area cordoned off for performers and pointed to Andre as she sang. And then the liquor in Fatima's system convinced her that she could hit the same notes Sade did. Fatima almost cracked a few beer mugs with the screeches she let loose. There were several. The audience howled with laughter each time. However, they heartily applauded when she was done. Fatima humbly returned to her seat.

"You weren't that bad, this time," Andre said.

"Thanks," Fatima said and gave him a peck on the lips.

"I need another drink," Andre said. Then he stood up and headed to the bar.

Fatima resumed work on her fourth margarita. As she took a sip she heard a voice behind her...

"Didn't I forbid your ass to sing in public?"

Fatima spun around and choked on her alcohol.

"Mama? What you doing here?"

"I can't hang out and have fun every now and then?" Pamela asked with a smirk. She sat down next to her daughter.

"No… but…"

"Hush and order your mother a gin and tonic."

A look of confusion was on Fatima's face as she walked to the bar. She was more confounded when she returned to the table ten minutes later and heard over the PA system:

"Singing next for us will be Andre Ellison. Let's show him some love?"

A round of applause went out. Fatima turned to see Andre take the mike from the hostess.

What in the hell? she wondered as the beat to K-Ci and JoJo's hit, "All My Life" began.

Andre couldn't sing worth a damn either. He strained to hit notes and more than once fell behind the pace of the lyrics displayed on the video monitor due to nervousness. His vocal transgressions were pardoned when he walked over to Fatima at the end of the song and bowed to one knee. All the women screamed in mutual elation.

Rivulets of sweat ran down Andre's forehead. His voice cracked as he slowly reached into his back pocket and retrieved the necessary diamond ring.

"Fatima, will you …"

"Yes!"

"Let the man finish!" Pamela scolded above cheers and applause from the audience.

"Sorry, Andre," Fatima said.

"What for? I got the answer I wanted."

The newly engaged couple stood and indulged in a kiss so passionate, Pamela grew hot and bothered as she watched. She took a swig of her drink.

"Isn't that romantic?" Marisol remarked as she leaned against her beau's shoulder. Raphael recognized the envy in her eyes so he kept his mouth shut.

After almost a minute of smooching Fatima and Andre finally detached from one another.

"I'm getting married!" Fatima yelled. She staggered and then sat back down. (Those four margaritas had her twisted.)

Pamela drained the rest of her drink and then motioned to her daughter.

"Come, give your mama a hug."

They embraced.

"I'm so happy for you, baby," Pamela whispered. "Anything you want for your wedding is on me… long as it's not over my Visa limit."

"Thanks, Mama."

"You're welcome. Now go and get your mama another drink."

One of the assets that helped Andre seal the deal on a relationship with Fatima was his apartment. Fatima loved his Park Slope neighborhood in Brooklyn. Andre lived on the corner of Fifth Avenue and Bergen Street, above a yogurt shop that made smoothies to die for. (She patronized the place so much she was given their employee's discount.) Andre's neighborhood had numerous bars within walking distance and different cafes to order delicious dishes from. However, it was the shopping that Fatima really had a hard-on for. The eclectic clothing found in the area's boutiques kept her credit cards maxed out.

Andre's two-bedroom apartment was stylishly decorated. The living room had a huge leather sofa, a flat screen television, and an antiquated oak writing table with a laptop on it. In the master bedroom was a huge, cherry oak sleigh bed that Andre regularly jingled Fatima's bells in.

He had her now in his bed with her legs thrown over his shoulders. He showed his future wife no mercy as he lovingly inched her backwards. Andre had the lights dimmed and Luther Vandross playing on his stereo. Strawberry-scented incense burned atop his Versailles-styled dresser next to the empty bottle of Cabernet Sauvignon.

This motherfucker's trying to split my spleen! Fatima thought as she gripped his neck. Her back was on fire from friction against the mattress, but she loved every minute of it. Andre placed tender kisses on her forehead while burrowing relentlessly inside her.

Is he on steroids?

•   •   •

Thirty minutes passed and Andre showed no signs of letting up. The Black Onyx oil he wore was more fragrant now that things were heated up. Between the delightful aroma that assaulted her nostrils and the wondrous battle that waged inside her womanhood, Fatima was going bananas. Waves of sexual satisfaction quaked through her body as euphoric tears fell from her eyes.

. . .

The last time Fatima was screwed this good she was a college sophomore. Tall, lanky, ponytailed Diego Maxwell from her statistics class had trouble with the concept of time series analysis and had begged Fatima for help with an upcoming exam. She obliged because he had looked so frantic pleading his case. The pair burned the midnight oil in the school's library three days straight. Diego was so happy to pass his exam with a D minus that he insisted Fatima join him for dinner to celebrate. (He was a political science major; he didn't give a rat's ass about statistics.)

Being broke in college was no joke. Fatima agreed to the free meal and drove Diego to a local steakhouse. One prime rib and three margaritas later, she was drunk. Fatima faithfully piloted her car back to Diego's apartment before she passed out. When she awoke the next morning, she found herself fully clothed in Diego's bed with strands of his hair in her face. Fatima curiously began to run her fingers through his mane and inadvertently stirred up his libido.

They spent a few minutes kissing before Diego began to undress her. Even though Fatima was still tipsy from the margaritas she'd polished off the night before, she was lucid enough to insist he wear a condom. She had no inkling that Diego was an avid reader of Indian literature. Nor that his favorite book was the Kama Sutra.

Also hidden from Fatima was the fact that Diego was well-endowed. She knew she was in trouble when Diego began to thrust his greatness upon her. He poked, prodded, and pushed Fatima around his bedroom for what seemed to her like an eternity. They were doing the tenth position listed in the pleasure manual when she begged for mercy. It was noon.

Fatima didn't even bother to eat when she reached her dorm. She showered, crawled into bed, and slept like a baby until morning. Feeling lonely and inspired later that evening, she drove back to Diego's apartment uninvited. She buzzed his door and was surprised when a young white woman answered, clad only in a long black T-shirt and sandals.

"Yes?"

"Uh… is Diego here?"

"He went to the store to get us some groceries. Something I can help you with?"

It took Fatima months to get over Diego.

•   •   •

When she heard Andre grunt happily, she knew he was done.

"Where'd you learn to screw like that?" Fatima asked after her heartbeat slowed down.

"That wasn't nothing," Andre chuckled. "Wait until we go on our honeymoon."

"Where would you like to go?"

"That's up to you, Fatima."

"I heard Maui's breathtaking."

"Fine with me."

"Great! We can work on picking out a wedding date tomorrow, after we finish my paper for school."

"School's another thing we need to discuss."

"Oh really?" Fatima said and sat up, attentive. Furthering her education would not be sacrificed. Marriage or no damn marriage. Her eyes said as much when she looked at Andre.

"I know how hectic it is for you working and going to school."

"And?"

"Maybe you should quit work after we're married and attend grad school full-time. "I can support us both, for now. What do you think?"

"Fuck yeah!" Fatima yelled. She smothered her fiancé with wet kisses. She was thankful to have found a good man and an adept lover in the same package. For the first time in a long time Fatima was worry free as she slept that night.

TWELVE

MR. OFFICER

The battle of good versus evil has been going on since the beginning of time. Ever since man figured out how much fun could be had with fermented grapes and lower body parts, the location of his eternal resting place has remained in peril. The souls of black folks in Harlem were not exempt; the dozens of churches found there were offset by an equal number of liquor stores.

Greater Harlem Baptist Church did its part in bringing folks to the Lord. Founded in 1963 by a Bible study group who gathered every Tuesday evening in a top-floor apartment on 152nd Street, they eventually grew large enough to buy a building on nearby Convent Avenue.

Reverend Lonnie Yizar was the church's seventh spiritual leader. He stumbled upon the job after the twenty-three-year-old newcomer to New York bumped into the previous pastor's daughter in a Brooklyn nightclub. Patty Redmond was fine as hell and could dance her little ass off. Once she bought the first couple rounds at the bar, the two exchanged numbers and began courting.

The Reverend Augustus Redmond had never been too keen on Negroes from Cincinnati. Lonnie was no exception. The man stuttered when he spoke, had absolutely no table manners, and worst of all, his ass was always broke though he claimed to work full time as a barber.

And yet this loser enraptured his Patty. Reverend Redmond tried not to dwell on what it was Lonnie did to keep a constant smile on his daughter's face. The pastor tried hooking Patty up with every single man in his congregation. (This even included his minister of music. That's how desperate he was.) But Patty only had eyes for Lonnie. Reverend Redmond reluctantly gave his blessing for Lonnie to marry his only child. It wasn't long after the nuptials that the newlywed got laid off from his barbering gig.

Reverend Redmond grudgingly paid the tuition for his son-in-law to attend divinity school in Virginia. He was determined to ensure his daughter's well-being and he knew that preaching was a recession-proof profession. There would always be wayward souls in New York City, especially when the economy soured. The pastor also knew he couldn't lead his flock forever and would eventually have to groom a successor.

Reverend Yizar's demeanor surprised everyone upon his return to Harlem with his degree in divinity. His speech was elegant, his table manners were passable, and he kept a pocket full of money his father-in-law never knew about. With practice, he eventually became a very good preacher. Yizar's reputation as a dynamic young speaker spread throughout the black church community and he soon began receiving invites all over the Tri-State area to preach. Sadly, as Reverend Yizar's fame traveled around the five boroughs and beyond, so did gossip about his womanizing. The infidelities grew worse once he succeeded Reverend Redmond four years later. Patty divorced him not long after he became the head minister.

·   ·   ·

As Fatima sat next to her mother and Nikki in Greater Harlem Baptist, bored to tears, she was motivated to pull out her cell phone and surf the Internet. The story of another financial planner being charged with embezzlement caught her eye. *Why do people always believe that a friendly man in a fancy suit won't steal their damn money?* She was in the process of clicking on the link to the story when she got busted.

"Put that away!" Pamela hissed then plucked Fatima's ear. (Old habits die hard.)

Fatima obeyed. She focused again on Reverend Yizar, who was in the midst of trying out a new sermon as he strolled around the pulpit in his tricolored, velvet-trimmed, silk pastoral robe. Whenever he raised his arms in a frenetic gesture, the congregation caught glimpse of the tailor-made dress pants he wore.

The title of the sermon that morning was "Running Away From a Bad Situation." With the exception of Fatima, Reverend Yizar held his entire flock in the palm of his hand as he stood tall before them, gripping the hand carved oak alter with the words: *Do This In Remembrance Of Me* inscribed across the front.

"I believe the words to that old Negro Spiritual went something like, Hush! Hush! Somebody's calling my name!"

"Yeah!" Greater Harlem Baptist yelled.

"I believe the song went on and asked, Oh my Lord? Oh my Lord? What shall I do?"

"Yeah!" Greater Harlem Baptist affirmed.

"See, what we have here… is a slave looking to run away from a bad situation, cause' slavery didn't pay much back then!"

"Got that right!" Greater Harlem Baptist shouted.

"And he's softly calling to another slave, to see if they want to come get in on some freedom too!"

"Gone and preach!" Greater Harlem Baptist continued.

"And now that fellow slave is debating on whether to escape too! Church, we should never hesitate to run away from a bad situation!"

Like your wife did! Fatima thought as the congregation exploded with applause. She was distracted from disrespecting the pastor further when her phone vibrated. Fatima slyly looked and saw that she had received a text message from Marisol. Not wishing to get plucked again, she opted to read it later.

It was another half hour before Reverend Yizar became winded and had to wrap up his sermon. When he called members of his flock who needed prayer to come to the altar, Pamela stood and joined the gathering crowd. Fatima quickly pulled her phone back out and read the message Marisol sent her: *Just scored us two tix to The Real Deal!*

After glancing up to make sure her mother wasn't looking, Fatima texted back: *Who cares?* She then put her phone away and refocused on the church service.

·   ·   ·

The sunny Harlem sky was beautiful later that morning as Fatima escorted her family back onto the grounds of The Dark Towers. Their Sunday dinner of baked chicken, fresh string beans, and candied yams was waiting to be cooked. Pamela stopped in her tracks when they neared the door to her building.

"Dammit, I forgot to buy onions."

"I'll get some," Fatima volunteered.

"Could you get some butter pecan ice cream, too?" Nikki asked.

"You got butter pecan ice cream money?" Fatima inquired.

"We just came from a nice service," Pamela said. "Don't you two start no shit," she growled. "Fatima, please get your sister the ice cream?"

Fatima headed to Majik Market at the intersection of Macombs Place and West 154th Street. As she neared the store, she saw a thin young black man strolling in her direction. Everything he wore was new; boots, baggy jeans, and gray hoodie. A cell phone was pressed to one ear while the other hand held a leash with a black pit bull attached. It was Jamaal Jackson.

Old hostilities resumed as the two recognized each other. Jamaal increased the slack on his leash, allowing his dog more room to roam. The pit bull sensed animosity in the air and growled. Fatima was nonplussed. She kept walking straight ahead.

"Better hold that damn dog if you want to keep it."

"Fuck you, ho'!"

"Your mama was a ho' first."

"What'd you say?" Jamaal asked, shoving his phone in his pocket.

"You heard me, bitch." Fatima replied, slowing her pace to show Jamaal she wasn't intimidated by him, or his pit bull.

Jamaal stood over the snarling animal. "You don't know who you fucking with," he hissed.

"And?"

"And?" Jamaal repeated. He used his free hand to raise the bottom of his hoodie. The silver revolver tucked in his waist glittered in the sunlight. Fatima wisely kept her mouth closed and picked up her pace.

"Yeah, that's right, bitch!" Jamaal jeered.

It pained Fatima to know her niece or nephew was going to have a thug for a father. *If only Nikki had used protection before she screwed that hoodlum!*

A few cars were double parked outside of Majik Market. All but two had a driver sitting at the wheel. New Yorkers were notorious for taking the gamble that they could double park outside a building, dart inside to handle their business and return in time to avoid a ticket. The police officer writing up a violation for an illegally parked Subaru was transcribing the license plate number when Fatima distracted him.

"Mr. Officer?"

The young white cop turned with a look of annoyance on his face. It was too late for him not to give this woman a ticket. He had already started writing it.

"Yes?" the cop said, ready for a confrontation.

"I was just threatened by a man with a handgun."

"Where at?"

"That block," Fatima said as she pointed behind her. "He's wearing jeans, a gray hoodie, and he's walking a black pit bull."

The cop walked to his patrol car and got on the radio.

Fatima entered the food mart and picked up a raggedy shopping basket. There were way too many people shopping along the cramped aisles of the small store. The space was so narrow between the rows of shelves that two average-sized people could not pass each other without one of them turning sideways.

Reaching the ice cream section, Fatima saw they were out of butter pecan. She selected her favorite instead, orange sherbet. The remaining onions in the vegetable section were sad. It took a minute to find two acceptable ones.

When she made it back outside she noticed a disturbance down the street. Three police cruisers, with their lights flashing, were parked in the oncoming lane of traffic. Fatima elbowed her way through a crowd of Harlemites and spied Jamaal's pit bull splayed on the pavement. The animal was soaked in its own blood. Angry citizens were cussing the police for killing the dog. Fatima's heart began to fill with hope, in spite of her recent church attendance, as she looked to see if Jamaal was also lying on the ground. She was disappointed when she spotted him in the back of one of the police cruisers, arms cuffed behind him. Jamaal was pissed as he yelled at the officers on the other side of the glass partition. The car containing his angry ass slowly began to back up and then turn around. Fatima pushed her way to the street as fast as she could to get a better glimpse. It was by chance that Jamaal turned his head in her direction. They made eye contact for only an instant, but it was long enough for Fatima to smile and wave his ass goodbye. She would never forget the look of hatred on Jamaal's face.

·   ·   ·

The next morning when Fatima got to work and turned on her computer, there was an email telling her that Juaneesha Bell was in the reception area. She didn't have an appointment, but Fatima knew Ms. Bell was relentless when it came to searching for employment. She had a good employment history and always complied with work activity requirements mandated by New York State while she received public assistance.

"Good morning, Ms. Bell. How are you?" Fatima asked once they were seated in an empty booth in the interview area.

"Fine. I found another job, Ms. Richardson."

"That's good. Where?"

"Always There Home Care."

Fatima wasn't too keen on the home health attendant profession. The work was noble and definitely necessary in every community, but the hours assigned were often crazy and the rate of pay minuscule. There was no incentive for agencies in the business to pay top dollar because new job applications came in weekly.

"I'm proud of you, Ms. Bell. Congratulations."

"Thanks. I'll need childcare for Tiphanie when she gets out of school."

"No problem. You have the forms to fill out?"

"No."

"I'll get them."

Fatima loved when her mornings started on a positive note. That usually meant things would go smoothly the whole day. She found the forms for childcare assistance and gave them to Ms. Bell.

"You still plan to return to school and get your nursing degree?" Fatima asked before she ended the meeting.

"Yeah. But, I have to save up for it first."

"If you wait until then it'll never happen, Ms. Bell. Get a student loan and pay it back when you can. I'm still paying mine off."

"Really?"

"I didn't have money to pay for college either. Most people don't."

"I'm gonna do it, Ms. Richardson."

"I hope you do, Ms. Bell."

"I am. You'll see."

.   •   •

Inez was in the hallway near the elevator texting on her cell phone when Fatima made it back upstairs.

"You wanna hang with us after work, Fatima? Kelly Morris is buying drinks for everybody. Probably clipped her old man again while he was sleep."

"That is so foul."

"Heifer, please. You'll be robbing Andre soon your damn self. All wives do it. Just remember… don't take the big bills."

"Why would I steal from my husband?"

"Taking cash out of Andre's wallet won't be stealing. You'll be retrieving communal assets."

"I'm not doing that."

"Free schools and dumb Negroes!" Inez sighed. "You coming with us?"

"Can't. My friend Marisol harassed me to attend a cable show taping with her."

"Which one?"

"The Real Deal."

"You going to waste your time at that ghetto-fest?"

"I tried my best to get out the shit, Inez… trust me."

THIRTEEN
THE REAL DEAL

Lincoln Studios was named for the nation's revered president. It was a popular movie house a decade earlier, but had succumbed to a bad infestation of bedbugs. The place was bought at auction by a group of visionaries who converted the building into a state of the art television studio that seated four hundred. This was ample space for the three hundred members of the audience, mostly female, which came to watch a taping of *The Real Deal*.

The program started as a late night talk show that aired every Wednesday on HCAT. (Harlem Community Access Television.) It became a local sensation after a few months. This was due to the high volume of drama the show's charismatic host delivered. Larry Little, or "LL", as he was known around Harlem, was a twenty-six-year-old media arts graduate from Hampton University.

Larry had always loved television. As an infant his mother would set him down in front of the idiot box and he wouldn't make a peep. It got worse as he aged. While most of his peers were reading hip-hop and sports magazines, Larry perused weekly television ratings in the *Hollywood Reporter*. Returning to NYC after college, Larry interned at a major television studio for a few months before deciding to create his own show.

His highly informative episode, The Real Deal About Child Support, earned Larry his first Community Access Cable Award (CACA) nomination. The fact that police raided the live taping and nabbed thirty fathers with outstanding warrants for non-payment of child support furthered the show's notoriety. *The Real Deal* was moved to Sunday nights at seven on Harlem Community Access Television due to its growing popularity.

Fatima and Marisol were seated three rows from the stage. Marisol had arrived early to get in line outside the studio. The set was minimally furnished. The host's chair in the middle of the stage was flanked by a leather couch on either side. To the far left of the area was a table holding deejay equipment. The young Latino who deftly operated the turntables was playing a series of hip-hop songs that everyone but Fatima knew the lyrics to. Two members of the production staff came out and briefly reviewed the rules for the show taping. After reminding everyone to turn cell phone ringers off, they disappeared.

When the theme song for *The Real Deal* began to play over the speakers, the audience began buzzing with excitement. Fatima was unfazed and sunk deeper into her seat. She watched Larry Little run onto the stage. The six-foot-tall, bald shaven brother was clad in a dark blazer, pink dress shirt, jeans, and black loafers. A platinum stud sparkled in both ears.

"How y'all doing?" LL asked his audience. Everyone, except Fatima, yelled with delight.

"Gotta bounce in thirty minutes," she said as she glanced at her cell phone. "I have another exam coming up."

Marisol kept silent and focused on LL.

"First, I want to thank you guys for coming! And second, I want to bring our guests on out and get this show started!" he yelled as the audience squealed with excitement. "Our topic for today is, Women Who Love Playas," LL announced.

Fatima shook her head in disgust at the topic.

"Make that twenty minutes."

Marisol was glad that her neighbor Shelia, who worked part-time for *The Real Deal* as a production assistant, had advised her which taping to attend. She ignored Fatima.

"So, without further delay, let's bring out our guests!" LL declared.

The audience clapped as they watched two young women trot onstage and sit on the couch.

"Welcome to the show, ladies," LL began after sitting in his chair. "Would you two introduce yourselves to the audience?"

The woman sitting furthest from LL was Michelle Clark. A rail thin, nineteen-year-old mother of twin three-year-old girls.

"My name is Michelle."

"Welcome to *The Real Deal*, Michelle."

"Thank you."

Sitting next to Michelle was Xiommara McDaniel, an eighteen-year-old employee at a major burger chain with a four-year-old son.

"My name is Xiommara."

"Welcome to *The Real Deal*, Xiommara."

"Thanks."

"Like I said earlier, our subject for today is, Women Who Love Playas."

A small chorus of boos echoed from the audience. LL turned to Michelle.

"You hear that, Michelle? Ladies out there are not happy."

"I hear," Michelle said timidly.

"You told me earlier backstage that the father of your children still has eyes for other women?"

"Yeah, he does."

The crowd booed again.

"So why are you still with him?" LL asked. He leaned close to Michelle.

"Cause she's stupid," Fatima mumbled. (Marisol fought to suppress a smile.)

"I… I love him," Michelle said. "Plus, he's the father of my kids."

"But he cheats on you. Doesn't that bother you?"

"Of course!" Michelle's voice cracked with emotion when she answered.

LL gave her a moment to compose herself. It was too early for guests to let loose with the waterworks.

"And what about you, Xiommara? Your man is doing the same thing?"

"Yeah," she answered hesitantly.

"They both stupid," Fatima mumbled.

LL scoured the notes he held in his hand for a brief second before continuing.

"It says here you even proposed the subject of marriage and that your baby's father turned you down?"

"Yeah," Xiommara repeated softly.

At least half the audience snickered.

"Hold up, people. I don't want my guests ridiculed. This is painful stuff these sisters are going through. They should be commended for having the nerve to get up here and share their stories."

Some of the guilty in the audience applauded, like LL knew they would.

"So what's this guy's excuse for not wanting to marry you, Xiommara?"

"He said he's not ready."

"Why are you still with him?"

Xiommara sighed. "I guess my reason is the same as Michelle's. I love him. Plus, he's the father of my son."

"Fifteen minutes," Fatima muttered to Marisol.

LL stood up and walked to the edge of the stage.

"Okay, audience! Are we ready to meet the gentlemen these young ladies are in love with?" he asked.

Some of the young men in the studio began clapping wildly.

"Come on out, fellas!"

The deejay promptly began to play the hook from George Clinton's hit, "Atomic Dog" as the two nineteen year olds strutted onstage and occupied the couch across from their women. Both young men were of average height and on the thin side, yet they wore oversized urban gear and large boots. Some men in the audience stood up and applauded. They were outnumbered by women who stood and jeered at the two cheats. LL cued his deejay to cut the music and then sat down between the opposite sexes.

"Welcome to *The Real Deal* fellas! The ladies in our audience can't wait to meet you. Please introduce yourselves?"

"I'm Kendall."

"My name's Sean."

"So... are you two really playas?" LL asked.

Sean and Kendall grinned uneasily. They were both rethinking their decision to appear on the show for a hundred-dollar gift certificate from Sneaker World. Their women had been compensated with gift certificates for double that amount from Rayneisha's Secret. A Brooklyn based business that sold racy lingerie.

"You can say that," Kendall finally said.

"Yep," Sean added.

"But your girls are not happy that you cheat on them."

"And?" Sean asked.

"She's the mother of your kids," LL reminded him.

"Michelle knows I love her," Sean said with a smirk.

"Then why the other women?" LL asked.

"They just be something to do," Sean explained.

All the women in attendance booed. Fatima sat up in her seat.

"This motherfucker is joking, right?"

"I don't think so, Fatima," Marisol said.

Back onstage, LL stood up from his chair.

"My audience seems a little disturbed by what you just said, Sean."

"I'm keeping it one hundred," Sean shrugged.

"Yeah, right?" Kendall said. The Casanovas gave each other a fist bump.

"Let me get some comments," LL said as he walked offstage and ventured into the studio audience. He stopped near a cluster of teenage girls from the Bronx.

"Anybody over here with a question or comment?"

One of the girls raised her hand. She revealed an expensive set of braces when LL handed her the microphone.

"You two ain't nothing but dawgs!" she said sternly.

Women whooped throughout the crowd while the guys onstage were unfazed.

"Don't hate the playa'! Hate the game!" Kendall said smugly.

This time, the men in the audience cheered. LL was in ratings heaven.

"Anyone else with a question, or comment?"

Fatima's arm shot up like the price of red roses the week before Valentine's Day. LL trotted over and handed her the microphone.

"I have a question for the women on stage," Fatima said turning to face them. "Can't you ladies do any better?"

The applause from the women was deafening. LL signaled Fatima to pause a few seconds before continuing. (He knew how to milk an audience response for maximum effect.)

"I mean, really? A man without a pulse could treat you two better than what you have up there now."

The ladies in the crowd howled. LL could have kissed Fatima at that moment, if he were still into women. Instead, he smiled and turned to the stage.

"Now, I know you guys want to respond to that!"

"Yo, I got a question for her ass," Kendall said.

"Sure, Kendall. But please, no swearing." (LL really didn't give a damn about cussing on his show. The more cuss words bleeped out in an episode, the higher the ratings.)

"Okay," Kendall said. "Yo, shorty, who you trying to diss? You don't know me like that."

"May I respond?" Fatima asked.

"Of course," LL answered. Fatima grabbed his microphone.

"I saw all I needed to know about you when you waddled out here looking like a clown, with your pants drooping off your butt."

Fatima paused until the laugher in the studio died down.

"Let me ask another a question?" she continued. "Do you know what a W-2 form is?"

"A what?" Kendall asked.

"A W-2 is a tax document most working people receive from their employers around January. It shows their wages earned and taxes withheld for the previous year," LL informed his guest.

"That don't ring a bell, do it?" Fatima asked.

There were snickers from the audience as Kendall scowled at Fatima.

"Let me ask one last question? Do you take care of your kids?"

"I takes care of all my children!" Kendall said defensively.

"All your children? How many is that?" Fatima asked.

Kendall clamped his jaws to prevent a few "motherfuckers" from slipping out his mouth.

"Come on, Kendall," LL coaxed. "How many children do you have?"

Kendall James would've charged into the audience and slapped the shit out of Fatima, if he wasn't afraid of violating parole.

"Four," he said faintly.

"Four kids already? You can't be more than twenty?" Fatima said.

"I'm nineteen," Kendall said proudly.

"Nineteen years old and never heard of a condom?" Fatima asked.

The studio audience roared with laughter. Even the guys laughed. Kendall shot Fatima a glare of hatred reminiscent of the ones southern Klansmen gave civil rights protesters back in the 1950's.

I gotta make sure this sister comes back! LL mused.

"Why don't you hush and mind your bizness!" Sean said in an effort to help Kendall out.

"You talking to me?" Fatima asked.

"Damn right," Sean replied.

Some of the audience gasped at the rude response.

"Watch the language?" LL said.

Fatima looked at Sean and smiled.

"Don't you even care if women think you're a dawg?" she asked.

Sean shook his head.

"Nope."

"Then you wouldn't have a problem if I offer to pay for you to get spayed or neutered?"

The audience went ballistic with laugher again. Sean was pissed.

"You clowning me!?"

"Hell yeah," Fatima replied.

"Watch the language?" LL repeated halfheartedly. He was in no hurry to take the mike away from Fatima. He could tell she was amped as she faced the two young ladies on the stage.

"And if I were you two sisters, I'd dump these fools!"

The women in the audience began clapping heartily. LL's smile grew as he took the mike.

"Can I have your name?" he asked.

"Fatima Richardson."

"Fatima, you seem upset about the men Michelle and Xiommara here have chosen."

"I see the results of what happens when young ladies make poor decisions at my job with Social Services every day. They have children early and struggle financially. Especially if they drop out of school."

"Michelle, did you finish high school?" LL asked.

The look of remorse on Michelle's face gave the answer.

"No, but I'm signed up to study for my GED."

"Glad to hear that, Michelle. What about you, Xiommara?"

Xiommara glanced at the floor.

"I dropped out after eleventh grade."

"Sister, you should really finish your education," LL said softly.

"My mother tells me the same thing," Xiommara sighed.

"Listen to her," Fatima implored. "Sex ain't going out of style no time soon. Save yourself for a guy trying to be somebody!" Fatima turned to the audience. "And that goes for the rest of you young ladies!"

The women in the studio stood and applauded. The men protested with their silence. Marisol wanted to pinch herself. Her scheme to get Fatima exposure with her message of safe sex worked far better than she could have imagined.

"Yo! Don't pay this ho' no attention!" Sean shouted above the clapping.

"I'm a ho' now because you're a poor excuse for a man?"

Another loud round of applause followed from the women.

"Hush up, bitch!" Kendall yelled.

The men in the audience clapped after his remark. (They were all thinking the same thing.)

"Your mama's a better bitch than me!" Fatima countered.

At that point, Kendall didn't care about a gift certificate for new sneakers or a possible parole violation. He wanted to put foot in Fatima's ass. He jumped off the stage and bolted into the audience. A second later, a member of *The Real Deal* security team nabbed him around his collar.

Fatima had to be restrained by Marisol as she tried to meet Kendall head on. (She reasoned she had a fair chance of winning a brawl against a fool with pants sagging off his ass.) She tried to twist free, but Marisol's grip was firm.

Throughout the audience, groups of men and woman fiercely debated. LL surveyed the pandemonium and grinned. Ratings for this show will be through the fucking roof! *I am definitely inviting this Fatima chick back to be on my show!*

FOURTEEN
HELL UP IN HARLEM

The last bona fide revolution Harlem experienced began in 1904 when a young black real estate entrepreneur named Phillip Payton Jr. took advantage of the glut of available low-priced housing in the then white-residents only locale. Through his Afro-American Realty Company, he moved countless Negroes uptown from the lower parts of Manhattan and made money doing so. The First World War brought blacks flocking north from southern states. They fled the predatory practice of sharecropping on farms down south to fill better paying factory jobs in big cities up north. This "Great Migration" helped further Harlem's Negro population.

White folks were not ecstatic living around so many darker people. They walked the streets of Harlem wondering to themselves what the hell was going on. Then they began to vacate. Their white flight allowed space for even more blacks to move into the community.

It was a very rainy weekend when *The Real Deal* aired its episode of Fatima trading insults with Kendall and Sean. The budding flowers of May welcomed the nonstop downpour that Sunday. But not the young folks in Harlem. Cooped up indoors, the choice for many of them was to turn on the boob tube. That led to an unusually high number of people watching LL's show. That led to hell up in Harlem.

The uprising didn't start with a bang. There was no loud proclamation trumpeted to gathered masses on 125th Street. No political group with banners marched noisily down Malcolm X Boulevard. Not a single soul took up arms and confronted the NYPD. (Which would have been suicidal.) The next revolution that hit Harlem actually began as a series of sensible choices made by some of its young female residents.

·   ·   ·

The white haze dissipated as soon as Jorge released the weed smoke from his lungs. The strong breeze circulating through Harlem carried it away. From where he sat, on a twenty-ninth floor terrace of a towering thirty story building, Jorge could see most of Central Park. The sun had just punched its way through a cluster of stubborn clouds and would soon warm up the city. It was a little after eight in the morning; the daily scramble of working New Yorkers getting to where they needed to be was at full throttle. Jorge's stomach rumbled, signifying that the munchies was approaching. He took an extra long pull from his blunt and exhaled. Another successful trip to "The Upper Room" had been completed.

Jorge's belly rumbled again. He grudgingly put out his joint, stood up, and drifted into the kitchen of the two-bedroom apartment. When he opened the fridge, he was reminded that there was nothing inside worth eating. His mother hadn't gone shopping yet and probably wouldn't until she got paid on Thursday. Jorge opened a cabinet and found dozens of canned meat products, but he dared not touch any. They all contained pork. Digging in another cabinet, he found a can of tuna hiding behind a half-eaten box of soda crackers.

Once his hunger was satiated, Jorge returned to the terrace and relit his blunt. He then planned his day. He needed to pick up a few job applications. That would keep his mother off his case about being twenty years old, still living at home, still unemployed.

But before Jorge did that, he had more important business. *Who can I get to come do me?* Jorge pulled out his cell phone and punched in some numbers.

"Hello?"

"What up, Rene?"

"Hey, Jorge."

"I'm chilling at the crib. You wanna come over? I got some good weed."

"No thanks."

What the hell? Ever since they were in middle school, Rene Harris never turned down Jorge when he wanted to screw her. She also never turned down good weed.

"You sick or something?"

"Actually, yeah. I'm sick of wasting my time with you. Call one of your other women. We're done."

The next sound Jorge heard was silence. He was perturbed at Rene's erratic behavior but refused to let her ignorance blow his high. She wasn't that fine to begin with.

Jorge searched his cell phone's contact list and decided to give Azure Walsh a ring. She was a real trooper. Always nagging him about spending more time with her. After getting her voicemail twice he sent a text asking for some ass. Jorge was puffing on a new joint when his cell phone beeped. He grinned as he picked it up. Her reply read: *Go fuck yourself!*

It seemed all Jorge's women were tripping. Never one to give up easily, he puffed on his joint and calmly clicked back over to his contact list.

.   .   .

Nineteen-year-old Joshua Edwards had sensed something was awry when seventeen-year-old Cheree Bridges came down to meet him in the vestibule of her building instead of buzzing him in as usual. He was traveling through her neighborhood that evening and had decided to pay her a visit… for some sex.

"What's up? Your aunt still home?" he had asked.

"She at work."

"Why didn't you just buzz me in?"

"We need to talk."

"Can't we *do it* upstairs?" Joshua asked with a sly grin.

"No," Cheree said flatly. She was not amused with his play on words.

"What's going on?"

"We ain't hooking up again until you find and keep a legal job, Joshua."

"I don't need no nine to five as long as I can get my hustle on."

"No. You need to focus on some long-term, legal goals."

"That's cool, but what's that got to do with us sexing right now?"

"Joshua, I wanna be with a man who's trying to be somebody."

"Cheree, you're only seventeen! Quit acting old!"

"I'm serious. You never wonder about your future?"

"I'm wondering about our future. Don't I do you right when we hook up?"

"I never complained."

"That's why you need to let me on upstairs."

"No dice."

"What if we go and get some pizza first? My treat this time?"

"We ain't doing nothing until you straighten up your act."

Joshua was pissed. After ten months of banging Cheree on demand, she had the nerve to tell him he couldn't hit it no more unless he agreed to new terms and conditions? That was some bullshit.

"This is some bullshit!"

"Sorry, but that's how it is now," she said.

"Naw, fuck that! Fuck you too!"

Cheree fought back tears as she watched Joshua storm off. She still wanted him. But she wanted a boyfriend with promise even more. With her head down, she walked to the elevators, her resolve still in place.

•   •   •

Barrington Davies was too busy working to notice none of his women had returned his calls. He'd set up shop at his regular spot on the corner of Broadway and 145th Street near the subway. As usual, he quickly started making sales. People returned to Barrington time and time again due to the quality of product he sold. The fact that he was the only seller in the area to offer a money back guarantee didn't hurt business either.

After watching too many young brothers like himself get serious jail time for pushing weight, Barrington choose the less illicit enterprise of hawking bootleg DVDs. The job was safer, the hours saner, and the penalties if prosecuted were far less severe.

His parents had scolded him for dropping out of school after almost passing twelfth grade the second time around. But at twenty years of age, Barrington had had enough of books, exams, and teachers. And since he loved cinema as much as he loved money, his choice of profession was easy. Each night Barrington counted a pocketful of money obtained from hustling Hollywood and added it to the savings account under his mattress. He was another participant in New York City's hidden economy, where business transactions worth millions of dollars went unrecorded and untaxed.

It was almost noon. Barrington had over two hundred dollars stuffed in his pockets when he realized neither Gloria, Melissa, nor Shamika had called him back.

Puzzled, Barrington checked his cell phone to make sure he had a signal. (He recently switched to a cheaper cellular plan and received the subpar service he paid for.) The phone indicated full signal strength. Barrington jammed it back into his pocket as he gave an old man a rave review of the bootleg Kung Fu movie he had displayed on the concrete in front of him.

Once Barrington made the sale, he whipped his phone back out and redialed Melissa's number. She was always down for some afternoon freaky-deaky since she worked nights at a hospital. He got her voicemail yet again. Undeterred, Barrington redialed Gloria. She didn't work at all and was usually home. He also got her voicemail again.

A customer wanting to know when the DVD of Chris Rock's new stand-up concert was going to hit the streets stopped him from calling Shamika again. The film was scheduled for wide release in theaters in a week, but Barrington had a copy in his knapsack.

He called Shamika after he made the sale, but she didn't pick up either. Something was amiss. However, Barrington wasn't about to waste time worrying over what the hell it was.

"A poor rat ain't got but one hole to run in," he mumbled as he scrolled down his phone's contact list to find another possible partner for sex.

·   ·   ·

Russell Hughes gripped the satin sheet on his bed so tightly he tore a small hole in it. The teenager sitting between his knees with her back to him, bucking wildly, was putting in work. He watched her long braids sway back and forth before him and smiled. The tattooed Monarch on her right shoulder glistened with sweat as it moved along with its owner.

Any doubts Russell had earlier about hooking up with Chelsea again were quelled; common sense often went ignored when the opportunity for sex arose. He had sensed something was up when she called him during her school lunch period Monday asking why she hadn't heard from him. The pause in their communication was not a fluke. Russell had been forced to cut expenditures when his T-shirt printing business slowed. And since Chelsea's love didn't come cheap, she was the first item deleted from his budget.

Chelsea refused to stay kicked to the curb. She'd giggled at the right moments during the brief conversation with Russell and mentioned how much she missed him. Before she hung up, he'd begged her to visit him the next day when she left school.

Chelsea bent forward and touched the floor with her hands. This allowed her more leverage to push herself back against Russell. Beads of perspiration ran down his forehead as he struggled to retain his composure. After a few deft strokes he couldn't fight the feeling any longer. His resistance went. And then he came.

"Ooh! Chelsea!" he moaned.

"You like?"

"Hell yeah!"

"Enough to buy me a laptop?"

"You can have whatever you like!"

Twenty minutes later, Chelsea was showered and squeezing back into her tight orange jeans when she looked up and found Russell staring at her. Buyer's remorse was on his face.

"What's wrong, Boo?"

"How much money you need?"

"The laptop I want only cost three hundred. I saved some money for it."

"How much you got?" Russell asked with a trace of hope.

"Almost a hundred."

"That's all?"

"I don't work. Remember?"

"Yeah, right," Russell answered as he reached across his bed and grabbed his wallet off the nightstand.

There was enough smell of hot sex in the air to keep his judgment cloudy. He slowly counted out two hundred dollars.

"Thanks, sweetie," Chelsea cooed as she took his money. She threw in a peck on the cheek for good measure. "What you doing the rest of the day, Boo?"

"Gonna take me a nap and then get back to work hawking T-shirts."

"I was wondering if you could give me a ride home?"

"I'm worn out, Chelsea."

"Can I have money for a cab?"

"What's wrong with the subway?"

"I need to get home as soon as possible. Don't want my moms to put me back on punishment."

Russell hesitated reaching for his wallet again. Chelsea decided to appeal to the brain in his other head.

"You do want me to be able to come see you again? Right?"

"How much more?"

"Twenty."

"Twenty dollars for a damn cab?!"

"You know these drivers all want a tip."

Chelsea gave him another peck on the cheek after she got her cab fare. She then picked up her book bag and turned to go.

"Wait! When we hooking up again?" Russell asked as Chelsea opened the bedroom door. (He was determined to make sure she worked off that laptop money.)

"I'll call next week and let you know," Chelsea answered sweetly. "Bye."

Nikki was waiting for her at the local pizza shop. She'd already shared some of her chocolate chip cannoli with Melody and was contemplating ordering a second one when Chelsea strolled in. Nikki noticed her eyes flash resentment when she saw Melody sitting at the table.

"Look who's here," Nikki said with a smile. Her eyes warned Chelsea to be polite.

"You know how crazy the subway is during rush hour, Nikki. The train was delayed twice."

"Hello, Chelsea. I love your new braids."

"Thanks, Melody."

"How's Russell doing?" Nikki asked.

"Let me show you," Chelsea said as she fished out her cell phone and deleted Russell's number.

"It's like that now?" Nikki asked.

"He's cries broke too much. I see you guys started without me?"

"I was starving," Nikki said.

The three got down to important business after they ordered slices of pizza.

"You guys see that cheap dress Cassandra had on?" Chelsea began.

"Yeah, right?" Melody added. "I'd hate to see what happens once it goes into a washing machine."

"You two need to stop," Nikki said when her friends giggled.

"Don't act all 'holier than thou,' Nikki. You the one texted me this morning about it," Chelsea said.

"Can we change the subject?" Nikki asked as she scanned Melody's plate for cannoli crumbs.

"You heard about Jamaal getting locked up on a gun charge?" Chelsea asked.

"No. What happened?" Nikki inquired.

"He got caught with heat on him. He's already a felon."

"Then he's gonna get serious jail time," Melody said.

"Exactly," Chelsea said. "He won't be around to assist you with the baby, Nikki."

"I'm not stressed. My moms and sister will help out."

"I saw Fatima on that cable show the other night," Melody said. "She lit into those two clowns."

"I saw that shit, too," Chelsea said.

The kid that delivered their slices kept his eyes glued on Chelsea the whole time he served the trio. He then pulled napkins out of the holder on the table for her before leaving.

"Y'all wanna hear some funny shit?" Melody asked as she smacked on her slice. "I heard there's some kind of pussy strike going on in Harlem now because of Fatima and what she said on that show."

"Really?" Nikki asked.

"Straight up," Melody replied.

"Who's doing it?" Chelsea asked.

"You mean, who ain't doing it?" Melody quipped.

Chelsea responded by sucking her teeth. Melody ignored her.

"First, I heard some girls in our building talking about it in the laundry room last night. Then, I heard two girls in my History class discussing it this morning."

"Ain't nobody in Harlem giving up fucking!" Chelsea laughed as she chewed her food. Two elderly women at a nearby table stopped their discussion and stared at the girls.

"Keep it down, Chelsea," Nikki hissed. "People can hear you."

"Fuck 'em," Chelsea replied.

FIFTEEN
STILL MAD AT ME?

The reggaeton music pulsating through The Harlem Bowl's speaker system made it hard for Fatima to focus. She was in a tight match and the stakes were high. Dinner and drinks at Gilmore's, the latest pricey neighborhood restaurant young people flocked to in droves, was on the line. Every pin counted. She slowly approached the foul line and released a nasty hook.

One brave pin remained standing defiantly in the far right corner of the lane. It taunted Fatima. She overcompensated with her angle of entry and tossed her ball into the gutter. Fatima swore under her breath as the pin was triumphantly spirited away by the racking system.

Raphael was silent as he stood up and prepared to bowl.

"Sick 'em, dawg!" Andre yelled to support his teammate.

"No doubt," Raphael answered.

Though he tried hard, bowling was not his forte. Basketball was his game. Raphael still had a jump shot most players of the sport would die to possess. And his crossover dribble had been legendary in high school. However, he couldn't bowl a strike to save his life. It pissed him off to see Marisol and Fatima achieve strikes so effortlessly.

"Give it your best shot," Marisol said encouragingly, while winking at Fatima.

They both knew he couldn't bowl worth a damn. Raphael scored five pins and returned to his seat. He reached for his beer, which he'd emptied earlier.

"I need a new beer," Raphael sighed.

"I'll grab one on the way back from the bathroom," Fatima said as she stood up.

"*Gracias*," Raphael replied.

Fatima maneuvered her way through the thick crowd of youngsters hanging out that Saturday evening and went to the lower level of the bowling alley, where the bathrooms were less crowded. The line at the snack bar on the lower level however, was a different story. She was the tenth person waiting to place an order. To pass the time she watched the music video playing on the television above the counter and was unaware that she too was being watched.

Seventeen-year-old Demetrious Byrd was brand new to the wide world of fucking. He had only gotten his first piece the previous summer from a girl he met at his cousin Peanut's house in Cambria Heights, Queens. The thin, pimple-faced girl was renowned as the neighborhood skeezer. It had only taken thirty minutes of begging, and the promise of a box of chocolates the next time he visited, to convince the girl to screw him.

Demetrious climbed out of her window that night smiling ear to ear because the albatross of virginity had finally been tossed from around his neck. The days of choking his chicken were over! Sex had been marvelous. And Demetrious couldn't wait to do it again… with a better looking partner.

His skill at seducing females in his own neighborhood gradually improved. And once he had the rudiments of screwing mastered, he went on a tear. Any decent-looking girl that crossed Demetrious' path was fair game.

And then Tyniesha Myers rudely told him to take the A-train straight to hell the other day when he called and asked for some more booty. They'd experienced a great bout of sex a week earlier, so he didn't understand what the problem was. Tyniesha then informed him she had watched a recent episode of *The Real Deal* and was now taking her life in a more positive direction.

Curious, and pissed, Demetrious viewed the episode in question online. Thus, he had no problem recognizing Fatima's ass in person at the bowling alley. He elbowed his homeboy Marquis, next to him.

"Ain't that the trick who was on television telling girls not to fuck no more?"

Marquis was not affected by the sex strike. He was still a virgin. Marquis also never watched television unless it was a sports event. He went along with his friend's claims nonetheless.

"I think you right, Dee."

Emboldened by Fatima's diminutive size, Demetrious stepped to her.

"I oughta slap your ass for that shit you talked on that cable show! My girl is trippin'!"

It took Fatima a couple of seconds to realize some teen was swearing at her and not some other kid.

"Excuse you?!"

"You heard me, trick!"

Fatima stepped out of line and looked up at the teen.

"I don't know what type of medication you on son, but I suggest you get the fuck out my face!"

At that point, everyone in line forgot about purchasing food. They all turned to view the sideshow. Marquis was as surprised as Demetrious, at the small woman's bold reply.

"She clowning you, Demetrious! You gonna take that?"

Demetrious had no choice but to get aggressive with an audience watching. He bumped against Fatima, causing her to stagger a few steps back.

"That big mouth of yours gonna get your little ass in trouble!"

Fatima was livid. She shoved Demetrious back, but the boy barely moved. It was at this moment that the old security guard hired to patrol the bowling alley came downstairs on his way to the bathroom. The growing crowd around the snack bar indicated a potential problem, so he went over to investigate. Demetrious was about to shove Fatima back when the security guard grabbed him.

"Hold up, fella!"

"Man, turn my fucking arm loose!"

The guard was way too close to retirement to get involved in a physical altercation and risk spending his golden years with a limp. He released the young man's arm, pulled out his cell phone and made a call.

"Hello, 28th Precinct? This is The Harlem Bowl. We have a situation. Can you send somebody over? Thanks."

With that, the security guard turned and proceeded to the bathroom. Demetrious was still mad, but he wasn't stupid.

"You lucky I don't feel like getting arrested, bitch!" he said and walked off to the exit.

Fatima was so heated that she hiked back upstairs instead of waiting in line at the snack bar.

"No beer?" Raphael asked when he saw her approaching empty-handed.

Fatima glared at him for a split second before she picked up her bowling ball. *Women*, Raphael thought, as he got up and went to get his own beer.

"Baby, you okay?" Andre asked.

"Fucking copacetic," Fatima muttered as she lined up for her shot. She heaved her ball and knocked the hell out of all ten pins.

Andre wasn't sure why Fatima was pissed so he decided to give her space.

"I need a beer too," he said and disappeared.

"What's wrong?" Marisol asked once Andre was out of earshot.

Fatima frowned as she sat and picked up her purse.

"Some punk downstairs had beef because his girl watched *The Real Deal*."

"Are you serious?" Marisol asked excitedly. Fatima glared at her.

"You happy about some moron getting in my face?"

"Of course not. I'm happy because it sounds like our idea is spreading."

"I didn't volunteer to argue with fools, Marisol."

Fatima placed her purse next to Marisol, minus her cigarettes and lighter.

"That young idiot got my nerves worked up, I need a puff. Keep an eye on my shit?" Fatima asked as she walked to the exit.

•   •   •

"You need to do something with your girl, she's out of control," Raphael said as he and Marisol rode home.

"Some guy threatened Fatima when she went to get your beer. She was upset," Marisol replied.

"That's no excuse for her to act bitchy to me, Marisol. Andre's gonna catch hell if he marries her. Wait and see."

"Can't we find something else to talk about?"

Dinner at Gilmore's had been postponed by Andre when he learned why Fatima was in a foul mood. Raphael and Marisol were heading home in his blue Chevy Silverado as they discussed the incident. Fatima had gotten on his damn nerves for the last time and he was letting Marisol know it. They were stuck in traffic after leaving The Harlem Bowl, which didn't help Raphael's mood.

"Naw. We need to discuss your girl," he griped, after cursing the traffic.

"What are you gonna say that you haven't said before?"

"Fatima's got issues," Raphael mumbled as he cut off a gypsy van.

"You've mentioned that before," Marisol answered.

"She needs to get help."

"That sounds familiar, too."

"Keep joking, Marisol."

"I'm not joking, Raphael. Fatima is my best friend. Just like Bluey is yours."

"Don't bring him into this."

"Why not? You don't think a man who beats his wife when he gets drunk has issues? That's the motherfucker who needs professional help. You should talk to him."

Traffic heading up Amsterdam Avenue was flowing again. Raphael was grateful. He wanted to get Marisol home before she started ranting about some of his other fucked up friends. He found a parking spot two blocks from Marisol's building and they walked to her apartment in tense silence. Once inside, Marisol headed to her bedroom. She needed a shower.

She had perspired a lot throwing those bowling balls. She was also heated that Raphael had the nerve to complain about Fatima's attitude, as screwed up as all his friends were. Marisol deposited her clothes on the bed and went into the bathroom. The sounds of a basketball game playing on the television in the living room echoed down the hall as she stepped into the shower.

As she scrubbed her neck, Marisol felt a draft waft across her soapy skin.

"Sorry, baby. I'll lay off your girl," Raphael said as he took the washcloth from Marisol and began cleaning her. No other words were spoken as Marisol tacitly responded to the gentle nudges Raphael gave her as he bathed her from head to toe. He lathered her breasts with care, lovingly wiped her butt, then kneeled and washed her feet with equal affection. Satisfied with his work, Raphael wrung the washcloth, draped it over the rim of the tub, turned off the water, and stood up.

"Still mad at me?"

When Marisol opened her mouth to reply, Raphael placed a finger over her lips. He then dropped back to his knees.

I need to argue with this motherfucker more often! Marisol thought when she felt Raphael press his tongue between her legs and pull her closer. Seconds later, Marisol had his skull in a death grip as she withstood a vicious tongue lashing. When she groaned in delight and began to secrete love, Raphael knew she was primed.

He silently picked Marisol up and carried her to the bedroom. He then found a towel and carefully patted her dry before depositing her on the bed. Marisol's desire for Raphael to be inside of her was maddening. She lay spread-eagle on her mattress and waited eagerly for him to apply his protection. Once he was done, Marisol's legs quivered in anticipated ecstasy when Raphael tossed them over his shoulders, lowered his head between her breasts and slid into her. He gripped her shoulders and began to play a game he called "hide the bone."

Advancing and retreating inside Marisol, Raphael was honored he was the one fortunate to sex her well-toned body. Every plunge he made into her was full of gratitude. Within minutes the peach shower gel Marisol had used began to release a scrumptious aroma when she started to sweat. The smell made Raphael hungrier for her. He tenderly sucked Marisol's aroused nipples to extract as much fruity flavor from them as possible.

This stimulated her even more. She rocked her hips in sync with Raphael's thrusts, and they fast approached a sexual crescendo. Raphael knew that he was serving Marisol good and plenty, but he still wanted proof.

"It's okay?" he asked her.

"*Si, Papi.*"

"Still mad at me?"

"*No, Papi.*"

For the finale Raphael decided to switch it up. He withdrew from Marisol and stood over the bed. Though she looked at him with uncertainty, he knew she'd comply. She allowed herself to be turned around, then Raphael bent her over and reentered her.

"Come here!" he growled as he pounded away. It took all of Marisol's athletic conditioning to withstand his loving assault from the rear.

"Don't stop!" she ordered as pleasure overruled pain.

Raphael held her by the waist and continued to wail away hard.

"You feel so good," he grunted and then liberated his load. The exhausted couple collapsed on the bed.

"I'm thirsty," Raphael said as he stood up and staggered out of the room.

Marisol gently rolled over and smiled as she looked up at the ceiling. When Raphael returned minutes later he had a bottle of water in one hand and his cell phone in the other.

"Did you check the box for the installation manual?" he asked as he glanced at Marisol with a look of annoyance. "I'll be there soon as I can. I'm at Marisol's. I gotta go home and change first."

Raphael grimaced as he listened on the phone…

"Hang tight, I said I'm coming!" He ended the call and sat next to Marisol on the bed.

"What's wrong?" Marisol asked.

"Zach's getting his butt kicked trying to install a tankless water heater."

"What's the problem?"

"The homeowner bought the damn thing reconditioned, so anything could be wrong. Don't know how long this shit might take."

"I understand," Marisol replied casually.

"Thanks, baby."

Raphael finished drinking his water and then walked over to the dresser and retrieved a washcloth from the top drawer. Marisol began to suspect deceit as soon as he left the room. She recalled him complaining a few days ago that Zachary had an upcoming vacation to South Carolina to play golf when he still hadn't repaid Raphael money he'd borrowed. She was sure Zachary's vacation had already started. Suspicious, Marisol got up and went to the bathroom. Raphael was at the sink washing off when she walked by him and stepped into the shower.

"You know, I read the most disturbing thing the other day."

"What's that?" Raphael asked.

"A report from the CDC stating that minority women in this country have an unusually high rate of herpes."

"That's jacked up."

"It sure is," Marisol said as she turned on the shower. "Don't know what I'd do if I caught that shit from someone," she said over the rushing water. "But it wouldn't be pretty."

Raphael ignored her threat.

"I'll call later and let you know how everything went," he replied and went to get dressed.

"Lock the door on your way out!" Marisol yelled.

Raphael began swearing as soon as he left Marisol's apartment. He hated when she hinted that he was being unfaithful. It couldn't be helped if women were attracted to him. And he'd be damned if he turned down a fine piece of ass like D'Jaris Anderson. She was way more liberal sexually than Marisol, always willing to try new ideas.

Earlier, Raphael had opened a brew and sat down to watch Cleveland beat up on the Hawks after returning with Marisol from bowling. His cell phone buzzed a minute later with a naughty selfie from D'Jaris. She wanted him to come up to the Bronx and dick her down again. Raphael figured the best way to meet D'Jaris in timely fashion would be to quickly knock off Marisol and then fake an urgent call from his brother.

After he climbed into his truck, Raphael cranked it and then reached under his seat to check for condoms. There was one left in the box. Raphael then called Zachary in Myrtle Beach and left a voice message informing him that they were currently working on a water heater in the Bronx if Marisol ever asked him about it. He then checked his side mirror and pulled into traffic.

SIXTEEN

MARISOL 101

Fatima was in the office break room preparing oatmeal with cinnamon when Inez and Drew entered.

"Look who's early, Drew? It's a miracle!"

"A miracle would be you shutting your big mouth, Inez," Fatima replied.

"How's those wedding plans coming?" Drew asked as she and Inez placed their lunch in the refrigerator.

Fatima's eyes lit up with excitement.

"We booked a fabulous place out on Long Island!"

"Details?" Drew asked eagerly.

"Well, the chapel is not too far from a secluded beach, so we're going out there to take wedding photos."

"Make sure you guys carry identification. Those white folks out there don't like your kind too close to their homes," Inez said.

"Hush!" Drew scolded her.

"Don't blame me when the cops show up," Inez chuckled.

Fatima glared at Inez for a second then continued.

"And the reception hall is bananas! After we return from taking photos on the beach, we're going to surprise our wedding guests by coming up through the venue's floor on a small stage elevator!"

"Wait, am I going to a wedding or a damn concert?" Inez asked. This time Drew shot her an icy glare.

"I need to know so I can wear the right dress."

"Don't hate on me because your country ass got hitched in a barn, Inez," Fatima snickered.

"You two need a reality show," Drew chuckled. "I'm going to get to work."

A few minutes later, when Fatima returned to her desk with her breakfast she found a note. Yvonni Graham was waiting in reception. The grin from clowning earlier with her coworkers vanished. Ms. Graham was one of her most difficult clients. The last time Fatima met with her, Ms. Graham raised so much hell that two officers walked over to deescalate the situation. Fatima sighed, wolfed down her food, then headed for the elevators.

Walking out of the elevator, Fatima reminded herself that Yvonni Graham was a stressed out young mother of two adolescent girls, and thus had a lot on her plate. If she got cussed out again, Fatima would try not to take it personally.

"How can I help you today, Ms. Graham?" Fatima asked after finding a vacant booth in the interviewing area.

"I want my case closed."

"Repeat that?"

"I need you to close my case. I'm moving to Florida."

"Really?" Fatima asked with restrained elation. "What city?"

"Mirmar. My sister lives there. She's going to hook me up with a job."

"That's good. How soon are you moving?"

"End of the month."

"Do you need help with the move?"

"My furniture's old, I'm going to sell what I can and leave the rest where it is."

"What about transportation? You need bus tickets to Florida?"

"I made that fucking mistake last year when I visited there. My sister and her husband's going to rent a van and come get us."

"Then I just need you to uh, write a brief letter requesting your case to be closed. Put down your new address if you know it."

"Okay."

Fatima could hardly refrain from turning backflips down the aisle as she walked to an ancient copier and robbed the metal behemoth's paper tray for a sheet. She wasted no time returning to her booth. Ms. Graham promptly wrote the request to close her case. She then pushed her letter to Fatima to review.

"Could you sign and date it?"

"Sorry," her client said before complying.

"That should do it, Ms. Graham."

Fatima grabbed the letter, ready to return upstairs, when Yvonni stopped her.

"Ms. Richardson?"

"Yes?"

For the first time since Fatima had the displeasure of knowing Yvonni Graham, she seemed at a loss for words.

"I just want to say… thanks for all the help you gave me."

"You're welcome, Ms. Graham."

"I uh, also want to apologize for all the times I cussed your ass out."

"No need. That's part of this job."

"I've been reading the bible lately, trying to get my life on the right track. I plan to make a fresh start down in Florida."

"I'm impressed."

"Most of the time when I was in here raising hell, I was really upset at myself and my situation. Raising two girls alone ain't easy."

"I believe you," Fatima said. "It's hard enough for a single person to make it in this city, forget about trying to raise children too."

"Exactly. And as much as I love my ungrateful kids, I sure wish somebody had started a pussy strike back in the day like you got going on in Harlem. No telling how different my life would be, if I hadn't gotten pregnant and dropped out of school."

Fatima was caught off guard. The sex strike thing was bigger than she'd imagined.

"Ms. Graham, I honestly don't know how to respond to that remark."

At that instant, Yvonni Graham ceased to be a job-related adversary. She was just another sister struggling to make it in the world.

"You're doing something that's needed," Yvonni said as she stood up. "Keep it up."

"Thanks. Good luck in Florida," Fatima said.

The two women then smiled and shook hands before they parted.

.   .   .

Fatima spent most of the afternoon reviewing new public assistance cases assigned to her. She did this while ignoring jokes from Inez about her upcoming "wedding gig" with Andre on Long Island. She was on her way outside for a smoke when her cell phone buzzed. It was Marisol.

"Hey, girl."

"Sounds like you're in a good mood, Fatima."

"Ain't I always?"

"Nope."

"What do you want?"

"I was eating lunch today when I came up with the perfect venue for our next rally."

"Next rally?"

"Of course."

"May I ask a question?"

"Shoot."

"Why are you so obsessed with this sexual awareness stuff, Marisol? You act like you on a damn crusade or something."

.   .   .

From the beginning of time, man has been obsessed with the urge to stick his penis inside a pretty woman. Marisol Aquino was a frequent object of that desire. When she arrived in America from the Dominican Republic at age seven, she couldn't speak a lick of English. Neither could her older brother, Luis. Only their mother, Mercedes, had a scant grasp of the language due to visiting family in Florida during her youth.

The nocturnal cab ride from JFK airport to the Bronx would always dwell in Marisol's memory. She had heard how big *Nueva York* was from classmates back in the D.R. who had obtained visas and traveled to the city. It was only when she crossed the Whitestone Bridge and was able to see Manhattan's brilliant skyline that Marisol comprehended the enormity of her new home.

The city's mass transit system was a thrill for her and Luis. They loved when Mercedes took them downtown on the subway to shop. It was a far cry from the way they used to travel around back home, she and her brother sandwiched between Mercedes and the operator of a loud, smoke-belching motorbike.

As soon as the subway doors would part, little Marisol would dash in the car and find a seat. She would then turn and kneel in her spot so she could gaze out of the smudged window. It fascinated her to see the sights as the train whizzed from station to station above ground.

Walking around the city was also exciting to Marisol. The numerous nationalities that composed NYC would enthrall any kid used to cohabiting with only a few other ethnicities on the island of Hispaniola. Observing the different hues of skin, dozens of foreign tongues, and wardrobes of other cultures daily took a lot of getting used to for Marisol. Her brother Luis was spellbound by the endless vehicles that cruised the jagged roads of the Bronx blasting hip-hop music.

Because their mother made them speak English every day, Marisol and Luis soon became competent in the language. Mercedes also made sure her kids brought home decent marks on their report cards. Whenever they complained how hard their schoolwork was, she'd remind them how fortunate they were to be in America, and that they'd better not "fuck it up." (Her mastery of English vernacular had improved as well.)

The population of Dominicanos clustered in the Washington Heights section of Manhattan was huge. The dozens of restaurants, hair salons, and grocery stores in the neighborhood that catered to Dominicans was the reason Mercedes and her kids visited the area frequently. It always made Marisol homesick for her birthplace, Santiago, when she saw old men playing dominos or heard merengue music playing. She vowed to live there herself one day.

Time went by and Marisol blossomed academically… and physically. She grew into a shapely woman and learned to ignore the unwanted advances and vulgar compliments she received daily from uncouth men. It got worse when her mother scrimped enough money to send her to Catholic School. Now Marisol had to wear skimpy skirts and jumpers to school again like she did back home. She was not happy about that shit.

Her happiness improved once she met Elpedio Leon. The twenty-year-old Latino music major at Columbia University had ears full of piercings, tattoos, wore shabby clothing, and was a chain smoker.

Marisol had walked by as he was busking with an acoustic guitar on the corner of Columbus Avenue and 96th Street for spare change. He sang U2's hit, "With Or Without You." Once Elpedio spied Marisol's shapely derrière as she headed down the block with two classmates, he serenaded her with Prince's love song, "Adore." Elpedio did such a good job wooing her (and making her classmates jealous) that he got Marisol's number. Clandestine rendezvouses soon followed.

Elpedio knew better than to get sprung over a young piece of ass, but it happened. After getting Marisol to relinquish her virginity, he wanted her morning, noon, and night. He wound up settling for weekend afternoons, when Mercedes thought her daughter was studying at the library. Instead, she was boning Elpedio in his apartment on Riverside Drive. Three months later Marisol became pregnant.

She tried to conceal the pregnancy, but her mother always checked to make sure her menstrual cycle arrived as scheduled. Mercedes confronted her daughter when she missed two cycles in a row. Marisol cried and fessed up. The last thing on Mercedes' "shit not to do" list was for her child to struggle and raise a baby at fifteen years of age.

Luis was sent to stay with relatives the next weekend as Mercedes and her daughter made a special trip to Rockland County to solve Marisol's dilemma. When Mercedes returned home she immediately put her daughter on birth control. She then forced Marisol to arrange a meeting with Elpedio.

As soon as he buzzed the lock for them to enter his building, Mercedes ordered her daughter to stay put. She went in and spoke with Elpedio alone. Ten minutes later, Marisol's mother walked out of the building with a scowl on her face. She hailed a cab and she and Marisol rode home in silence.

After her phone calls went unanswered for two weeks, Marisol snuck over to Elpedio's apartment one evening. He no longer lived there. And she never heard from him again. Marisol didn't think he was jailed for statutory rape, because she was never contacted by New York's judicial system. And she was not stupid enough to ask her mother what was said or done to make Elpedio disappear. It took a long time for Marisol to get over losing both a child and her first lover.

The dual shames of becoming impregnated at a young age and having an abortion haunted her. On many occasions Marisol had almost revealed her blemished past to Fatima, but she was fearful of being morally judged.

·   ·   ·

"I have no idea what you're talking about, Fatima."

"Whatever, Marisol."

"Anyways, like I was saying, I know a great place to hold our next rally."

Fatima was jonesing for some nicotine, so she cut the conversation short.

"Can we discuss this later? I got some business to take care of."

"Sure, I'll buzz you around eight?"

"That'll work."

Soon as Fatima ended the call and grabbed her cigarettes, she spied Ella Watkins approaching her. *Dammit!*

"Hey, Fatima."

"Hi, Ms. Watkins."

"Call me, Ella."

"Sorry, I keep forgetting."

"I was on the Internet last night when I came across something you might be interested in," Ella said and handed Fatima a sheet of paper.

"What's this?"

"Information on e-cigarettes. This ad claims they're better than traditional cigarettes. No foul smell, no ashes. It's not quitting entirely, but it's a step in the right direction."

"I'll check it out," Fatima said halfheartedly.

"Great."

Fatima then stood up from her desk and waited for Ella to leave… she didn't.

"Fatima?"

"Yes?"

"You… uh, got an extra two dollars so I can get some snacks from the vending machine? I didn't get a chance to eat lunch yet. Been busy doing paperwork."

"I think so," Fatima said opening her purse. "Here."

"Thanks," Ella said as she took the money. "I'll get you back next week."

When Fatima was sure that Ella was gone she tossed the printout in her trashcan and headed to the elevators.

There was already a group of coworkers outside the building chatting between puffs. Fatima lit up and joined the discussion about the possible layoffs due to a budgeting shortfall. After a few pulls on her cigarette, her mind and body relaxed.

She chuckled at the idea of somebody inventing fake smoking. As far as Fatima was concerned, an electronic cigarette was akin to a battery-operated boyfriend. No matter how pleasurable or convenient it was, it could never take the place of the real thing.

SEVENTEEN
SWINGING IN THE PARK

Sandwiched between 120th and 124th Streets and bordered by Fifth and Madison Avenues is a twenty-acre tract of land known as Marcus Garvey Park. It was named in honor of Marcus Mosiah Garvey Jr., the Jamaican born Pan-Africanist who founded the Universal Negro Improvement Association in 1914 to promote social political and economic freedom for people of African descent. He moved to New York City in 1916 and held legendary rallies and parades in Harlem to inspire and motivate members of his race.

Fatima was late to her own rally because the MTA was once again doing construction over the weekend. Subway service was therefore jacked up. As she hurried into the park from 124th Street, she spied a rusted shopping cart shoved in a cluster of overgrown bushes. It was jammed with tattered clothes, paper bags, old shoes, broken toys, and blankets. A large plastic bag full of recyclable cans and bottles sat nearby in another clump of thick brush. Fatima stopped appraising the homeless person's possessions when her cell phone rang. It was Marisol. Again.

This is the last time I'm getting talked into this bullshit! Fatima thought as she answered the call.

"Walking into the park now."

Fatima ended the call before Marisol could respond. She'd been calling since dawn expressing her consternation about the weather, insufficient advertising, and the subpar public announcement system loaned to them. Fatima just wanted to get the shit over with.

After this engagement, Marisol would have to accept her refusal to give more damn speeches to teens about sexual behavior. Fatima was certain she could find another way to contribute to the cause besides preaching to horny adolescents. She gingerly stepped over a used condom and an empty liquor bottle as she hurried across the park.

Fatima was dressed in a white blouse already damp with perspiration and a pair of faded black jeans. She hastily wiped away trickles of sweat from her forehead. The July humidity was extremely high. Fatima heard the hip-hop music blasting from speakers before she saw the crowd. An army of teens was amassed near the historic Mount Morris Fire Watchtower. She recognized Marisol pacing frantically back and forth on the portable stage the NYC Parks Department had graciously provided.

Shaconda was onstage near Marisol, stocking a cooler with bottles of water. What Fatima didn't see onstage was the lectern that she had specifically asked for. It made Fatima feel protected. She liked feeling that there was something between her and the crowd.

"You can quit worrying now, Marisol," Fatima said as she hurried onstage.

"Hello, Fatima," Shaconda said as she opened a bag of ice and dumped the cubes into the cooler.

"Hi, Shaconda. Thanks for bringing water."

"No worries. Glad to help out."

Marisol grabbed Fatima's arm and guided her to the far side of the stage.

"We have a slight problem."

"What's wrong?"

"Our other scheduled speaker cancelled. But, we do have a hip-hop group scheduled to arrive and perform in about an hour. Could you, stretch your speech out, and help fill the gap in activities?"

Fatima would've slapped Marisol if there weren't so many witnesses.

"You're fucking kidding me, right?"

"I'm dead serious. Maybe you can do a question and answer session after you're done speaking?"

"Maybe you can have your damn head examined?"

"Come on, Fatima? *Please*, for me?"

"Marisol, you're a royal pain!"

"I love you too," Marisol said and then gave her a peck on the cheek. "Have a seat while I get things started."

Fatima grabbed a bottle of water and sat in one of the plastic chairs nearby. She sipped the cold liquid and surveyed the scene. The crowd of young people numbered over four hundred; the majority of them female. To the right of the stage was a series of square tables covered with pamphlets on health issues. Fatima was surprised to see on one table a large illustration showing the proper application of a condom. She was sure that if Marisol had her way, there'd have been free prophylactics for the crowd to take home. However, since Marisol enjoyed employment with the Board of Education, that was not the case.

There were different colored balloons tied to a stretch of fencing in the area, most likely the work of Shaconda. A fifty-five-gallon steel drum that had been converted to a transportable grill sat some distance from the stage, belching smoke like a metal dragon. The overweight brother sweating in front of the grill was busy cooking his ass off. Teens were lined up near him to get the free hotdogs, burgers, and chicken wings that the event's lone sponsor, a well-known commercial bank recently sued for making predatory home loans to minorities, had sprung for.

Marisol stepped to the microphone and cleared her voice before using the PA system.

"Can I have everyone's attention?"

The majority of the crowd ignored her and continued chatting.

"Hello? Can I have your attention?" Marisol said. She received the same weak response. Her NYC teaching skills then kicked in.

"Hey! Please settle down so we can get started!"

Startled, the crowd hushed and focused on her.

"That's much better," Marisol said softly. "First of all, my name is Ms. Aquino, and I want to thank everyone for coming out this afternoon. We have a lot of information on sexual awareness that we want to give to you today, so the sooner we get started, the sooner we'll be finished. And, we'll have a performance from that new rap group right here from Harlem, The Young Turks!"

The females in the crowd screamed at the mention of The Young Turks. They were the biggest sensation to hit Harlem since prepaid cell phones. The suave, handsome leader of the group, Omar X, was the star of countless young women's wet dreams.

"Now, without further adieu, I wish to present a dynamic young orator. If you saw her speaking on *The Real Deal* recently, you know this sister does not have a problem with telling the truth."

Several women in the audience clapped.

"She works for Human Resources and sees a lot of the hardships that our community has to deal with, which is why she's here to speak today. Ladies and gentlemen, let's put our hands together for a special young lady, and *very* special friend of mine, Ms. Fatima Richardson!"

The audience gave Fatima a decent applause when she stood up. Marisol's sugary introduction was not going to smooth things. Fatima let that be known by rolling her eyes at her when they traded places at the microphone stand. More beads of sweat ran down Fatima's brow as she surveyed the crowd before her. She longed for a cold margarita in one hand and a cigarette in the other.

"How's... how's everybody doing?" Fatima asked nervously.

The crowd mumbled back an assortment of weak responses.

"Good," Fatima continued. "I'm glad to see we have such a nice turnout. Hopefully, when we're through today, you'll have heard and seen some things that you'll remember for the rest of your lives."

The crowd murmured with bored anticipation. Fatima reached into her jeans pocket to pull out a few thoughts she had jotted down while stuck on the subway when someone in the crowd caught her attention. It was seventeen-year-old Lynn Spruill. A golden complexioned girl with a mini afro, dressed in a T-shirt and short shorts. She had a finely detailed leopard tattooed on her left arm. The animal stretched from shoulder to elbow. When Lynn turned her head to speak to the girl standing next to her, Fatima saw beautiful Japanese calligraphy etched down the back of her neck. It was too much to ignore.

"One of the uh, main ideas that we want you people to come away with today is that, you need to think, before you act."

Fatima plucked the microphone from its stand and walked to the edge of the stage where Lynn was standing.

"Excuse me, young lady?"

"Me?" Lynn asked guardedly.

"Yes, you."

Fatima didn't miss the suspicious look displayed on the teenager's face.

"I'm not trying to put you on blast, dear. Can I ask a question about your tattoos?"

"I guess so."

"Why did you get them?"

"Why'd I get these?" Lynn repeated.

"Yes."

"To be honest, I got this one on my arm because my sister got herself a nice panther done on hers."

"And the one on your neck?"

"Those are the Japanese kanji symbols for Love and Peace," Lynn answered. "I like the way they look."

"May I ask you one more question?"

"Okay…"

"You ever think about how many long-sleeved blouses you're going to have to buy if you decide to work in Corporate America with that leopard on your arm?"

"I've… never given that any thought," Lynn admitted.

"You might want to."

Fatima saw the look of annoyance growing on Lynn's face, so she turned away before she got cussed out and strode to the opposite end of the stage.

"I am aware of the tattoo craze that everyone around here seems to be enjoying. But you know what?" Fatima whispered, as if she were about to divulge a deep secret. She paused a few seconds for effect. "There used to be a time when the white man branded people who looked like us with free tattoos because they owned us. Now you guys pay for that mess."

The profoundness of her statement registered with the crowd. Murmurs passed through the audience.

"What? You guys haven't learned about slavery in this country yet?" Fatima asked with a sly grin. "Look it up online."

Standing a few feet behind her friend, Marisol relaxed. Everything was going to be fine. She was sure Fatima could keep the crowd captivated until the musical act arrived.

"Sorry for getting off track about tattoos, but that needed to be addressed. I don't want you guys doing things that you might regret later. The reason I'm standing here today, at the urgent request of Ms. Aquino, is to talk to you people about sexual awareness."

Giggles echoed throughout the crowd.

"Before anyone gets excited, I will not be telling you guys what goes where and how. That's your parents' job. But here's something I will tell the young ladies who walk around with low riding jeans on, showing off your goodies. I don't need to see the crack of your butt! Nobody else needs to see it either."

Loud giggles swept over the crowd.

"Look, when you girls dress like ho's, some boys treat you like one."

Nobody laughed. Marisol smiled.

"What I also need to tell you folks about, is how HIV is devastating our community. And also, how catching an STD such as herpes, will be with you forever. Like some of the tattoos you people have."

The crowd laughed once again.

"I'm serious!" Fatima said and looked over the sea of faces staring up at her. "I especially want to talk to the young ladies here today, because you're the ones who have the most to lose if you make the wrong choices." The crowd grew quiet. "Let me see the hands of all the young ladies here who call yourselves having a boyfriend?"

Half of the women in the crowd complied.

"Dang! That many of you girls are in love? I should ask how many of you with hands up are engaged in sexual activity—but I won't go there... yet."

Once more the crowd laughed.

"I will ask this, though. What do you 'young ladies in love,' know about your boyfriend's sexual health?"

Fatima glanced around. Her eyes fell upon one of the first girls she saw raise a hand to indicate she had a beau. She pointed at the thin sixteen-year-old, who was fighting a losing battle with acne.

"I saw you raise your hand. Do you know your boyfriend's status?"

Poor Tracie Stevens looked petrified, like a deer caught in the headlights of an oncoming tractor-trailer.

"I... I think he's still on probation," she stuttered.

The crowd cracked up with laughter. This encouraged Fatima. Nervousness was now a thing of the past. Adrenaline flowed through her. She began to pace back and forth across the stage, like a veteran politician stumping at a fundraiser.

"That's not exactly the answer I was looking for, but I thank you for your honesty, sister."

Fatima spied another teen who'd raised her hand.

"How about your boyfriend? Do you know his status?"

"His status?" fifteen-year-old Wanda Hardy asked.

"Yes, his HIV status."

"No, I don't."

"Don't you think you should?"

"I guess so," Wanda answered.

"You *guess* so?"

Everyone in the crowd waited for Fatima to scold Wanda for not being aware of her boyfriend's health condition. She didn't.

"Sweetie, please do yourself a favor and ask him about his HIV status," Fatima said softly.

"I will," Wanda said.

Shaconda was awestruck as she watched Fatima. She whispered to Marisol, who stood next to her.

"Isn't she good?"

"She's remarkable," Marisol replied.

Fatima was hyped up as she spoke. However, she soon lowered her voice and slowed her pace.

"Listen, ladies, one of the worst mistakes you can make at this point in your life, is to become a teenage mother. This could lead to you dropping out of school." Fatima paused again for effect… "And while we're on the subject of motherhood, can I ask a question? What is the deal with these jacked up names you guys are giving your kids? Naming them after cars, and liquor?"

The crowd laughed.

"Don't you all realize that as soon as certain employers see your child's jacked up name on their job application, they will not get called in for an interview?"

The laughter ceased.

"And poor LaQuanda, Lexus, Tykwon, or Alize won't ever have a clue that they were discriminated against because of their 'ghetto' sounding name."

Fatima surveyed the crowd. Teens were pondering the point she'd just made. She lowered her voice again, almost to a whisper.

"Here's a newsflash, folks. Names like Lisa, Mary, Christopher, or David, still work. Keep that in mind."

.   .   .

Twenty-one-year-old Effrom Daniels had recently returned to Harlem after spending the past fourteen months in Stone Mountain, Georgia. He'd moved there because the cost of living was cheaper. Also, he'd heard how the ratio of black men to black women in the Atlanta area was stacked in his favor. Effrom was also encouraged to leave New York due to an outstanding warrant. It was an assault and battery charge he felt was unjust, because the drunken fool at The Silhouette nightclub had bumped into him first.

Soon it dawned on Effrom that Atlanta was no New York City. The public transit system was whack. The humidity was horrific. The weed was weak. And the women he met were fine, but bossy because of their high salaried jobs.

After a long ride back home via Greyhound, Effrom was not pleased to find insanity going on in Harlem. He had telephoned three of his former flames with the hopes of hooking up. The two girls whose phone numbers still worked had both instructed him to drop dead after he asked them for some booty.

Hot and horny, Effrom was hoofing it up Madison Avenue, sipping on a cold, citrus-flavored malt beverage. He smiled at every young female he passed. He was hoping for a friendly smile, or at least a questionable glance back from one of these females in return. He received nothing but frowns. The fact that many of them were wearing sundresses and showing mad skin didn't help Effrom's dilemma. As he neared Marcus Garvey Park he noticed an event taking place. His curiosity was aroused further when he smelled food so Effrom crossed the street to investigate.

He thought he'd reached the Promised Land when he saw a gathering of mostly young women. The large Sexual Awareness Forum banner hanging on a fence told him what was going on. Effrom walked to the rear of the crowd and eyed all the female bottoms in front of him. Meanwhile onstage, Fatima was whipping the women into a frenzy.

"The onus is on you ladies to make the right choices about your bodies now!"

"Yeah!"

"Because later might be too late!"

"Yeah!"

"Am I right, or am I wrong?!"

"Right!"

"You ladies need to T-B-A! Think, before you act!"

"Yeah!"

"You don't have to sex every cute boy you meet!"

"Amen!" Shaconda yelled.

Marisol glanced at her, surprised by the teenager's passion.

"Keep your legs closed and your schoolbooks open!" Fatima preached.

"Yeah!"

"Listen, having sex, paying rent, shopping for girdles... you girls'll be doing grown up stuff soon enough. Don't rush it! Because sex ain't all that anyway!"

Many young women in the crowd applauded. Many young men in the crowd hissed their disapproval. Fatima remained undeterred.

"I know some of you out there don't like what I'm saying... but I'm here to tell you guys the truth!"

Effrom couldn't believe the bullshit he'd stumbled upon. Some short, dreadlocked heifer actually preaching against fucking? *In Harlem?* That was outrageous! He drained most of his alcoholic drink and then hurled the bottle toward the stage.

Kip DiFranco, a twenty-three-year-old rookie photojournalist for the weekly news rag *Manhattan Daily Press*, was near the stage when this occurred. He was given the undesired assignment of covering the Sexual Awareness Forum because of his lowly status at the publication. A tall Caucasian, Kip stuck out in the crowd like January snow on Vermont macadam. He'd been fantasizing about what Marisol Aquino looked like naked when he saw a bottle slam into the girl standing next to her.

Shaconda yelled when she felt the jagged pain from the pieces of glass now embedded in her shoulder.

Hot Alabama summers spent at her grandmother's house had conditioned Fatima to react quickly on hearing a buzzing sound. (Mosquitos down there loved Northern Negro blood.) The loud whooshing Effrom's bottle made as it hurtled toward Fatima allowed her to duck just in time.

The crowd gasped on seeing the blood on Shaconda's arm.

"Whoever threw that? Bring your fucking ass up here to my face!"

The crowd gasped again at Fatima's profanity-laced response. Kip quickly raised his camera and snapped photos of her enraged face. He then snapped pictures of Fatima and Marisol attending to Shaconda.

"Should we call an ambulance?" Marisol asked as she soaked napkins with bottled water to place on the wound.

"We got ambulance money?" Fatima asked. She frowned as she watched the dark stain on Shaconda's sleeve spread.

"Not really," Marisol replied.

"Let's take her to Harlem Hospital in a cab," Fatima said.

"Okay," Marisol replied.

"I hope we find the bastard who threw that bottle," Fatima grumbled.

Kip was still taking photos of Shaconda getting aid when people near him began to murmur.

"Yo, that was foul," some girl mumbled.

"Bitch needed to hush with all that noise," a young man countered. Two girls next to him responded.

"Why she gotta be a bitch?" the first girl demanded.

"You shouldn't have shit to say, if she wasn't talking about you," the second one added.

"I'll say what the fuck I want! Y'all best get out my face!"

Hearing the threat, Kip abandoned the drama onstage and turned his camera to the argument nearby.

"You don't scare me!" the first girl countered.

"You'll fear my foot in your ass!" the young man replied.

"Don't let them ho's clown you!" a young man behind the quarreling trio shouted.

"Who you calling a ho'?" the second girl asked as she turned and faced the interloper.

"You, and your mama," he replied.

The second girl then hauled off and slapped him. Her bigger foe briefly registered shock on his face and then punched her in the jaw. The young lady fell flat on her ass.

"Don't be hitting no girl!" several young women yelled as they surrounded the young man. The group began shoving him about, so he swung on them too.

Then all hell broke loose.

A dozen girls bum rushed the young man. Numerous males, previously watching the spectacle, rendered aid to their comrade. Kip wished he had a video camera instead of his single lens reflex to record the boatload of 'motherfuckers', 'ho's', 'bitches', and other cuss words that flew back and forth as the teens fought.

Fatima was calling a cab on her cell when she heard the ruckus. She turned and saw the huge commotion going on in front of the stage.

"Marisol, look!"

Marisol was shocked to see the brawl when she turned around.

"Fatima, you gotta break that up!"

"Me?"

"They'll listen to you!"

Unconvinced, Fatima hurried to the microphone and snatched it up.

"Hey! Everybody, please calm down!"

Her pleas went unheeded. Fatima watched in alarm as more young men unwisely tried to rescue their peers from the fierce ass-kickings the young women were doling out.

"Stop this fighting!"

Fatima was again ignored. She was about to advise anyone not participating in the fight to safely vacate the area, when a can of grape soda splattered at her feet and doused her blouse with the sticky beverage. Fatima's jaw dropped in disbelief. Before she could say a word, she spied another teen aiming his soda can at her. She easily dodged the projectile.

"You sumbitch!" Fatima yelled and then leapt off the stage after the kid.

Fortunately, two of the volunteers Marisol had recruited to help with security at the event intercepted Fatima. As she let out a string of expletives at her assailant, Kip captured her angry mug on film.

Realizing things were out of control, and that police could soon be arriving, Effrom decided to leave the vicinity. He was three blocks away, stepping into a bodega for another citrus-flavored malt beverage, when he heard the first NYPD squad car scream past the store toward to the park.

•   •   •

Most teens present that sultry afternoon agreed the male combatants in what was being hailed as "The Battle of Marcus Garvey Park" suffered more casualties. They were outnumbered and outgunned. Men's name-brand clothing got ripped, their faces were badly scratched, and countless male gonads were injured during the conflict.

Fatima was still fighting mad as she was extracted from the crowd and shoved into a cab by one of the security personnel. She rode with Shaconda to Harlem Hospital's emergency room, where the poor teenager received sixteen stitches to close the gash in her shoulder. Marisol was left with the task of trying to restore law and order to the event.

Her pleas over the PA system for calm fell on deaf ears, as Fatima's had earlier. The scuffle in the park attracted throngs of local residents and passersby. Many of them documented the clash on their cell phone cameras, resulting in a phalanx of inner city paparazzi who would later post the images for posterity.

The high-pitched wails of approaching police cars snapped the fighters back to reality. All teens involved in the scuffle hauled ass before the first pair of handcuffs could be pulled from a NYPD utility belt. When The Young Turks arrived half an hour later and saw all the police cruisers, they assumed there had been a shooting in the area and returned home. Their manager would be tasked with collecting their performance fee from Marisol Aquino.

EIGHTEEN
VIRAL!

Fatima stayed in bed on Sunday. She was physically and mentally exhausted. After introducing herself to Shaconda's stressed-out parents in the emergency room, she had apologized profusely for their daughter being injured at the park. Once Shaconda was treated and released a few hours later, Fatima returned to her apartment and went off the grid.

She unplugged the landline phone her cable company refused to allow her to disconnect because it allegedly came free with her cable package, and turned off her cell phone. Her moms, Andre, Marisol, and whoever else could wait until Monday to reach her. Fatima did leave her bed once Sunday afternoon to shower and grab an order of shrimp fried rice from the Great Wall of Harlem, a local popular Chinese eatery, and a pack of smokes from the corner bodega. After she finished eating and puffing on two cigarettes, she crawled back into the sack and dozed off again.

Fatima woke up late for work Monday morning. She took a quick shower and then scurried around her apartment getting dressed and then ran out. She was two blocks away when she realized she'd forgotten her phone. Fatima cussed all the way back home to get it.

She turned it on when she exited the subway station near her job an hour later and was surprised to see fifteen voice mails waiting, along with a bunch of text messages. Fatima turned the phone back off and slipped into her office undetected. She was greeted with a copy of Sunday's edition of *The Manhattan Daily Press* in her chair. Her snarling face and other fight scene photos were plastered on the front page under the caption: Swinging in the Park.

Fatima wanted to die from embarrassment.

"Only you could get them fools to fight like that. Shame I wasn't there to see it," Inez chuckled from across the aisle.

Fatima held her tongue and sat down. Now she knew why she had all those phone messages.

"You just gonna ignore me?"

"I'm trying to, Inez."

"Let me say one more thing, and then I'm done?"

"Go for it."

"Listen Fatima, quit trying to be Ms. Malcolm X and leave them damn teenagers alone before one of those fools hurt you."

"I'm way ahead of you, Inez."

All morning long coworkers and even clients snickered and pointed at Fatima as she performed her duties. She was in the break room, devouring an overpriced tuna wrap for lunch when her cell phone rang. It was Marisol calling.

"You saw the paper?"

"I did, Marisol."

"A video of that fight was posted on the Internet, too."

"Are you serious?"

"It went viral."

"That's fucking great!" Fatima yelled.

She had forgotten she was among coworkers. An elderly clerk, renowned in the office for his religious faith, glared at her with holy indignation.

"Let me call you back, Marisol." Fatima hung up before Marisol could reply.

She was eating the remnants of her wrap when her phone vibrated. It was a text from Andre. Apparently he was also an object of ridicule at work because of Fatima's fracas at the park and wanted to discuss the situation with her. Fatima turned off her cell phone.

It's going to be a long ass day! she thought as she bit into her wrap again.

• • •

"Quit fidgeting! And suck in that gut!"

"I did, Mama."

Fatima knew her day could not get any worse when she left her job that evening. Verification of her not being clairvoyant was confirmed when she met her mother at Irma DeLuca's dress shop on Amsterdam Avenue. She'd fallen in love with a strapless mermaid wedding gown that came with a pleated chiffon bodice and had draped petal technique detailing.

Fatima had found it on the website of a well-known Chinese-American fashion designer. The gown was listed there for seven thousand dollars. Irma DeLuca told Pamela she could make the exact dress for fifteen hundred. A deposit of half the cost was required before work would begin. The Italian seamstress from Hoboken, New Jersey had a solid reputation in Harlem because she designed a lot of the church choir robes in the area. It was a no-brainer.

"Eating cheesecake like it's going out of style! Know you got to fit your ass in a wedding dress next May!" Pamela chastised. Fatima held her tongue and peeked at the pudgy mass a few inches below her breasts as she stood on a small stool. Irma DeLuca eyed it as well.

"Bambino?" she asked in her still heavy Italian accent.

"Hell no! Wrong daughter."

"Watch your damn mouth, Fatima! And apologize!"

"Sorry, Mrs. DeLuca."

"It's no problem," Irma said while taking necessary measurements. "Plans for the wedding okay?" she asked.

"So far, yes. My wedding coordinator is helping me with a lot of stuff."

(That was an understatement. Fatima had to remind Marisol that she was not the person getting married and thus, a geometric china pattern was a no go.)

"Which church you get married in?" the seamstress asked.

"Greater Harlem Baptist," Pamela proudly stated.

"That is, Reverend Yizar?"

"Yeah," Fatima answered.

"Good man."

Fatima held her tongue once again.

"By the way, Fatima, Reverend Yizar is giving you a real big discount to perform the ceremony."

"How come?" Fatima asked bluntly.

"You trying to get smart?"

"I only asked a question, Mama."

Irma gently grabbed Fatima by the hips and nudged her to the left. "You turn now."

Fatima turned as instructed. She now had her back to her mother.

"Fatima, could you do your mother a little favor?"

"What kind of favor?" Fatima asked suspiciously. She tried to turn around, but Irma shoved her ass back the other way.

"Nothing major. I just kinda sorta volunteered you to be the keynote speaker for our Youth Day service at church next month."

"You did *what*?" Fatima yelled as she spun and faced her mother.

"Please!" Irma exclaimed.

"Turn back around, Fatima!"

"Why'd you do that?" Fatima moaned as she turned around.

"I'm doing you a favor. Trying to get you closer to the Lord."

"I'm only twenty-five. I've got plenty of time for that."

Pamela took a menacing step toward her daughter before she remembered there was a witness in the room.

"You wanna get buried in that dress? Say something stupid like that again!"

"Sorry, Mama."

"You're going to speak at that damn Youth Day service, and you're going to smile while doing it! We clear?!"

"Yes," Fatima sighed.

"Good, now keep your ass still for Mrs. DeLuca."

Fatima craved a cigarette… badly. She fought the urge because she didn't want to hear her mother's mouth about her smoking.

"We're done now. You are going to look lovely in your wedding dress," Irma said.

"I hope so," Pamela replied sarcastically.

Fatima ignored her mother's comment.

"Now, I need you to do me a little favor," Irma said.

"What is it?" Fatima asked cautiously.

"Promise me you won't fight more boys in the dress I make for you?" she teased.

Fatima was livid as she stepped down off the stool. She marched past the women and grabbed her pocketbook from the chair she'd hung it on.

"Where you going?" her mother asked.

"I need a cigarette!" Fatima said as she stomped out of the shop.

Standing at the curb in front of the shop, Fatima took a couple of pulls on a cigarette to ease her stress. Seemed like everyone knew about that fucking fight! As she took another puff, two prepubescent girls walked by. They were trailed several feet behind by three young men. It was hard for Fatima not to notice the boys whispering amongst themselves as they studied the skinny derrières before them. The tallest member of the group then cleared his voice and spoke:

"Yo, Cathy! Wait up!"

The girl in question turned to see who called her. Once she recognized the boy, a grin spread across her face. She then held a brief discussion with her walking partner. Cathy's friend continued across the street alone while she remained.

The tall youth quickened his pace to join Cathy and they strolled up the block. When he put his arm around Cathy and hugged her, his two friends high-fived each other. Fatima sighed and pulled deeply on her cigarette.

•   •   •

She came home that evening drained. She also had a headache. Fatima took two aspirin, ate a slice of leftover pizza, and then climbed in bed. As she waited for the pain to subside, her cell phone rang. She saw who it was calling and answered, though she wasn't in the mood to talk.

"Hello, Andre."

"You okay? I've been trying to reach you since this morning."

"I have a migraine."

"Then I'll be brief. I trust you saw that newspaper?"

"That's why I have a migraine."

"What happened, Fatima?"

"Long story short, some asshole threw a bottle at me while I was addressing the audience. Shit got out of hand after that."

"Obviously."

Fatima waited for Andre to continue.

"Do you know how embarrassing it is for a coworker to show you a newspaper with a picture of your fiancée on the front page, trying to fight kids?"

"No, but I'm sure you'll let me know."

"Don't be flippant."

"Andre, I've had a tough day."

"So have I."

Whatever grief Andre experienced couldn't come close to the shit Fatima had to deal with. She started to tell him that but decided against it. The thought of having to deal with further bullshit made Fatima's headache throb more.

"Andre, let's have this discussion another time? I can't do this right now."

Fatima ended the call before Andre could reply. She felt bad about hanging up on him, but her head felt worse and she needed to rest.

•   •   •

Fatima woke up early the next day feeling only slightly better. She picked out her clothes for work and then made bacon, scrambled eggs, and toast. She took her breakfast into the living room and clicked on the television. She was sitting serenely, sipping fresh java and enjoying her meal, when the local news show she regularly watched aired the video of the Marcus Garvey Park brawl. She scalded her leg when she dropped her coffee cup.

"*Fuck!*" Fatima yelled as she jumped up. With eyes still glued to the newscast, she saw herself, in high definition, being restrained by the two volunteers while she desperately tried to reach the boy who threw the soda at her. And all around her teens were either kicking ass or getting their ass kicked. Fatima's headache returned.

She clicked off the television when the video ended and slipped out of her coffee stained pajamas. Fatima then took two aspirin, a sip of water, and a shower. After drying off and putting on fresh pajamas, she picked up her cell phone and left a message for her supervisor that she would not be at work. She then turned off her phone, climbed into bed, and went to sleep.

The next morning Fatima was in bed debating whether or not to call out sick one more day. She didn't want to go to work, but knew that the longer she stayed out the more crap she'd have to do when she did return. A few minutes later Fatima crawled her butt out of bed. She turned her cell phone on and then went into the bathroom. As soon as she sat on the toilet her cell rang. Only Marisol had bad timing like that. Fatima returned her call five minutes later.

"Good morning, Marisol."

"Where have you been, Fatima?"

"Home."

"I've been calling since yesterday!"

"I turned my phones off. What's up?"

"I have a meeting with my principal today about that fight in the park."

"Damn."

"She saw my mug in that video when it aired on the news yesterday."

"You in trouble?"

"Not really, it wasn't a school sanctioned activity, and it wasn't on school property. All she can do is talk shit, which is nothing new."

"I guess that's good."

"How'd it go at your job yesterday?"

"I called out sick after I saw that shit was on the morning news."

"You going in today?"

"I'm afraid so."

"Come on Fatima, how bad could it be?"

.   .   .

Inez was waiting for Fatima when she arrived at work.

"Hi there! We missed you!" Inez sang.

"Please, don't start?" Fatima pleaded as she sat down at her desk.

"I got to. That shit was crazy!"

Fatima mentally prepared herself for a salvo of wisecracks.

"You know, we could have used you and your girls down in Mississippi back in the sixties. Y'all could have put foot in the Klan's ass like y'all did them boys!"

Fatima frowned at Inez, but it didn't faze her.

"What you got against folks up in Harlem fuckin' anyway?" Inez asked.

Fatima turned in her seat, reached across her desk, and picked up her metal stapler. She then closed her eyes and bowed her head. She made the sign of the cross with the stapler when she was done praying. This made Inez uneasy.

"Okay, I'll stop for now. But this shit ain't hardly over."

"Thank you!" Fatima sighed. She was thankful that her prayer had been answered and she didn't have to go upside Inez's head.

NINETEEN
YOU HEAR ME STUTTER?

Summers in The Dark Towers were always brutal. Even though the sun had gone down an hour ago, it was still blazingly hot in the Richardson apartment. The ancient air conditioner in the living room window was clanking loudly and chilling nothing. Fatima unlocked the front door and walked inside the humid apartment to find Nikki and Melody spending Saturday night on the sofa watching the idiot box.

Nikki was recently diagnosed with gestational diabetes. Excessive nausea and vomiting prompted her mother to take her to the clinic for another prenatal visit. When the obstetrician asked if diabetes ran in Nikki's family Pamela sadly nodded. Their clan was cursed with the disease. Nikki was immediately put on a diet that excluded soda, fruit juice, and sweets. The restrictions were killing her. The daily walks she had to take for exercise were also burdensome. And then Nikki's mother made her quit her part-time job. To be young, pregnant, and broke was a major inconvenience.

"Hi, Fatima."

"Hey, Melody. What you guys watching?"

"*The Beautician,*" Nikki answered.

The Beautician was the latest reality show to dominate television ratings. It followed the antics of Brooklyn based, thirty-seven-year-old hairdresser Denise Alston, aka Nasty Niecy. After winning a million dollars from a scratch-off lottery ticket, Nasty Niecy cussed out her underpaying employer and then opened her own beauty shop across the street from her ex-boss. Every other word that came from her foul mouth had to be censored as she put customers, begging family and friends, and her two boyfriends in check. This of course contributed to the cable show's runaway success.

"Why you girls looking at that garbage? You two don't have anything better to watch?"

"There's a new version of your fight in the park online. Wanna see it on my laptop?"

"Wanna see my foot up your pregnant ass?"

"Why you here, anyway?" Nikki asked, ignoring her sister's threat.

"To borrow a Bible. Mama got me speaking at church in a few weeks."

"You really gonna do it?" Nikki asked.

"Your mother gave me no choice. She back from the casino?"

"Bus left Connecticut late. Mama won't get here until after midnight."

"What day you preaching?" Melody asked. "I wanna see that shit," she chuckled.

"Melody... don't start," Fatima warned. She then walked across the room to the bookcase and began Bible hunting.

"I'll let you know when," Nikki whispered. "I wanna see that shit too."

"I heard that," Fatima cautioned.

"How's that Global Economics course?" Nikki asked, switching subjects.

"The course is easy. It's the students that's giving me problems."

Fatima found a dusty, seldom used, New International Version on the lower shelf of the bookcase. It wasn't the version she preferred, but it would do. Fatima tucked the Bible into her bag and sat across from the girls in the old leather recliner.

"What's wrong with your class?" Melody asked.

"I'm tired of bastards pointing at me and snickering on campus."

"That pussy strike you started is being talked about all over," Nikki said.

"I didn't start no pussy strike!"

"That's not what the media is saying," Melody said.

"Damn the media!"

"Showing that fight video on television didn't help things, either," Nikki said.

"Don't I know it," Fatima mumbled.

She'd already received a dozen phone messages at her house from various news organizations seeking interviews. She even received voice mails on her cell phone. Fatima was very selective whom she gave her phone numbers to, but a certain Latino gym teacher was obviously not so picky.

"You're not excited about being recognized, like a celebrity?"

"Not at all, Melody."

"A lot of guys in Harlem ain't happy about this sex strike, either," Nikki said.

"Fuck 'em," Fatima said dryly.

"My cousin said she ain't never giving up screwing," Melody said.

"Good for her," Fatima said as she watched Nasty Niecy rip a weave off a customer's head when the lady inquired about paying for it on installment.

"Can't see how y'all watch this!" Fatima said in disgust. She got up and grabbed her bag.

"You out?" Nikki asked.

"I have a date with my fiancé. Need anything before I leave, Nikki?"

"Besides a job?"

Fatima sighed as she pulled her purse out of her bag.

"Here. And don't spend this on foolishness."

"Thanks!" Nikki said as she snatched the fifty-dollar bill from her sister.

"Later, Melody."

"Bye, Fatima."

"Love you," Nikki said sweetly.

Fatima opened her mouth to give a smart reply but remained silent and left the apartment.

•   •   •

The Great Migration that began during the First World War gave thousands of unpolished rural blacks from the south a chance to pass themselves off as sophisticated urbanites in the streets of Harlem. Yet racism refused to be left behind at the train depots of Atlanta, Birmingham, Greensboro, Jacksonville, and countless other stations below the Mason Dixon line. It was awaiting Negroes as they climbed out of the subway stations in upper Manhattan. To briefly forget the slights they endured daily because of the color of their skin, the people of Harlem required diversionary entertainment.

The Apollo Theatre, Savoy Ballroom and Small's Paradise were just some of the venues where Harlemites could go and enjoy themselves back in the day. Legendary performing idols, recognizable by first name alone; Billie, Cab, Chick, Count, Dizzy, Duke, Ella, Fats, Louis, Miles, and Sarah performed at these locales. Harlem's musical tastes would morph from jazz, to rhythm and blues, and then hip-hop as time marched on. The community's thirst for live shows would always be unquenched.

This was why Fatima and Andre were lined up with dozens of other patrons down the sidewalk of Lexington Avenue near 125th Street, waiting to get inside Café Bulawayo. The restaurant had opened at the beginning of the summer and was the place to be uptown Saturday night. Café Bulawayo served great authentic South African cuisine. Its barbecued boerewors sausage, mealie bread, and spicy chutney kept the place packed.

And while Café Bulawayo's food was to die for, it was the sounds of Dingane Brown, the kick-ass house band that played a hypnotic mixture of hip-hop and Xhosa beats the people came nightly to hear. The eight-piece band included two very talented drummers and a female deejay from South Jersey who wrecked the turntables on the regular.

"This line is hardly moving," Fatima complained.

"We'll be inside soon," Andre said. "And then we can discuss a few things."

"If you say so," Fatima replied. (She had stalled discussing the fight video with Andre for as long as she could and was ready to get the shit over with.)

The area around them was filled with trash, despite the valiant efforts of men and women paid to remove rubbish daily. Candy wrappers, paper cups, empty soda bottles, shopping bags, and cigarettes butts provided a crude obstacle course for Fatima and Andre as they slowly advanced toward the entrance.

They were just about to be waved through the front door when Tayzohn Lopez recognized Fatima. The twenty-year-old, six-foot five,

Latin behemoth was forty pounds heavier than Andre and had plenty of muscles from working manual labor jobs due to his limited education.

"You that bitch who started that fight!" he rudely exclaimed.

Fatima's blood pressure soared.

"What the fuck you just say?!"

"Bitch, you fucking up the game for us!"

Tayzohn's loud accusation generated onlookers. Most of whom were also waiting in line to pay for good food and hear good music. A good street fight too would be a bonus.

Andre was in a difficult situation. He was a stern believer in non-violence. He also didn't see the need for unnecessary roughness while dressed in a new pair of designer slacks. He also had on expensive Italian loafers. Why get them scuffed up over foolishness? But nevertheless, Fatima had accepted his proposal for marriage. Andre was bound by duty to defend her honor.

"My man, I need you to apologize to my woman."

Tayzohn looked at Andre and sneered.

"And if I don't?"

"Then, you'll have to deal with me."

"Really?" Tayzohn asked. He then stepped close to Andre.

Ain't this some shit? Andre silently pondered. It was too late to back down.

"You hear me stutter?" Andre asked.

He was about to talk more mandatory smack when he felt a straight right slam into his jaw. If Andre hadn't staggered into Fatima's arms he would've hit the ground. He was upset for leaving his guard down. The last fist fight he'd had was in the third grade with a girl over a basketball. (She won. They later attended their high school prom together.)

Andre lunged wildly at Tayzohn and received another straight right to the jaw. He scraped his palm on a piece of glass when he hit the sidewalk. The sharp pain enraged him. There was no way he was going to take an ass kicking in front of his woman… without getting in some good licks himself. With startling speed Andre again charged Tayzohn, catching him around the waist and driving him hard against a parked utility van.

Tayzohn rained blows on Andre's back, but Andre refused to let go of him. He managed to shove Tayzohn hard against the van a few more times. Tayzohn desperately tried to scoop Andre up and slam him against something solid, like the pavement, but the motherfucker refused to turn him loose.

All the time Andre and Tayzohn were scuffling, Fatima had been hysterical. Not because she was watching her man take a beat down, but because two brothers restrained her from joining the fight out of concern for her safety. Fatima unleashed a flurry of profanity as they held her arms, but they were unimpressed, having been called far worse back home in Newark, New Jersey.

The crowd of onlookers grew. This aroused the curiosity of a passing NYPD patrol car. When the two policemen swooped in on Andre and his adversary, they didn't halt to hear versions of who was guilty and who was not. That was for a judge to determine. Andre went peacefully into the rear of his patrol car. Tayzohn had to be tasered before he could be cuffed and stuffed into the patrol car of a backup police unit that was called to assist. Fatima almost received a pair of silver bracelets too, had the Jersey boys not held her from attacking the police as they detained her fiancé.

Andre was pissed as he sat in the back of the patrol car. The handcuffs on his wrists were too tight and his thumbs were numb due to poor circulation. His jaw felt like it was on fire and he couldn't feel his lower spine at all. Andre's trousers had a hole ripped in one knee, but his Italian loafers were in okay condition. He would have no problem cleaning his blood off them.

The ride to the police precinct was fifteen blocks away. Andre was booked and placed in a holding cell while an officer searched their database for past criminal activity or outstanding warrants. Three hours later he was released with a date to appear in court. Fatima was faithfully waiting outside the building. She dropped her cigarette when she saw him walking her way.

"You alright?"

"Do I look fucking alright?" Andre asked. He walked past Fatima and headed for the corner. She followed.

"Where you going?"

"To get my car and go home."

Andre raised his hand to hail a passing cab. The driver ignored him and sped on by.

"What about me?"

Andre slowly turned and scowled at Fatima.

"Thanks to *you*, I need an attorney to ensure I don't get a criminal record."

"Andre, you know I didn't start that altercation."

"Yeah, but that pussy strike, or whatever you guys are doing, had a lot to do with it."

Andre signaled another cab. This time the driver, a young immigrant from West Africa, pulled over. Andre opened the rear door and hopped in. He then faced Fatima.

"Are you coming?"

"Are you going to be rational?"

Andre closed the cab door and nodded to the driver to pull off. He didn't return Fatima's phone calls for three days.

.   .   .

When Andre did call Fatima back the following week, he requested she meet him that night at Susie's Sushi, a Japanese eatery around the corner from his apartment. He said they had a few important items to discuss before they became man and wife. Fatima agreed to the summit.

Andre was sitting at the small bar area sipping on a bottle of Sapporo beer when she walked in.

"Hi, how was class this evening?" Andre asked. He lightly kissed her cheek.

"Boring as usual."

"You want something to drink?"

"I'll just have water."

Andre stood up and escorted Fatima to a nearby table. After they ordered a serving of California rolls he got straight to business.

"Fatima, first of all, I want to apologize for being mad at you the other night. I was wrong."

"Apology accepted," Fatima said with a smile.

"The reason I was so upset about getting arrested is that it may blow my chance for a job I interviewed for last week."

"You interviewed for a new job?"

"I'd have twice the responsibility I have now. And… twice the pay."

"Twice the pay?"

"I'm one of four finalists for the position. I'd have my own office, my own assistant, and eight people working under me."

"Really?"

"I was going to tell you about it the other night, once we sat down in Café Bulawayo."

"That's great," Fatima said. "You'll get the job. I know it."

"Blowing a golden opportunity like that was on my mind the entire time I sat in that jail cell," Andre sighed.

"I'm sorry about the other night, too."

"I know it wasn't your fault," Andre said as he took a sip of his beer. He then took hold of Fatima's hand. "On a positive note, I've retained a good lawyer. She guaranteed me she'll get my charges thrown out. She'll need to talk to you about what went down that night."

"No problem," Fatima said before sipping the water with lemon she ordered.

"Now, we need to discuss this uh, sex stoppage you've got going on."

"For the last time, I didn't start no damn—"

Andre held his hands up in surrender.

"Okay! But as we both know, that's the opinion of some people out there in the streets. You have to fix that."

"What do you suggest?"

"You go to the media and say to them what you just said to me. You didn't start this sex strike, and you have no affiliation with it now."

"I think you're right."

"I know I am, Fatima. If you do that, it'll be a lot safer for the both of us until hopefully, we get to leave."

"Get to leave? Where to?"

Andre took a long swallow of his beer and then set the empty bottle on the table. He then looked uneasily at Fatima.

"The new job I was telling you about… it's in Philly."

Fatima leaned across the table.

"I'm sorry, I thought you said Philly, as in the state of Pennsylvania?"

"I did."

"I can't leave New York! My family and friends are here!"

"Philly is only a two hour ride from New York City."

"I've driven to Philly. Got parking tickets both times," Fatima replied.

Andre ignored the cynicism.

"What I'm thinking, if I get this position, is that I'd move out there and find us housing in a nice neighborhood. Then you'd come out once you finish school."

Fatima silently prayed then and there that Andre didn't get the position. She took another sip of water once she was done. When Andre opened his mouth to further plead his case, Fatima interrupted.

"Our food's here!" she announced cheerfully.

Andre chose to let the matter rest… for the moment. After saying a quick blessing over their meal, they ate in silence. Fatima was glad for the reprieve. As she dined, she reminded herself to follow Andre's advice and disassociate herself from that pussy strike. What he suggested was sensible. But Andre was crazy as hell if he thought she was moving to goddamn Philadelphia.

TWENTY

PREACH IT GIRL!

Fatima was frustrated. She'd been pouring over her mother's Bible for almost an hour and still hadn't found adequate scripture for the worshippers at Greater Harlem Baptist. She searched for something to do with youth battling great odds and succeeding. The obvious choice was the story of young David versus the giant Goliath, but Fatima wanted to stay away from that tired tale.

She was splayed on her couch, sipping a glass of chilled merlot as she flipped through the pages of the Good Book. Fatima jotted down every idea that came to her in a notebook and ran with it… until she hit a mental roadblock. When her cell phone interrupted her, she frowned before answering.

"Yes, Marisol?"

"Are you home? I'm outside."

"Okay."

Fatima pushed herself off the couch and buzzed her into the building.

"Why are you here?" she asked when Marisol walked in.

"Greetings to you too, Fatima."

"Why are you here, Marisol?"

"I was in the area, so I decided to stop by."

Fatima lowered her eyes and scanned the floor around Marisol.

"What's wrong?"

"I'm making sure you don't drop any of your bullshit on my floor."

Fatima locked the front door and returned to the couch. Marisol sat in the armchair across from her.

"So, what you doing?" she asked.

"Looking up scripture for church tomorrow. I'm the guest speaker for Youth Day."

"You?"

"Yeah, me," Fatima answered curtly. "Is that a problem?"

"I think it's cute."

Fatima shot Marisol an icy glare.

"What subject are you speaking on?"

"Inspiring youth. I need a good story from the Bible that relates to it."

"What about the Three Hebrew Boys?"

"How can I tie that into a message for today's youth?"

"You could uh, mention how Harlem is like a huge fiery furnace, and how youth in the community are surrounded by hot temptations every-where and—"

"Marisol, that's stupid."

"I was trying to be helpful."

"Thanks anyway," Fatima said. "Now, again, why are you here?"

Marisol opened her mouth to spew more bullshit, then saw the skep-tical look in Fatima's eyes. The gig was up.

"I need a big favor."

"What else is new?"

"LL wants you back on his show."

"Do you want Andre and me to marry, or not? I'm confused."

"LL will donate five hundred dollars to GASP if you appear on *The Real Deal* again."

"What the hell is GASP?"

"Girls Against Sexual Promiscuity."

Fatima drained the rest of her wine.

"GASP?" she then asked Marisol, fighting to keep a straight face.

"LL asked me for the name of the organization to make a donation to if you appeared on his show again. That's what I came up with."

"You are really scaring me, Marisol."

"Will you do it?"

Fatima remained silent as she got up and walked into the kitchen. She returned with her bottle of merlot and another glass. She poured wine into the glass and handed it to Marisol.

"Thanks."

Fatima then refreshed her own glass.

"This is good. Where'd you get it?" Marisol asked after sipping the vintage.

"A wine shop near Andre's place."

"How is he?"

"Andre's fine. He wants me to distance myself from this... this pussy strike. Which is what I am going to do."

"But we need you."

"I did tell you how pissed Andre was after he got arrested for defending me from that asshole?"

"You did."

"Yet you still ask me to do stuff for your cause? Look, I don't know how you and Raphael roll, but I try to make Andre happy."

Marisol took a quick sip of wine. Fatima almost missed the tear that slid down her face.

"Hey? What's wrong?"

"We broke up."

"You and Raphael? When?!"

"A few weeks ago."

"You didn't even tell me?"

"It's not something I feel the need to broadcast."

"What happened?"

"I caught him cheating."

Fatima drained her glass and then reloaded.

"Any details?"

"I was at Raphael's place and dropped my MetroCard for the bus behind his bed as I was getting dressed. When I looked under it to retrieve my card, I found a large, gold-hooped earring. You know I don't wear gaudy shit like that."

"Did he offer an excuse?"

"Said it was his sister's."

"So?"

"His sister's a minister in Cincinnati. She doesn't wear gaudy shit like that either."

Marisol took another swig from her drink.

"I can't figure men out, Fatima."

"I know, girl. They spend nine months waiting to get out of a woman and the rest of their lives trying to get in as many women as they can."

Fatima topped off Marisol's glass with more wine. "Will you take Raphael back if he begs for forgiveness?"

"*Nada.* I'm moving on. I've registered with Black People Hook Up."

"The Internet dating site?"

"Yes. A music teacher at my school got engaged last month to a guy she met online. If that lunatic can find a man over the Internet, anybody can."

Fatima spilled half her drink when she laughed.

"That is so foul," she snickered.

"It's also true."

"Any bites?" Fatima asked as she sopped up the spilled wine with napkins.

Marisol pulled her cell phone out and opened up her email.

"Look," she said and handed the phone to Fatima.

"Wow! Didn't know New York had that many desperate men!"

"Gimme my damn phone!" Marisol said as she snatched it back from Fatima. They then shared a fit of the giggles. The alcohol was working. As Fatima laughed she glanced at her mother's Bible. The fact that she was fixing to fuck up sunk in quick.

"I have to get back to work, Marisol."

"Okay," Marisol said as she drank the rest of her wine. "I can take a hint."

Fatima followed her to the front door.

"Keep me posted on your Internet dating?"

"Will do, Fatima."

Fatima locked her front door and sat back down in the living room. She sighed deeply then smiled at getting out of appearing on that damn cable show. As she opened the Bible her cell phone vibrated. It was a text message from Marisol: *Please say yes to The Real Deal?* Fatima texted her back: *Marisol, why doest thou torment me so?*

.   .   .

Birdman loved the smell of Harlem in the morning. He was sitting on a wet bench outside The Dark Towers when Fatima cruised by looking for a space to park her car. She lucked out and found one three blocks away.

"What you doing out here so early?" Fatima asked when she walked back to the housing project. She was dressed in a gray herringbone pant-suit and had her locks tied up in a black, African print headwrap. It was a little past seven.

Fatima had nodded off on her couch while studying the Book of Job. The heavy rain that started afterward, and the wine she had consumed ensured that she slept like a baby. She was fortunate to have set the alarm on her cell phone beforehand to wake her up early on Sunday.

"I'm watching folks go to jail," Birdman said. He was wearing an once-white undershirt and a pair of tattered jeans. The new gray canvas sneakers he wore clashed with the rest of his outfit.

"Say what?"

"See that beige car across the street?" Birdman indicated the automobile with his cigarette. "The passenger side window is rolled down with an open pocketbook on the front seat."

"An 'okeydoke' car?"

"Exactly. I passed it earlier when I went to get me some cigarettes."

"The police still doing that?"

"Evidently."

"How many arrests?"

"I've seen two so far. The cops are in that old green van on the corner."

"I hope people can walk by that car and not try to steal shit that ain't theirs?"

"Two fools failed so far," Birdman said. He then studied Fatima's wardrobe.

"What brings you out this early, looking all dark and lovely?"

"I'm the guest speaker at my church this morning."

"You?"

"What the fuck is wrong with everybody? Yes! Me!"

"Okay, damn, calm down. Here…"

Birdman pulled out his pack of smokes and offered Fatima one. She took it.

"Thanks, Gregory," Fatima said as she lit it.

Birdman was silent as he watched a gaunt teenager walk by the police's bait. The kid slowed down, peered into the car and smiled. He wisely continued on his way.

"I heard Jamaal caught some serious time on that gun charge, Fatima."

"Good for him."

"When the judge gave him four years on a criminal possession of a weapons charge, Jamaal smiled and told her that he could do that standing on his head."

"That was stupid."

"The judge thought so too. She added two more years to his sentence. Told Jamaal that should be enough time for him to get back on his feet."

"What an asshole," Fatima said. She took several long puffs on her cigarette and then tossed it to the ground.

"I have to go get my Moms. Thanks for the smoke."

"You welcome, Fatima. Good luck at church."

.   .   .

Pamela was plucking her eyebrows in the bathroom when she heard her front door close.

"Fatima?"

"Yes."

Pamela walked into the living room clad in her favorite Sunday suit. It was a turquoise, satin three-piece number.

"You look nice," Pamela said after giving her daughter the once over.

"Thanks."

"I trust you won't disappoint your mother today?"

Fatima held her tongue.

"You eat?" Pamela asked. (She recognized the silent treatment.)

"I had a couple pieces of fruit."

"I'll treat you guys to brunch after service," Pamela said with a smile. She then stepped into the hallway. "Let's go, Nikki! We don't have all morning to wait on your ass!"

The closer Fatima got to church, the more nervous she became. And the traffic didn't help. She was on St. Nicholas Avenue when a taxi cut her off to make an illegal left turn.

"Stupid motherfucker!"

"Fatima!" Pamela moaned and then hung her head in despair.

    •   •   •

Fatima's penchant for profanity was the result of an ill-fated decision her mother made twenty-four years earlier. As a single working mom, child-care was always an issue that caused Pamela angst. The daycare center Fatima's mother wanted her child to attend was priced out of the household budget. And being from down south, there was no kinfolk Pamela could beg to watch her child at a reduced rate. The answer to her problem was literally over her head.

Keisha Woolfolk was a nineteen-year-old high school graduate who lived one floor above the Richardson family. She was well groomed, well mannered, and soft-spoken. The fact that Keisha attended college in the evenings made her a perfect candidate to babysit little Fatima. Plus, Keisha was inexpensive. Things went well… for the first year.

Then one day Pamela and her toddler were strolling down the cereal aisle of a grocery store and young Fatima spied her favorite food in the world, Crispy Cocoa Snaps! When Fatima grabbed a large box of the sugar-laden breakfast cereal and held it out for Pamela to put into their cart, her request was denied. Her mother placed the box of cereal back on the shelf.

"Dammit!" little Fatima yelled. She started to cry. Needless to say, Pamela was mortified. A few shoppers nearby heard the tot use profanity and deduced that Fatima's potty mouth came from her unfit mother. It took Pamela another month to realize that Keisha was the cause of the cussing. But by the time she was able to find another affordable babysitter it was too late.

Fatima had taken to cussing like a rat to a Manhattan sewer line. The toddler enjoyed sitting in the living room and shouting "mudderfucky" or "sumnabit" at everyone she saw on television. And no matter how many times her mother popped her hand for swearing, little Fatima would cuss again when she felt the need.

As time marched on, Pamela was regularly summoned to parent-teacher conferences to discuss Fatima's aptitude for foul language. The poor woman gradually realized that physical chastisement and heavy prayer for her daughter were futile. Fatima was around eleven when her mother finally said, "Fuck it," and gave up trying to fix her daughter's potty mouth.

·   ·   ·

"Fatima? Watch what you say as you're speaking up there?" Pamela requested as the family got out of the car near the church. Fatima looked at her mother with disbelief.

"Mama, please? I got this."

Twenty minutes later, Fatima actually began to hyperventilate as she sat up in the pulpit looking over the congregation. *When did Greater Harlem Baptist have this many damn people show up in the morning for Youth Day?* Fatima needed another cigarette. Bad. The swarm of butterflies in her stomach felt like they were trying to re-enter their cocoons. The Greater Harlem Baptist Youth Choir had just wrapped up a soul-stirring rendition of "Oh Mary Don't You Weep" led by a young girl who sounded eerily like Aretha Franklin. While they received a thunderous round of applause, Reverend Yizar approached the lectern. He was decked out in an elegant black pastoral robe with gold embroidered sleeves.

"Let's give our youth choir another hand? Amen!" The congregation clapped again for another two minutes.

"This Sunday morning, we've been blessed to hear words of inspiration from a dynamic young lady, who is rapidly becoming a force to be reckoned with in our community... as well as in our local parks."

Members of the congregation snickered at the pastor's allusion to Fatima's public brawl. She was not amused.

"Nevertheless, I'm proud that Greater Harlem Baptist can claim her as one of our own. Ladies and gentlemen, I present to you, Ms. Fatima Richardson! Hear ye her..."

Fatima was mindful not to roll her eyes at Reverend Yizar as she passed him. Her legs felt rubbery as she ambled toward the large lectern. Standing behind it she was horrified to realize she couldn't see over the damn thing. Her talk would have to be delivered out in the open. That would be hard with her mother and Nikki plopped in the front row staring up at her. And she couldn't give a talk holding notes in her hand. That would be too amateurish. Fatima would have to recite the information she remembered and wing the rest. *Dammit!* She thought as she reluctantly placed her notepad on the lectern.

"First and foremost, I would like to give all honor to God. Secondly, I would be remiss if I didn't mention that my mother is the reason I stand before you folks today. Thank you, Mommy dearest."

Fatima glared at her mother and smiled. The audience lightly applauded. Pamela beamed with pride.

"Last, but not least, I would like for you all to bear with me, as I attempt to bring a few words of encouragement to the youth present here today."

"That's alright!" a member from the back of the congregation said.

"Earlier this week, as I was turning the pages of my Bible in an effort to find something of relevance to speak about this Youth Day, I stumbled upon the Book of Daniel. And, when I got to the third chapter of Daniel, I stumbled across the three young men named, Shadrach, Meshach and Abednego. I believe you folks know them as, The Three Hebrew Boys?"

"Well?" another member of the congregation uttered.

"Now, my Bible tells me that King Nebuchadnezzar, of Babylon, had a golden image made for all his subjects to bow down and worship. And, apparently, these three brothers wasn't feeling that."

A light chuckle traveled through the church.

"Matter of fact," Fatima continued, "they wasn't feeling the king's edict at all. And, as I read a little further, I discovered that when Nebuchadnezzar found out that these cats broke the law, and refused to bow down and worship his golden image, he had them tossed into a fiery furnace."

"Yes, he did," Pamela added loudly.

Fatima's butterflies still fluttered in her stomach as she tried to remember the main idea she wanted to take from the story of The Three Hebrew Boys.

"And you know, when we think about it, we can compare their situation, to the situation that our youth face today, in Harlem and elsewhere. The Three Hebrew Boys literally caught hell. Our youth today are also out here, catching hell."

The sound of hands clapping swept through the congregation, indicating agreement with Fatima's statement.

"Our youth are catching hell from the education system. They're catching hell from the criminal justice system. They're catching hell from the rampant racism we all have to deal with in this, this modern day Babylon."

There was more applause. The butterflies Fatima had felt previously flew away in defeat.

"I came by Greater Harlem Baptist this morning to tell you that, in the same way the Three Hebrew Boys didn't despair when they were tossed in that fiery furnace? Our youth should not lose hope either."

"Preach it girl!" several members yelled as Fatima edged her way over to where the Youth Choir was seated.

"Young people, not only do you need to believe in God, but you also need to believe in yourself."

"Amen!" more church members responded.

"See, if you can believe? Then you can achieve," Fatima said as she turned and walked back toward the center of the pulpit.

"Church, just as precious metals are placed into the fire to be purified? We too, have to go through our own trials by fire."

"Amen!" Pamela said. (She was so proud of her eldest child.)

"Because, that's the only way we can come forth as pure gold!" Fatima said.

Greater Harlem Baptist was flooded with all the "Amens!" that rained down from the congregation. Fatima was knocking them dead! Even Reverend Yizar sat up in his large wooden chair and took notice...

This girl's good! And she got a nice ass on her!

Fatima got caught up in the spirit as she delivered her message. She pontificated about the high unemployment rate for young people of color. She ranted about the lack of positive role models for today's youth. And she railed on the entertainment industry's "golden images" that distracted young people from the real issues that mattered.

Fatima mentioned culprits such as ignorant reality shows on television, time-wasting home video games, and the mindless music played on inner-city radio stations that glorified criminal activity and sexual promiscuity. The more Fatima spoke, the more members of Greater Harlem Baptist shouted their approval.

"So, just like the Three Hebrew Boys, don't bow down and do the things you know isn't good for you! Am I right church?"

"Yeah!" half the congregation yelled back.

"Preach!" Reverend Yizar yelled. (Fatima ignored him.)

"Think before you act! Don't steal what don't belong to you! Don't sell drugs! Don't drop out of school! Don't be pressured into having sex!"

Hearing that, Nikki shrank down in her seat the best she could. The rest of Greater Harlem Baptist was in a frenzy. Folks were jumping up and shouting. Young people were clapping enthusiastically. Even church elders were nodding their valued endorsement.

The organist, Sister Denise Greene, joined the affair by accentuating Fatima's message with "preacher chords" on her instrument. Fatima got so worked up that sweat and alcohol seeped from her pores.

"Young people, don't worship new sneakers, or designer clothes! Don't bow down and try to make fast money!"

"Tell it!" one of the church members hollered.

"Worshiping fast money will get you into quick trouble! Am I right, or am I right?" Fatima asked as she wiped perspiration from her brow.

"You right!" Pamela shouted.

"And young people, when you see trouble up ahead? Move out the way! I mean, why get caught up in some dumb shit if you can avoid it!?"

The entire church gasped in astonishment when they heard what came out of Fatima's mouth. Everybody froze. It was as if someone had taken a giant remote control and paused the whole congregation. Pamela, Nikki, and Reverend Yizar's jaws were all wide open in disbelief. Fatima panicked...

"I meant, uh, why get yourself into a problem, if it can be avoided? And also, why go on, and—"

Seeing worry on her beloved pastor's face, Denise Greene cranked her organ up and the Youth Choir sprung into action with a heartfelt rendition of "Standing In The Need Of Prayer" as Fatima turned and retreated from the pulpit. She hastily exited the church through a rear door.

Fatima nervously paced back and forth in front of the building a few times before she realized that she was being watched.

"You okay?" a fashionably dressed black woman asked as she walked down the front steps of the church. She appeared to be in her late forties. Fatima noticed the streak of silver hair running through her carefully coiffed dark mane.

"Not really," Fatima said.

"I'm Roxanne Carter," the woman said holding out her hand. Fatima shook it warily.

"Fatima Richardson."

"That was an interesting message you delivered up there."

Fatima was too humiliated to reply. The woman then pulled out a cigarette and fired it up. As she inhaled, she noticed the desperate look on Fatima's face.

"Would you like one?"

"Do you have one to spare?" Fatima asked anxiously.

TWENTY-ONE
LOIS

Fatima didn't sleep a wink that night. The incident at church kept playing in her mind over and over. She'd never be able to show her face there again. The wedding plans would have to be altered, and to make matters worse, her own mother had refused to speak to her when service let out.

At six in the morning, Fatima's alarm clock interrupted her fretting. It was time for another day at work. Before rising from her bed, she asked the Lord again to accept her apology for cussing in his holy sanctuary. She also prayed for enough strength to make it through another day at her damn job. After getting a pot of coffee going, Fatima hunted around her apartment for the possibility of a misplaced cigarette… to no avail. Trying to quit smoking was going to be the death of her.

An hour and a half later she rushed out her door to catch the subway. As Fatima passed her Beetle, she noticed it was sitting low against the curb. Further investigation revealed that some asshole had flattened all four tires. She swore under her breath the entire subway ride to work.

.   .   .

"Please tell me you didn't really use profanity in church?" Inez asked when Fatima walked past her cubicle. She was too pissed about her tires to wonder how Inez's nosy ass knew what had happened at Greater Harlem Baptist.

"Not in the mood right now. Somebody slashed all my tires last night."

"Sounds like divine retribution. Did you call the police?"

"What for?" Fatima asked sarcastically. She dropped her belongings on her desk and plopped down into her chair. She then leaned forward and placed her head in her hands.

"Morning, Fatima. Are you okay?"

Fatima looked up and found Ella Watkins looking down at her.

"My blood pressure's high right now."

"That's part of the nicotine withdrawal, girl. Fight it."

(Nicotine was not on Fatima's mind. Financing four new tires was.)

"Thanks, Ella."

"You try those e-cigarettes, yet?"

"Yes," Fatima lied in an effort to get the woman to leave.

"How are they?"

"Never tasted anything like it."

"Good. Stick with it, Fatima."

"I will."

Fatima closed her eyes and thought hard on where to find inexpensive tires in New York City. She drew a blank.

"Fatima?"

Ella was still there.

"Yes?" Fatima asked slowly as she opened her eyes.

"You have an extra two dollars on you? I want to get me a cup of coffee and a bagel, but I'm a little short. Inez suggested I ask you when you came in."

Fatima bit her tongue as she opened her purse for the cash.

"That's a nice blouse you have on," Ella threw in for good measure.

"Thanks," Fatima mumbled.

"Bless you," Ella said. She took the money and disappeared.

Fatima made it through the rest of the morning without further aggravation that wasn't job-related. Marisol called around eleven and offered to treat her to lunch at the Cue' and Brew Grill, which was a few blocks from her job on Flatbush Avenue. Fatima was in no fiscal condition to turn down a free meal.

She arrived a few minutes ahead of schedule and was shown a seat near the bar. Seated at the bar were three men combating the summer heat by guzzling beer. Fatima was perusing the endless variations of chicken dishes on the restaurant's menu when Marisol strode in. She wore a bright yellow, flowered sundress that highlighted her gorgeous legs and onion-shaped ass. The men sitting at the bar all paused.

"How's everything?" Marisol asked once she sat across from Fatima. She strategically shifted in her chair and turned her back to the gawkers nearby.

"Some fucker flattened all my tires."

"Get out!"

"I'm so pissed right now, it ain't funny."

"I don't blame you."

"What are we going to order?" Fatima asked.

"Let's see," Marisol answered as she looked over the lunch specials.

•   •   •

Elroy Murdoch was a prim and proper news reporter who possessed an uncanny ability to wrangle the most asinine opinions from New Yorkers he met in the streets during his Man With a Microphone interviews. The middle aged brother had a loyal following at WRAP news radio. Listeners loved to hear Elroy's nasal voice ask an unsuspecting passerby a question about a current news event and hear their ignorant reply.

For weeks Elroy had been hearing rumors of a Lysistrata type, sex stoppage taking place uptown by young women. Armed with his microphone and his trusty assistant producer, Harry, he hit the thoroughfares of Harlem in search of a scoop. Elroy dutifully slogged along Amsterdam Avenue, Broadway, Lenox Avenue and 125th Street shoving his microphone into the faces of young women and asking about the booty boycott.

More than a few girls cussed Elroy out. Many girls however, were happy to rant about the strike. One of these girls was Shaconda Miller, who also gave him Marisol Aquino's cell number. It was not a coincidence when Elroy walked through the door of the Cue' and Brew Grill as Fatima and Marisol were eating.

"Hello, Ms. Aquino," Elroy said when he approached her table.

"Hi," Marisol said weakly.

Elroy turned to Fatima.

"You must be Ms. Richardson?" he asked with a wide grin.

"And you are?" Fatima said to the man dressed in dark slacks, a white dress shirt, and a crooked bowtie.

"Elroy Murdoch. I'm with WRAP news radio."

"Is that right?" Fatima asked as she focused on the microphone Elroy held.

She smelled a setup.

"If I was to cuss your ass out right now, would I be wrong, Marisol?"

Marisol saw the anger in Fatima's eyes and remained silent. Elroy sensed something was amiss, but he didn't care. He was there for an interview.

"Ms. Richardson, could I ask you some questions about this sex strike you got going on in Harlem? It'll only take a few minutes."

"I do not have any sex strike going on," Fatima growled.

Harry the assistant was a dedicated employee at WRAP. But the station didn't offer combat pay. He slowly backed away from Fatima's table. However, Elroy was not about to be denied a story that involved sex, or the lack thereof.

"Ms. Richardson, could I please just get a few comments from you?"

Fatima ignored him and looked angrily at Marisol instead.

"If I was to cuss this idiot out, would I be wrong, Marisol?"

"Uh, Mr. Murdoch," Marisol began, "perhaps now is not the best time to talk to my friend. She's having a bad day."

Elroy didn't care about any female problems. He was trying to get a scoop.

"Look, Ms. Richardson, how about I ask three questions and then leave?" Elroy said as he held his microphone out to Fatima.

"How about getting that thing out my face, before I make you eat it?"

The assistant tapped Elroy on the arm and gestured it was time for them to move on.

"Maybe another time?" Elroy asked Marisol.

"No!" Fatima answered.

Elroy excused her foul manners to a bad case of the cramps and left without another word.

Fatima read Marisol the riot act as the two finished eating their hot chicken sandwiches.

"That stunt you just pulled was fucked up."

"Fatima, I only wanted to get us more—"

Fatima raised her hand and cut her friend off.

"Marisol, I'm done. If you wish to continue this anti-sex crusade, that's cool."

"But you have a gift. People listen to what you tell them."

"You know, Marisol? You're right."

Fatima opened her purse. She dug through it and pulled out a business card. She then grabbed her phone and began dialing.

"What are you doing?"

"Making a phone call."

"I get that," Marisol said dryly.

"Hello? May I speak with Roxanne Carter please?"

Marisol's eyes widened.

"*Black Awareness,* Roxanne Carter?"

Fatima ignored Marisol and shifted in her chair, turning her back to her.

"Please tell her Fatima Richardson called? Thank you."

Fatima ended her call and turned back to Marisol.

"When did you meet Roxanne Carter?"

"We talked last Sunday after I uh… spoke in church."

"Why didn't you tell me?"

"You'd be sweating me to do her show, like you are with LL and *The Real Deal.*"

"Fuck that clown," Marisol said. "*Black Awareness* is a legit TV show!"

"You're so loyal," Fatima said cynically. Before Marisol could reply, Fatima's cell phone rang.

"Hello? Hi, Ms. Carter."

Fatima saw Marisol staring. She turned her back to her once more.

"Yes, I'm calling to let you know I've changed my mind. I'll do your show."

When Marisol squealed in delight, Fatima shot her a disapproving look.

"When would you like me to come in for the taping? Next Tuesday evening? I'll see you then."

As soon as Fatima ended her call, The Latino Inquisition began.

"Where are you taping at?"

"The studio's in Midtown."

"What's the topic?"

"Don't know yet."

"How long will it take?"

"Couldn't tell you."

"Can I come?"

"Hell no. You can watch the show when it airs like everybody else."

"Whatever, Fatima."

Both women walked out of the Cue' and Brew Grill on a high note. Marisol was happy Fatima would be getting the exposure that their movement deserved. Fatima was pleased Roxanne Carter had returned her call. Her plan to publicly renounce her involvement with the pussy strike was all set.

.   .   .

Lois Ellison owned a spacious two-bedroom Co-op in The Astoria, a lovely building complex in Jamaica, Queens. She moved into her home when her son Andre was eight. The fifty-two-year-old retired NYC correction officer was contemplating selling her property and beating a retreat to Charlotte, where her pension checks would stretch a lot further.

When the door buzzer rang Lois extinguished her cigarette in the ashtray on the kitchen table and stood up. The door buzzer sounded again before Lois could reach the intercom.

"Who is it?"

"Fatima."

"Come on up!" Lois said as she pressed the button to the entrance door seventeen floors below her.

She was ecstatic about her future daughter in law. Fatima and Lois were both Sagittarians. They both loved Old School music, menthol cigarettes, and a well-mixed margarita. Fatima entered Lois' front door carrying a brown paper bag.

"Hey, Mrs. Ellison."

"Didn't I tell you to call me, Lois?"

"Sorry. I'll be more comfortable doing that after Andre and I are married."

Fatima walked into the kitchen and placed the bag on the table. Lois trailed behind her.

"Are those pork buns I smell?"

"Yes Ma'am," Fatima said. She reached into the bag and pulled out a carton of Chinese food.

"Didn't I tell you I'm trying to lose weight, Fatima?"

"You did."

"Are they baked?"

"They are. I got us shrimp rolls, too."

"I'll grab the plates," Lois said with a sly grin.

It only took twenty minutes for them to polish off their food.

"Wedding dress fit okay?" Lois asked as she washed the dishes.

"Still a little tight, but I'm working on it," Fatima said as she grabbed a dish rag and wiped off the table.

"That Chinese food didn't help."

"Didn't hurt either. Especially, since you ate most of it."

They looked at each other and laughed.

"I feel like a cigar now," Lois announced when she was finished with the dishes.

"You smoke cigars?" Fatima did little to hide the surprise in her voice.

"It's my new vice."

Lois opened her refrigerator and pulled out a small humidor.

"You in?" she asked.

"I've never smoked a cigar before."

"Cohibas, from Cuba!" Lois said as she pulled out two cigars.

"I don't know," Fatima said warily. "Andre's on my case now about smoking."

"I won't snitch. Take a few puffs and see if you like."

They sat at the table and lit up. Minutes later, the Ellison kitchen was clouded with cigar smoke. The buzz Fatima felt from her cigar relit memories of smoking good weed. That was something she hadn't done since she landed the job working for HRA.

"How we doing on seating arrangements?" Lois asked after taking a long pull on her stogie.

"Pain in the ass," Fatima answered.

"I know. I remember the hell I went through when Andre's father and me got married. I had to remember who wasn't speaking to who, who owed who money, who drank too much liquor. All kinda shit."

"Really?"

"Yeah, girl. That reminds me, Andre's dad is coming with a female guest. Put a few tables between me and that asshole?"

"We already did."

"Thanks. You see Andre's new apartment, yet?"

"No. I'm meeting him in Philly next week."

"He told me it's in a nice area."

"I was surprised he actually took the job."

"You don't want to leave New York, do you?" Lois asked.

Fatima weighed her response before she answered.

"No."

"Andre knows this?"

"He does. But this new job is paying him ridiculous money."

"Money isn't everything, girl."

"True, but Andre's so happy," Fatima said and then puffed on her cigar. Her head was floating above the clouds. "I have to be a team player and move down there after graduation."

"You two need to talk that issue out now. Andre's dad was offered a big promotion once, on the condition he relocated out of state."

"What happened?"

"I told that Negro he'd be moving to Texas by his damn self."

"That was the end of it?" Fatima asked.

"You see any damn cactus outside this building?" Lois asked while tapping her cigar into the ashtray.

"I don't want to stand in the way of Andre's career," Fatima sighed.

Lois placed her cigar in the ashtray. She then reached across the table and took Fatima's hand.

"Fatima, listen. Do not move to Philly if you're not going to be happy. Because if you're miserable, Andre will be miserable. I guarantee it."

TWENTY-TWO
ROXANNE & PHILBERT

Roxanne Carter's sparkling personality, hard work, and ability to get to the crux of a news story allowed her to survive the dog-eat-dog world of local television news anchoring for twenty years. It also allowed the divorced mother of two teenaged boys the financial ability to have her sons educated at a prestigious boarding school in Kutztown, Pennsylvania. The kids hated being away from New York, but their mother didn't care. There was only so much trouble two young black men could get into in Kutztown.

The time not spent raising her family allowed Roxanne the flexibility to work the various schedules her career required. This included her Tuesday evening taping of *Black Awareness*, an hour-long show that discussed important social issues affecting people of color. Thousands of Black New Yorkers tuned in each Sunday morning to be updated on current events impacting their lives.

The Harlem based news anchor had picked up chatter from her fourteen-year-old niece about a sex strike going on. Her niece also told her that the leader, Fatima Richardson, was in that Marcus Garvey Park brawl. A few weeks later, Roxanne was forwarded an email blast from a sorority sister who attended Greater Harlem Baptist Church. It announced that Fatima Richardson would be speaking there on Youth Day.

After watching Fatima make an ass of herself in the church that morning, Roxanne had deduced she would not be hanging around in the pulpit. She'd guessed correctly.

· · ·

Mahogany Media Studios was a state-of-the-art production facility in Manhattan owned by an astute Korean businesswoman. Fatima was impressed by the lavish décor. The bathroom was equipped with Japanese style, porcelain basins. The kitchen area, next to the conference room, had granite countertops and stainless steel appliances. And to top things off, the plush green room Fatima waited in contained a large edible arrangement of fruit that resembled Yankee Stadium.

An elderly white woman came in as Fatima was munching on centerfield and offered to apply makeup. When questioned, the woman informed her that the powder was necessary to make her face appear more natural under the lights of the talk show set. Fatima relented.

Roxanne walked in seconds later, dressed in a bespoke beige suit. She wore a white scarf printed with small butterflies as an accessory. Roxanne smiled warmly as she gave Fatima her official hug.

"Thank you so much for making it!"

"You're welcome," Fatima answered.

"Everything okay?"

"This food here is great."

"Thanks. I have to go speak to my director about a few things, then we'll get started."

"Okay," Fatima replied as she grabbed a piece of dugout from the fruit display. Roxanne left the room just as Fatima's cell vibrated. It was Marisol trying to reach her yet again. She declined the call. Marisol was hyped about the exposure her crusade would receive from being discussed on *Black Awareness,* but she was in for a rude awakening. Fatima was going to distance herself from the pussy strike on-air and then get on with her life.

A young blonde production assistant with a LA accent led her into the studio. Fatima was surprised to see another guest sitting at the set's clear, triangular discussion table. She'd thought she would be doing the show on the solo tip. The brother reminded her of Steve Urkel from the television sitcom, *Family Matters,* except he was shorter and his glasses thicker. He appeared to be Fatima's age and was dressed in a conservative dark blue suit. He wore a black tie that appeared to strangle his thin larynx.

Fatima had dressed conservatively herself by putting on a white blouse, dark gray slacks, and a pair of black low-heeled pumps. She had taken time the night before to re-twist her locks. She also wrapped her hair in a dark gray *gele* before she left home for the show's taping. Fatima smiled at the brother as she took her seat. The man nodded and continued texting on his cell phone.

Gazing around the small studio, Fatima noticed the two sets of low hanging hair lights above their table. More lighting was scattered above those. There were two cameras twenty feet away from the table on opposite sides of the room. Behind Fatima hung a large Afrocentric themed panel with the *Black Awareness* logo on it. The LA production assistant now approached Fatima with a small wireless mike in her hand.

"Let's just get you miked up," the woman said as she clipped the audio device on Fatima's blouse.

"Now, use your natural speaking voice when you talk and try not to make any unnecessary noise. These microphones are very sensitive."

After wiring up the other guest, the production assistant left the room. She returned several seconds later carrying three bottles of water.

"You guys will probably be needing these," she said cryptically and placed the water on the table.

A minute later Roxanne sat down and was also miked up. She turned on her megawatt smile once she was hooked up.

"Now, I want the both of you to call me Roxanne and, I'm sorry, have you two been formally introduced?"

"No," Fatima answered.

"Fatima Richardson, I'd like you to meet, Philbert Phelps."

What a fucked up name! Fatima thought.

"Pleasure to meet you, Mr. Phelps," she said with a tight smile.

Philbert Phelps hated his name. He was christened after his maternal grandfather. (He hated him also.) His classmates picked on him because of his funny sounding name, plus he was short. But being no punk, Philbert stood up for himself each time… and usually got knocked down. He compensated for his physical shortcomings and dreadful name by hitting the books hard. In time he became a bright, articulate student. This earned him a full ride to Tufts University, the prestigious research institution outside of Boston. He graduated with full honors.

Philbert adjusted his glasses as he gave Fatima a long look. He instantly analyzed her to be another uncouth, belligerent, black woman who was most likely also sexually frustrated.

"Nice to meet you, too," Philbert replied. *With your ghetto ass.*

Roxanne briefly explained how the videotaping process would go. When she was finished, she turned matters over to her set director, who counted down for the show's taping to commence. Roxanne then faced the camera to her right and turned on her charm.

"Good Sunday morning, New York. I'm Roxanne Carter and this is… Black Awareness." Roxanne smiled for five seconds and then continued.

"This morning I have with me two dynamic young activists who are striving to have a positive impact on the lives of youth in their communities."

Roxanne turned and faced Fatima.

"Fatima Richardson is a case worker with the city's Human Resources Administration." Roxanne smiled at Fatima and continued. "She's also associated with an extraordinary movement in Harlem that involves young ladies in that community consciously abstaining from sexual intercourse. Welcome to the show, Ms. Richardson."

"Thanks for having me," Fatima replied. She was anxious as she awaited her chance to renounce her affiliation with Marisol's movement.

Roxanne then turned and faced Philbert.

"Philbert Phelps is a political journalist for *Urban Warrior* magazine, and the founder of the community action group, Concerned Black Men of Harlem. Welcome to the show, Mr. Phelps."

"Pleasure to be here, Roxanne."

Roxanne turned back to Fatima.

"I want to get straight to this, sex strike if you will, that's going on in Harlem, Ms. Richardson. How did all this come about?"

Fatima felt obliged to answer the question. Then she would announce her separation from the movement.

"Actually, a sex strike was not planned. I was invited to speak at a high-school function earlier this year, and in my speech, I disclosed a story of a teen I knew who shocked everyone by becoming pregnant."

"Another unfortunate statistic," Roxanne observed.

"Exactly," Fatima said. "The fact that the father of the unborn is a reputed drug dealer in the community makes the situation more unfortunate."

"I see," Roxanne said.

"So, I kind of gave the teens some 'real talk' about life while I was speaking that day, and before I knew it, there's this sex strike up in Harlem."

Fatima shrugged her shoulders for emphasis and the sound technician cussed her from his booth because the noise she made rattled in his ears.

"That's amazing. Mr. Phelps, have you heard about the sex strike that's going on in Harlem?"

Roxanne smiled at Philbert as she questioned him. He adjusted his glasses, smiled back, and then leaned forward.

"First of all, I want to say how much I appreciate this opportunity to be on your program. Second, I wish to say that undertakings like this… sex strike is one of the reasons why I formed Concerned Black Men of Harlem."

Both Roxanne and Fatima gave him a puzzled look.

"For too long, young men of color in this society have been demonized by others, who find delight in keeping a proverbial foot on the black man's neck. And it pains me to see sisters, like the one across from me, add to their suffering."

No, this motherfucker didn't!

Fatima was not about to let some Brainy Smurf looking Negro go off on her.

"Excuse me?" Fatima asked, barely suppressing an expletive. Philbert ignored her.

"I've been informed, by some of the young men that my group mentors, of the appalling vitriol that Ms. Richardson here has been spewing in Harlem. I also had the misfortune of watching the video of that violent incident she caused at Marcus Garvey Park."

This shit is going to be good. Roxanne mused. She hadn't planned for a confrontation between her guests, but drama always helped the ratings. She smiled coolly. Meanwhile, Fatima grew hot sitting at the table. The lights radiating above her were not helping. She opened her bottle of water and took a sip as Philbert continued his attack.

"The last thing that Harlem needs is another person or group, trying to divide the community anymore than we already are."

"Would you like to respond to that, Ms. Richardson?" Roxanne asked.

"Yes. First and foremost, Roxanne, I'm amazed at how your guest has chosen to attack me, unprovoked."

Philbert eyed Fatima indifferently as she spoke.

"Second, I think it's mighty small of Mr. Phelps to sit here and try to belittle me. Everything I've ever said in my speeches was nothing but the truth."

Roxanne turned back to Philbert.

"Mr. Phelps, I believe that one of the activities your group does is give career counseling to youth?"

"That's correct. We find out what their interests are and give them the positive encouragement they need to purse their dreams. Motivation like that is needed to help them overcome the negative obstacles they encounter in society, such as Ms. Richardson and her ilk."

Fatima took another sip of water before she responded.

"Sorry, but I'm not a problem that our young men need to be aware of. They need to be aware of 'The Trap.'"

"Could you elaborate on that?" Roxanne asked.

"Gladly. There's a cycle of poor choices young men should be warned about that does far more damage to their future than, to hear Philbert tell it, I could ever do."

Philbert tensed up when his first name was called. Fatima observed it.

"There are a lot of young men in our community who, for whatever the reason, make the unwise decision to drop out of high school. Wouldn't you agree?" Fatima looked at Philbert when she asked her question.

"Yes," he answered.

"And with little education, their job prospects are low. So, what do many of them do to make money? They sell drugs."

"The reason they sell drugs is called economic desperation," Philbert said.

"No, *Philbert*. The reason they sell drugs is called economic stupidity. If you see three of your peers get locked up for selling drugs on the corner, what makes you think you won't get jail time doing the same thing?"

Philbert ignored Fatima as he composed himself. The bitch was pushing it with using his first name. She didn't know him like that.

"That's a good point, Ms. Richardson," Roxanne said. Fatima nodded and continued.

"And once they get out of jail with no skills, no money, and a criminal record. Who's going to hire them? No one. So what occupation do they gravitate back to? Selling drugs. Young men of color need to avoid this trap."

.   .   .

For the next fifteen minutes, Fatima and Philbert traded statistics, opinions, and foul looks. Their contentious discussion was like nothing *Black Awareness* had ever taped before. When Roxanne asked Philbert for his opinion of the role racial prejudice plays in the plight of young people of color, he puffed out his diminutive chest and smirked.

"Actually, we warn our youths about the perils of using race as a crutch. Far too many people of color blame white folks for their own shortcomings. Racial bias is no excuse for underachievement."

By this time Fatima was determined to get in little Steve Urkel's ass like a reverse-flow enema. She jumped on him, even though she partly agreed with his response.

"Are you kidding me, *Philbert*? Do you know what the white man does when he sees young black boys standing on the corner peddling drugs? Or, young black girls pushing around baby strollers?"

"No, enlighten me," Philbert said flippantly.

"He claps his hands, *Philbert*. He knows those people will not be competing against his children for good jobs. So, it's in his best interest to keep people who don't look like him suppressed. This is why racial bias continues to thrive in this society."

"Interesting observation," Roxanne said. "Any response, Mr. Phelps?"

Philbert readjusted his glasses and sat up in his chair.

"Roxanne, the dearth of intellect today in black society is a tragedy. The rubbish your guest here just presented is so logically flawed, it's on the verge of being comical."

Philbert turned and gave Fatima a broad grin.

Take that… bitch.

Fatima was nonplussed.

"There's nothing funny about watching our young people struggle, and being in denial as to the reasons why. Hopefully, with a tiny amount of effort, *Philbert* can leave the fantasy island he's on and join the rest of us here in the real world. Also—"

"Fuck you!" Philbert snarled. He'd had enough wordplay about his small size. Also, memories of his drunk grandfather calling him "Tattoo," in reference to the pint-size character on the television show *Fantasy Island* was still painful.

"Mr. Phelps!" Roxanne shrieked.

"Cut!" the set director yelled.

During the ensuing ruckus, Fatima searched for an item to bash in Philbert's head with if things got ugly. She spied a small metal wastebasket next to the camera two operator that would work. But tempers cooled and the taping continued without further drama.

Roxanne thanked Fatima and Philbert and handed them both a *Black Awareness* calendar when the show wrapped. She then invited Fatima to join her in a small office for a quick chat.

"Ms. Richardson, thanks again for coming."

"It was my pleasure, Ms. Carter."

"You can still call me Roxanne. What you're doing is sorely needed in our community. Speaking to these young folks and 'making it plain,' as Malcolm X used to say, is exactly what they need. All this 'politically correct' bullshit we're forced to do in the media dilutes the real message."

Fatima registered a look of surprise on her face. Roxanne smiled.

"Born and raised in the South Bronx, baby." Roxanne then held out her right hand, which contained a check.

"I want to donate to your organization."

"My organization?"

"I received a call yesterday from your colleague? Marisol Aquino?"

Fatima laughed in spite of herself as she pocketed the check made out to GASP for one thousand dollars. She made a mental note to curse out Marisol later.

"Thank you," Fatima said as Roxanne escorted her to the exit.

"The show airs next week. If there's anything else I can do for your group, do not hesitate to ask."

"I will, Roxanne. Thanks again for the contribution."

Fatima walked outside Mahogany Media Studios to the intersection of Madison Avenue and 48th Street. She took in the chaotic scene of people and traffic in motion and smiled at how brilliantly she'd handled that dick, Philbert Phelps. And then she realized that he'd inadvertently kept her from disavowing her involvement with that damn sex strike.

Fatima's mother still would not speak to her. Her phone calls went un-answered, her voicemails were not returned and her text messages were ignored. Whenever Fatima did visit the Dark Towers, her mother would go to her bedroom, slam the door and turn up the volume on her television.

The last time Pamela had gotten this mad at her was when Fatima had acted out during her middle school's annual winter play. The eighth-grade production of *A Raisin In the Sun* was running smoothly until the kid playing Joseph Asagai walked onstage and panicked when he looked at the audience.

Fatima was cast as Beneatha Younger. She had learned her lines and was eager to impress friends and family. After the nervous boy for-got some of his dialogue and stammered with the lines he did remember, Fatima lost patience and yelled at him to quit fucking up. Half the au-dience gasped. The rest nearly died from laughing so hard. It was after Easter before Fatima's mother finally forgave her for that transgression.

·   ·   ·

Pamela did put her current grudge on hold long enough to send word via Nikki that Fatima's presence was required at The Dark Towers while their mother went on a casino trip. Fatima obeyed. While traversing the yard to her family's apartment she ran into Quinn carrying groceries into the adjoining building.

"What you doing here, Fatima?"

"Babysitting my pregnant sister. And you?"

"I moved in with my sister to save money for school. That tuition is kicking my ass."

"What about student loans?"

"I have a felony. Not eligible."

"Management know you're here?"

"I'm on the hush. Felons aren't allowed to live here."

Quinn shifted the bag of groceries he held in his massive arms.

"Haven't seen you in a minute, Fatima. Why don't you meet me at the spot in a little bit so we can chat more? I gotta go put this food up."

"That's cool."

Fatima made sure Nikki was comfortable before she went to meet Quinn at their old hangout. She left her propped up on the living room couch watching another reality show. The air conditioner was dialed to full blast, again doing more clanking than cooling. A jar of unsalted peanuts was on the coffee table along with a bottle of water and the other half of Nikki's tuna salad wrap.

Quinn was on the rooftop when Fatima opened the broken access door. She joined him looking down on Harlem, where dozens of cars were inching along the congested street.

"Must be an accident down there," Fatima said.

"Or police activity."

Quinn turned to Fatima.

"You remember the first time we came up here?"

"Of course."

"Whatever happened between you and me, Fatima? I thought we made a good couple."

"I did too, until I caught you banging ole girl in the stairwell."

"Oh yeah," Quinn muttered. He reached into his pockets and pulled out a spliff and his butane lighter. He fired up the joint.

"Your ass going right back to jail."

"Not even," Quinn said as he blew smoke from his nostrils. "My parole officer is mad cool. She lets me know ahead of time when I need to turn in a urine."

"Your test don't come back dirty?"

"I buy urine and hand it in to her."

"Be careful. I had a client who did the same thing."

"And?" Quinn asked.

"His parole officer informed him that he was four weeks pregnant, before she sent his ass back upstate."

"That's jacked up," Quinn said, taking another hit of his spliff.

"Don't say you haven't been warned."

The quasi serenity atop The Dark Towers was suddenly disturbed by the sound of hip-hop music blasting from below. Fatima looked down and spied the culprit. It was a dark green Jeep sitting under a street light. A second later, Fatima spied Melody getting into the vehicle.

"I wonder where she's going?"

"You know that chick?"

"She's a good friend of Nikki's."

"Yo, I hear that girl's fucking out of both pants legs."

"What?"

"One of my boys told me he tapped her last week. I think her name is Mandy, or Mindy, some shit like that."

"Melody."

"That's it. Rumor has it she's got a mean head game."

"I didn't need to hear that, Quinn."

"My bad. I warned my boy to keep his Johnson wrapped if he's going to deal with her. I see her hopping in and out of niggas cars around here."

"I need to talk to her."

"Might not be a bad idea."

Quinn took another pull on his spliff and exhaled.

"Fatima, every time I think about you, I realize how bad I fucked up."

"No use crying over spilt milk, Quinn."

"I'd give anything to get with you again."

"Negro, please!"

"I'm for real, Fatima."

"No dice."

"I can love you way better than that lame ass Andre."

"I'm marrying lame ass Andre."

"What?"

"He proposed to me."

"You said, yes?"

"That's correct."

"Damn," Quinn sighed.

"What's your problem?"

"All the good sisters getting taken off the market."

"We're not going to sit around on the shelf until we expire, Quinn."

Quinn took one last pull and then extinguished the joint.

"I guess I should congratulate you."

"That would be polite."

Quinn took Fatima into his arms and gave her a hug.

"Congrats, Fatima."

"Thanks."

Quinn tenderly lowered his hand along Fatima's spine as he held her. "Is it possible, we can hook up, just once more?"

"*Nada.*"

"No one has to know," Quinn pleaded. The yearning in his voice was real.

"Quinn? Let me go before I toss your ass off this rooftop?"

Regret covered Quinn's face, but he complied.

"Will you at least come see me play again? Before you go and get married and whatnot?"

"What venue?"

"We're in negotiations now to book a spot in the East Village. I'll contact you when it's finalized."

"I'll come check you out."

"You promise?"

"Promise."

"Don't lie to me, Fatima."

"I'm not the one who does the lying. Remember?"

"Oh yeah," Quinn muttered.

.   .   .

When Fatima walked back into her family's apartment Nikki was stretched out on the couch. The wrap and water were finished. The jar of peanuts had lost half of its content. Fatima sat at her sister's feet.

"I need to ask you a question, Nikki."

"What's up?"

Nikki's attention was still focused on her reality show. Fatima grabbed the remote on the coffee table and clicked off the television.

"Hey!"

"I need to talk to you, not at you."

Nikki did little to mask her displeasure as she sat up on the couch.

"You have my undivided attention."

"I want to ask you about Melody."

"What about her?"

"You two still tight?"

"Yeah. Why?"

"I just heard something disturbing about her."

"That she's fucking everybody?"

"You heard too?"

"She tells me."

"You serious?"

"Melody ain't the cutest girl you gonna find in Harlem, Fatima. She knows it herself. She wants attention from boys like other girls do."

"She's going about it the wrong way."

"I know. She thinks if she keeps giving it up, eventually she'll find someone who'll fall in love with her."

"That's stupid… and dangerous."

"I've already had that conversation with her. Feel free to try it, yourself."

"I will," Fatima said.

"Anything else, before I watch the rest of my show?"

"What are your plans after you have the baby?"

"I'm going to raise it."

"In terms of your education, smart ass."

"To graduate high school next year and go to college. Same as before."

"Good," Fatima said as she reached for the jar of peanuts. "When your mother speaks to me again, I'm going to talk to her about putting you on some type of birth control."

"Fatima, I made one mistake, I won't make another one."

"Damn right, you won't," Fatima said before loading her mouth with peanuts.

"Can I watch my show?" Nikki asked, clearly irritated.

Fatima kissed her teeth as she picked up the remote and clicked the television back on.

•   •   •

Philadelphia, Pennsylvania is roughly a hundred miles from New York. All the way down the New Jersey Turnpike, Fatima tried hard to convince herself that relocating to The City of Brotherly Love wouldn't be that bad. She made good time in her trusty Beetle because there was no traffic congestion. A rarity for that highway.

Fatima had called out sick Friday morning to get an early start on her first weekend with Andre in Philly. His new real estate development job was located in Center City West on Market Street. Fatima parked in a public garage not far from his office. Andre was waiting for her on the ground floor when she stepped off the elevator.

"Hey, baby. You got here quick."

He kissed her and then escorted her to his office building.

"You're going to love this city. There's a lot to do here."

"I'll take your word for it," Fatima said weakly as she looked around.

Andre's corner office on the 29th floor was fabulous. It had the works; large oak desk, leather executive chair, soft leather couch and a huge antique credenza. Fatima was impressed.

"This joint is nice."

"I even have a good view of the Schuylkill," Andre said proudly.

"The who?"

Andre guided Fatima over to the window.

"That's the Schuylkill River over there."

"New York City has rivers too."

"Come on, Fatima. Work with me? These people made me a ridiculous offer for employment that I couldn't refuse."

"Sounds like you working for the mob."

Andre ignored her comment. "Come, I want you to meet my boss."

He led her to an even bigger office with even better furniture. There were photos of well-heeled Negroes hung on the walls. Many included the classily dressed female who sat at her large desk surveying Fatima.

"Fatima, this is Mrs. Lorena Trapp. Mrs. Trapp, this is my fiancée, Ms. Fatima Richardson."

The first thing that struck Fatima about her was her eyewear. The designer glasses Mrs. Trapp wore told Fatima the woman had serious money. Months earlier Fatima had tagged along with Marisol to a vision center in SoHo and had priced the exact pair of glasses while Marisol took an eye exam. The cost for the frames were over six hundred dollars.

Mrs. Trapp's bob hairstyle was short with sexy bangs. Her light makeup was expertly applied, making it hard to guess her age. The crow's feet around her eyes indicated that she was indeed mature. The three gold bangles on her wrist jangled loudly when she stood from behind her desk and reached to shake Fatima's hand. The pink paisley blouse and black skirt she wore were both made from fine material and her fancy heels made her a foot taller than Fatima.

"Pleasure to meet you, young lady," Mrs. Trapp said with a smile.

Her perfect set of teeth indicated she visited the best dentist her money could buy.

"Nice to meet you too," Fatima said.

Mrs. Trapp released Fatima's hand and looked at her oddly for a second.

"Something wrong?" Fatima asked.

"I've seen you somewhere before."

"I haven't been to Philly in a minute," Fatima said jokingly.

Andre jumped into the conversation.

"I've been telling Fatima about all the good things Philadelphia has to offer. Fine, inexpensive restaurants, historical landmarks, exciting sports teams."

"Well-mannered Eagle fans," Fatima said nonchalantly.

Andre ignored that comment too.

"Affordable housing," he continued.

"Where do you two plan to live?" Mrs. Trapp asked.

"We'll be staying at the apartment I leased in the Loft District for now. But we do intend to buy a home," Andre said.

"They have nice properties in Chestnut Hill and Elkins Park. And the homes out in Mt Airy are simply beautiful! That's where I live. I have a neighbor who's a great realtor. Let me know if you need her services."

"Sure," Andre said. "We'll probably start looking at homes after Fatima finds a job here. She's finishing her Master's back in New York."

"Really? What are you studying?"

"International Studies," Fatima answered.

"I see," Mrs. Trapp said. "My youngest daughter is finishing up her last year at Meharry Medical College, in Nashville."

Fatima detected the hint of snobbery in the woman's voice. She ignored it.

"Good for her."

"My family has a long history of kinfolk attending Meharry."

"Isn't that special?" Fatima said dryly.

Mrs. Trapp looked oddly at Fatima again.

"You were in that video."

Andre looked down. Fatima played dumb.

"I'm sorry?" she said to Andre's boss.

"You were in that awful riot, in New York."

"It wasn't really a riot," Fatima said.

Mrs. Trapp did little to mask her disdain. She turned up her nose as she looked down at Fatima.

"On that stage, cussing like a sailor!"

"You'd cuss too, Mrs. Trapp, if somebody had just tried to take your head off with a bottle."

"As bad as black folks are already portrayed in the media, you people are out in public fighting each other like savages. Shameful!"

"*You people?* That's what you called me?" Fatima asked and stepped toward Mrs. Trapp.

"Baby, how about we go for lunch?" Andre said as he grabbed Fatima's hand and pulled her along behind him. "There's a Japanese place near here that makes great sushi!"

•   •   •

A few minutes later they were seated at the Kyushu Steak House on South Broad Street. Fatima still wore a frown as she dipped her Godzilla roll into a light green sauce and took a bite.

"Good?" Andre asked.

"It is."

"Wait until the sushi arrives."

Fatima finished her roll and grabbed another.

"This almost makes up for meeting that snooty ass boss of yours."

Andre was silent as he enjoyed his appetizer.

"She talking about, *you people*, like her ass is no longer black."

Andre sipped his water and forked another Godzilla roll for himself.

"Glad I won't have to see Lorena Trapp again, no time soon."

"She's coming to the wedding," Andre mumbled.

Fatima finished chewing her roll. She then wiped her hands clean with her napkin.

"What did you just say, sweetie?"

"I invited Mrs. Trapp to our wedding."

"When did you plan on sharing this information with me?"

Andre knew he was in trouble from the way Fatima smiled at him.

"Now?" he answered weakly.

"Why'd you invite her?"

"When I mentioned that I was getting married soon, she was excited for me. I told her where our wedding venue was on Long Island, and she told me that she grew up not too far away, in Sag Harbor."

"Oh, so she comes from money."

"She has family and property there. Mrs. Trapp kept harping about how happy she was for me, and how nice the venue was we had chosen, and how she's up in Long Island all the time on weekends, I kinda had no choice but to invite her, Fatima."

"Un-invite her."

"I can't do that."

"Cool, I'll do it."

"You can't disinvite her either. She's my boss, that wouldn't be kosher."

"Andre, you saw how that bitch stuck her nose up at me. Why the hell would I want to see her at my wedding?"

"I never imagined you two wouldn't hit it off."

Fatima saw the look of remorse on Andre's face. But it didn't matter.

"Well, we didn't. I prefer not to see that bitch at my wedding."

"It's my wedding too, Fatima."

"What's that supposed to mean?"

"It means I have some say in who attends as well. It wouldn't be in my best interest if I were to disinvite my new boss at my new job."

"Forget that job. You know how I feel about moving to this damn place to begin with."

"Don't start that crap up again?"

"Okay, let's get back to this crap about that trick coming to my wedding."

Andre was pissed. He'd had enough. He reached into his wallet and pulled out some bills.

"What are you doing?" Fatima asked.

"Paying for our meal before I go back to work. I'm not going to sit here and argue. We can continue this later when I get home."

"You're really leaving?"

Andre dropped the money on the table and then popped another Godzilla roll in his mouth. He washed it down with the rest of his water and then reached into his pocket and retrieved a key.

"Enjoy your meal. I'll re-text the directions to the apartment, to make sure you find it," Andre said as he placed the key beside Fatima's plate.

"If you leave me at this restaurant, I'm going back home. Shit on this."

"Why you have to be so difficult, Fatima? Would it kill you to let me have my way, once in a damn while?"

Fatima was taken aback by his question.

"Who you think you're speaking to like that?"

"Just me and you here at this table."

Fatima bit her tongue momentarily and then changed her mind.

"You think I'm going to sit here and let you pop shit to me? You must have bumped your head."

"Maybe I bumped my head when I asked you to marry me."

"What did you say?!"

"I didn't stutter."

Fatima was livid. She wanted to take her glass of water and toss it in Andre's face, but she'd already drank it all.

"That's it! The wedding's off!"

"Don't do me no fucking favors," Andre replied coldly. He stood up and walked off.

Fatima's Japanese waitress missed the commotion while she was outside, behind the restaurant sneaking a cigarette. When she arrived at Fatima's table with sushi that was ordered, she was startled to find the young black woman sitting alone… on the verge of tears.

"Can I get that order to go?" Fatima asked softly. She was determined to not let a single tear fall from her eyes.

TWENTY-FOUR

DAMOCLES' DEN

The episode of *Black Awareness* aired as scheduled and despite masterful editing, Philbert Phelps still wound up looking like a dick. They deleted the part where he demanded Fatima get sexed, but they could not erase the acrimony the guests had shown before and after his outburst. Fatima had bested Philbert, point blank. His friends and family began clowning him as soon as the program finished airing.

His professional reputation was at stake and therefore the bitch had to pay. One of the first nuggets of wisdom Philbert discovered during his formative years in school was that the pen was mightier than the sword. On numerous occasions he'd been tormented by someone bigger than himself and had retaliated by scribbling a mocking limerick on the bathroom walls of the school. In both the boys and girls facilities.

These humorous writings usually highlighted some physical defect or mental deficit Philbert's oppressor possessed. He shrewdly signed all his work with the moniker: *The Shithouse Poet*. Philbert had seen several school bullies brought to tears from the taunting they received from other classmates who'd read his witty writings. His craft grew better with time and became amusement to everyone in the schools he attended, the exception being custodians.

The same Sunday *Black Awareness* aired Philbert shut himself in his bedroom with a fifth of Bacardi and his laptop. He emerged hours later with a manifesto for black males, titled, "Brothers Gonna Work It Out."

Philbert took Fatima and her kind to task with a masterful attack on the large sum of black women who he deemed as serving no purpose on earth than to disparage the black man.

Philbert put all types of sisters on blast; the "angry" black woman, the "fine but crazy" black woman, the "manipulative" black woman, the "scandalous" black woman and the "needy" black woman. He posted his writing on the Internet at 3:00 AM Monday morning. By 9:00 PM that night there were hundreds of comments from members of either sex supporting or lambasting Philbert's opinions.

.   .   .

That same Monday night one of Fatima's friends forwarded her an email that contained Philbert's manifesto. She was pissed to see her name mentioned often.

"No, that shrimp motherfucker didn't!" Fatima kept mumbling as she read. She knew the buffoon would be upset when he saw how foolish he looked on *Black Awareness*, but she had no idea how far he'd go to take revenge. Fatima had received dozens of text messages and phone calls commending her performance on the show. Marisol had called three times while the show was being aired; she was delighted the way Fatima had dominated Philbert.

Fatima herself couldn't be pleased because she was missing her man. Badly. She'd been sure Andre would've caved in and called, but she hadn't heard from him since he stormed out of the restaurant in Philly. Demanding schoolwork, and Nikki's impending childbirth also weighed heavily on Fatima's mind.

However, all of those issues had to be pushed to the side as Fatima formulated a proper response to Philbert's cyber attack. She tried to find where he lived so she could roll up on him and kick his little ass, but she failed to locate a name and matching address online. Fatima was stirring a pot of oatmeal on her tiny stove the next morning listening to Al Green croon about "Love And Happiness" on the radio when the solution materialized. Surely Philbert had a significant other somewhere. Since he had gotten personal with her... Fatima would get personal with him.

During her lunch break Fatima went online and typed in Philbert's full name to conduct another search. She found several websites containing articles from his magazine gig and also information about his community action group, which appeared to be doing great things with the male youths of Harlem. Fatima was finishing the last scoops of her low-fat Greek yogurt when she spied a link to a popular social website. She clicked on it and hit pay dirt.

Some young, skinny Chinese woman had a Facebook page that contained numerous pictures of herself and Philbert. The woman was three feet taller than him. In every photograph Philbert was hugging, kissing, or laughing with his Asian girlfriend, Mili Wong. Fatima was ecstatic. She emailed the link for Mili Wong's webpage to herself and then began to fish for more ammo online. Inez's griping interrupted her trolling.

"If I get one more damn 'address unknown' for another baby daddy, I'm gonna slap somebody!" Inez said as she reviewed a new case that was transferred to her.

"Let it go," Drew said with a laugh.

"How you gonna screw somebody, have their child, and not know where they live at?" Inez said. "That don't even happen in Hollywood!"

Fatima had no luck finding more dirt on Philbert so she signed off the Internet. (Which she was not supposed to be using for personal use in the first place.)

"I love how their amnesia goes away once they break up with the baby daddy. They call and give you his full name, address, place of employment, and his blood type," Fatima mocked.

"Speaking of love, are your wedding plans all set?" Inez asked.

Fatima froze. She wasn't foolish enough to inform her coworkers about her wedding cancellation yet. That would have made her the subject of office gossip until Easter.

"Uh… yeah. We all set," she stuttered.

Inez smelled a lie.

"Everything okay?" she asked.

"Why wouldn't it be?" Fatima replied defensively.

"No need to get stressed," Inez said.

"Nobody's stressed!" Fatima said.

"You're not having second thoughts about it?" Drew asked.

"If she knows what I know, she better have third thoughts too," Inez quipped.

"Don't you two have stuff to do, besides worry about my damn wedding?"

Everyone was silent as the tension elevated. Fatima was about to apologize and try to laugh the shit off when the phone on her desk rang.

"Ms. Richardson speaking. How may I help you?"

"This is reception. You have a client here whose lights just got turned off."

"I'll be right down."

It was the first time Fatima was happy to have a client with an emergency come into the office unscheduled. Her client, Michael Cooper had ignored notices from his utility company about paying them. It was time consuming for Fatima to get the utility company to reconnect his service, but the respite from her coworker's prying questions was worth it.

Fatima took a ten-minute smoke break after she finished helping Mr. Cooper. (Since breaking up with Andre she had escalated to smoking like a chimney.)

She was back at her desk writing up a narrative for Mr. Cooper's case when her work phone rang again.

"Ms. Richardson speaking. How may I help you?"

"This is Fatima Richardson?"

"Yes, it is."

"Better watch your back, bitch!"

"Excuse me!?"

The line went dead. If Fatima had caller ID on her work phone she would've jeopardized her employment. She'd been cursed out plenty of times on the job; that came with the territory. But something about the venomous tone in the male voice that cussed Fatima hit a nerve. She was highly pissed. It was time for another cigarette.

She was in front of the office building relaxing with a cigarette in her hand when she heard a familiar voice behind her.

"You back at that nasty habit?"

Fatima turned and gave Ella Watkins a cold stare. The woman was at the entrance door with a small pizza box in her hands. (Fatima was sure she didn't pay for the food with her own money.)

"I felt like smoking so that's what I'm doing."

"I was just trying to help you to quit, Fatima."

"If you really wanna help me, you can pay back all the money I've lent you."

Ella scowled and walked into the building. Fatima felt remorse for being disrespectful, but her nerves were on edge. Plus, the bitch owed her thirty dollars. That was almost money for three packs of cigarettes! Fatima decided to worry about Ella Watkins later and enjoy her nicotine now.

·　　　　·　　　　·

When Fatima came home from class late that night she heated up some leftover spaghetti and cracked open a bottle of red wine. After dinner she knocked off a cigarette and then booted up her computer. Fatigue was kicking Fatima's ass, but she was on a mission. She located Philbert's girlfriend's social website page again and selected an adorable picture of the couple kissing each other to copy and paste.

She then opened the photo editing software on her computer and altered the picture by converting it to black and white and giving it a sepia tint to make the picture look ancient. Fatima superimposed the words: *'You Too, Philbert Phelps?'* across the top of the photo. Next, she extended the bottom of the photo digitally and typed in a caption that read: *Another fake, so-called conscientious brother exposed! No (little) surprise here!* Fatima smiled at her handiwork. She posted the revised picture on various social media sites Negroes were known to frequent. She was about to log off her computer when the phone rang.

"Have you spoken to him?"

"No, Mother. I haven't."

The instant Pamela found out from Nikki that there would not be a wedding, Fatima received a pardon from her mother. Pamela was not only horrified at the thought of her daughter losing a decent, straight, gainfully employed black man; she was distraught over the deposit money in danger of being forfeited. It didn't help Fatima's cause any when her mother found out the origin of the quarrel with Andre.

Pamela had a long, heart-to-heart talk with her pending son in law and received all the facts. She then hung up and immediately called Fatima.

"Let that snob Andre works for come to your wedding, girl! Are you fucking kidding me?!"

"Can we not do this now?" Fatima had begged her mother. She was painting her toenails at the time and needed to concentrate.

"Fatima, if you don't call that damn boy and tell him that you were wrong, I will break my foot off—"

Fatima hung up on her own mother. Yet that did not deter Pamela from calling daily with unwanted advice. It was driving Fatima nuts. She was on the verge of threatening to speak at another church in Harlem if her mother didn't leave her alone.

"Fatima, please stop being silly? Call that boy and tell him you were wrong."

"Ma, please?"

"Baby, you are screwing up."

"I'm busy right now. Can we talk later?"

"What if I tell Andre you lost your cell and you need him to call your house phone?" Pamela asked, she was desperate.

"Goodnight, Mother. We'll talk soon."

Fatima ended the call and then lit another cigarette. She also poured herself more wine. Pamela was a piece of work! Fatima had spoken to Andre's mother twice about the breakup. Those conversations had been constructive. Fatima was able to vent, plus get a little moral support. Andre's mother was not happy either about the split, but she was calmer about it. Lois told Fatima that she'd pray for them and that she was positive things would work out in the end because they were meant to be together.

Fatima wasn't happy at the prospect of losing a good man like Andre either, but the comment he made about possibly being crazy when he'd asked her to marry him had stung. Sometimes pride was stronger than love.

Exhaustion crept up on Fatima so she clicked off her computer and clicked on her stereo. She then slumped back on her couch with her drink. As luck would have it, the local R&B station's "Quiet Storm" program was flooding the airwaves with love songs. Hearing the last verses of "Here We Go Again" by The Isley Brothers made Fatima take a long sip of vino. Goapele's "Closer" poured through her speakers next. Fatima emptied her glass. And then the station played the singer Monica's version of "Misty Blue." Tears moistened the blouse Fatima wore before she realized she was crying.

The urge to hear Andre's voice was overwhelming. Luckily, Fatima still had her dignity. Why should she call first when he was the one who started shit by inviting that arrogant bitch to their wedding? Fatima picked up her remote and tuned the stereo to a jazz station. She was not about to waste time pining for Andre.

She smashed her cigarette in the ashtray and then lay on the couch. A minute later she received a text message. Fatima's heart raced with hope. Was it him? She slowly sat up, picked up her phone, and read the message: *Come check me out at Damocles' Den tomorrow… Quinn :-)*

•   •   •

Damocles' Den occupied the basement in a corner building on St. Mark's Place and Avenue A. In a past life it was a popular speakeasy. It now functioned as a must-visit spot in the East Village for tourists wanting to hear decent jazz.

Fatima and Marisol held tightly to the long metal handrail installed as a liability precaution and carefully descended the steep narrow stairs that led to the subterranean venue. The further they went down the stairs, the more enchanting Quinn's saxophone sounded. When they reached the bottom they were smiling in anticipation of having a good time.

Damocles' Den consisted of twenty small tables spread around a highly polished wooden floor. The ceiling was low, which matched the lighting delivered from the small votive candles all around the room. It took Fatima a minute for her eyes to adjust to the dim surroundings. She finally spied Quinn and his fellow musicians in a corner of the club. They were jamming "Street Life" by The Crusaders and Quinn was grooving away on his solo. The mostly white patrons in the room were in awe as he played. Several shouted happily, motivated by over-priced liquor from the bar.

Fatima was proud of the way Quinn commanded everyone's attention. Her first lover looked sexy as sweat trickled from his brow. The white dress shirt he wore was opened at the top and revealed a well-developed chest. Quinn had hit the weights during his stretch in prison.

"How many please?"

The women turned and beheld a Latino barely out of his teens. The smile he gave was solely for Marisol.

"Two," Fatima said.

The host didn't respond.

"Two," Marisol repeated.

"This way, please."

The host seated them near enough to the stage that Marisol's ass caught every band member's eye when she turned and sat down at their table. The drummer lost count of the beat, the pianist hit a wrong key, and even Quinn missed a note. The audience still applauded wildly when the set was over. Quinn shook a few hands in the crowd and then made a beeline to Fatima.

"You made it. Thanks for coming."

"Thanks for the invite, Quinn. This is my friend, Marisol."

Quinn smiled as he eyed the fine woman.

"Pleasure to meet you," he said.

"Likewise," Marisol replied. "You guys are really good."

"Thanks. You ladies want anything to drink?"

"I'll take a margarita," Fatima said.

"I'm good," Marisol answered.

"I'll bring your drink after I get a quick smoke in, Fatima."

"Mind if I join you, Quinn?"

.   .   .

The street outside the jazz club was bustling with people walking around with cell phones pressed against their ears. Fatima and Quinn ambled over to a broken streetlight and lit up.

"You guys killed them in there," Fatima said after taking a drag. "Those white folks were going nuts."

"Fatima, I never let those applause go to my head. If I had a nickel every time a white woman clutched her pocketbook tight when she walked by me, or some white dude double clicked his car alarm when I was in the vicinity, I'd be rich now. Wouldn't have to play another fucking note on my horn."

"Damn, dude. That's deep."

Quinn took a drag from his cigarette and continued. "You sisters don't know how good you guys have it."

"Now you talking crazy," Fatima said sarcastically.

"Let's change the subject. What's up with your girl?"

"Marisol?"

"She's hotter than fish grease."

"You joking, right?"

"I'm serious. I've accepted the fact that you and I'll never be together again. Is Marisol spoken for?"

Fatima took another pull on her cigarette. She didn't want to lie and say Marisol was still with Raphael. Yet, she couldn't stomach the thought of Quinn dating her best friend either.

"You need to ask her that question."

"Come on, Fatima. Either she is, or she ain't."

"Ask her... and see what she says."

"We like that now?"

"Like what?"

Quinn took another hit from his cigarette and threw it on the sidewalk.

"If I didn't know better, I'd swear you were trying to cockblock me."

"Who, me?" Fatima asked with feigned indignation.

"Yes, you," Quinn chuckled. "Let's get you that drink."

Quinn waited for Fatima to take a few more drags on her cigarette before holding the door open for her to reenter Damocles' Den. He found his drummer sitting at Marisol's table, running his mouth, when he got back downstairs.

"Marisol, I see you've met my homeboy, Black Mack Mallory," Quinn said.

"Yes. He knows a lot about my country, the Dominican Republic."

"That's because he took his wife to Punta Cana for their honeymoon."

Black Mack grinned sheepishly at Marisol as he stood up and beat a hasty retreat. He'd cuss Quinn's ass out later for throwing him under the bus.

"You sure you don't want anything to drink, Marisol?" Quinn asked.

"No thanks. I have to work in the morning."

"What type of work you do?"

"I teach physical education."

"Really?" Quinn smiled. "Is that how you maintain such a lovely physique?"

"Should I go get my own margarita?" Fatima asked.

"Going now," Quinn said stiffly and walked off. Marisol fired away with questions once Quinn was out of earshot.

"What's up with your boy?"

"Quinn?"

"He married too?"

Again Fatima faced a dilemma. She didn't want to lie to Marisol, but she was not going to hook her up with Quinn either.

"He is definitely not married."

"What's that supposed to mean?"

"You need to ask him that."

Marisol studied Fatima closely for a few seconds.

"I thought you two were just friends?"

"That's what we are."

"I don't want to get in the way of you and Quinn hooking up. However, you need to make sure it's worth possibly losing Andre over, Fatima."

"I'm not trying to hook up with Quinn."

"Then why are you being so cryptic? Is he single?"

"Far as I know, yes. But… he's got baby mama drama."

"Baby mama drama?"

"Yep."

Quinn returned a minute later and handed Fatima her drink as he sat next to Marisol.

"Thanks," Fatima said and grabbed the glass. She downed most of it on the first sip. Quinn eyed her in disbelief.

"You okay?"

"Copacetic," Fatima answered.

Quinn turned to Marisol. "So, you're a gym teacher?"

"Yes… and Fatima's closest friend."

"You know her fiancé?"

"I do."

"Is he okay?" Quinn asked. "I don't want him messing Fatima over."

"Andre's a great guy. You don't have to worry about that."

Fatima grabbed her drink again and drained it.

"Good," Quinn said. He then stood up. "Gotta get back for our next set. Will you ladies be staying?"

"We'll be here," Fatima answered.

"Then I shall return," Quinn said. He nodded at Fatima, then smiled at Marisol before strolling back to his band.

"He is too fine! How much 'baby mama drama' does he have, Fatima?"

"I heard it's nonstop."

TWENTY-FIVE

THIS IS GOING TO BE BIG

Fatima's living room was crowded with baby shower paraphernalia. She had dozens of balloons, rolls of streamers, packs of party favors, bags of tableware, boxes of candy bars, and a three-tiered diaper cake. The baby's estimated time of arrival was less than a month away. Nikki had decided against knowing the gender before its delivery so Fatima had to select a neutral color for the event. She chose her favorite, lavender.

The Dark Tower's community center was rented for the occasion and Fatima had only one evening to make preparations. She'd planned to take a day off during the week to get everything ready, but work had been hectic. She skipped her Friday college classes and went straight home after work to get shit done.

Fatima was placing wrappers on the four-dozen cupcakes she ordered when her doorbell rang. The thought of pretending she wasn't home flashed through her mind. However, she took one last pull on her cigarette, crushed it out in her crowded ashtray, and went and buzzed her mother in.

"You went all out for this," Pamela said when she looked around the apartment.

"I've seen my share of half-assed baby showers."

"What would you like me to help with?"

"I need these blown up," Fatima said. She handed her mother a bag of balloons and returned to her own task.

"I stopped by Mrs. DeLuca's and paid your dress off. It's hanging in Nikki's closet," Pamela said casually.

"Thanks," Fatima sighed. "I'll give you back the money next weekend."

"I don't want your money. I want your ass to call Andre."

"Please, don't start."

"You have a lovely wedding dress. Use it."

"Mama!" Fatima groaned.

Pamela expelled hot air into a balloon and tied it.

"Why can't you call and say you're sorry," she asked as she reached for another one. "Won't be the first time you had to apologize to a boyfriend!"

Fatima knew what her mother was alluding to. She rolled her eyes.

.   .   .

Eleven-year-old Ronnie Suber was a heartthrob with dark curly hair whose family had moved three floors below the Richardsons. Just the sight of him made ten-year-old Fatima grow moist. Not a slow leak when it came to affairs of the heart, Fatima stepped to Ronnie one summer morning as he rode his new bicycle in front of The Dark Towers and started up a conversation. The topic of music came up and they discovered they liked the same rap groups. That made them compatible.

No one could tell Fatima shit once they became a couple. She rode Ronnie's bike whenever she wanted, he bought all the junk food her young heart desired, and it thrilled her to no end to run her fingers through that dark curly hair of his when they kissed.

Other girls hated on Fatima back then, so she fiercely protected her property. She'd threaten any girl who grinned too long up in Ronnie's face. But as soon as she'd put one young trick in check, another would make a play for him. Those heifers were like flies at a cookout.

And then one afternoon she came home with her mother and Nikki from shopping in the Bronx to see a light-skinned, red headed hussy zip past her on Ronnie's bike. Fatima was on the girl faster than a New York City cockroach. She tossed the bag of fresh bread from Arthur Avenue she held and chased her rival down. Fatima bulldogged the girl from behind, rolled atop of her, and pounded her reddish skull into the pavement.

She was shocked when Ronnie screamed for her to leave his cousin alone. He ran and snatched Fatima off the girl and then seized his bike, which was damaged when his cousin crashed it on the sidewalk. The boy cussed Fatima out in front of her mother. Pamela then whipped Fatima's ass in front of Ronnie because she'd ruined three loaves of bread.

Though she apologized profusely to Ronnie afterwards, he wanted nothing more to do with Fatima. His family broke their lease and moved out of The Dark Towers the following month. It took Fatima awhile to get over her heartbreak.

"Mama, can't we talk about something else?"

"You know what's going to happen?" Pamela said. "You're going to leave that man by himself in Philly too long, and then getting him back will not be an option."

(The same thought had crossed Fatima's mind more than once, but she'd never divulge that to her mother.)

"Andre ain't the only game in town," she said defiantly.

"I hope he hasn't said the same about you already."

Fatima kept quiet and concentrated on wrapping her cupcakes.

"Look, baby," Pamela said as she took Fatima's hand. "If you let Andre get away you'll regret it. I promise you will."

Fatima reached for her cigarettes with her other hand. The pack was empty. Flustered, she stood and grabbed her purse and keys.

"Where you going?"

"To get me some smokes."

"You and those damn cigarettes."

"You want me to bring you back something, Mama?"

"Yes. Would you come back here with some common sense?"

.   .   .

Fatima was fuming as she walked to the bodega. She knew her mother was being a pain in her butt out of love. Fatima also knew her mother was right about Andre. He was indeed a good catch. Andre was smart, hardworking, and trustworthy. Nonetheless, Fatima held him guilty for their present dilemma. Andre couldn't pop shit to her without there being any consequences. The boundaries for their relationship had to be set... if they still had one, that is. Fatima conceded that she'd misjudged Andre. She had no idea it would take him this damn long to apologize to her.

The sun had yet to set on Harlem. Plenty of people were out and about getting their weekend started. As she neared the bodega, Fatima passed a group of middle-aged black men having a heated debate over which local team had the best point guard, the New York Knicks or the Brooklyn Nets. One of them eyed Fatima and scowled.

"Yo, it's that trick who started that sex strike!"

Fatima's nerves were already on edge from her mother's nagging plus a lack of nicotine. She went immediately from zero to a hundred.

"Was I fucking with you?" Fatima asked as she stepped to the Negro.

The brother had more than a few gray hairs in his goatee, yet he was clad in a large T-shirt, sagging jeans sans belt, and unlaced boots. A Kangol bucket hat sat tilted on his head and a gold Cadillac medallion hung from his neck. The man was astonished at Fatima's boldness.

"No," he stammered as he adjusted his Gazelle eyewear.

"Then why you fucking with me? Out here looking like a damn Run DMC reject!"

The rest of the men howled with laughter. Fatima continued into the store and got her cigarettes. When she exited and passed the men again they were debating the best way to make a tuna casserole. The one she'd confronted earlier pretended not to see her. Fatima smiled. She'd checked him just like she'd done Philbert Phelps.

Two days after she posted her altered picture of Philbert and his woman online, Mili Wong's Facebook page vanished. Fatima had revisited the social media sites that she'd posted the photo on and saw that the majority of feedback questioned the sincerity of the leader of Concerned Black Men of Harlem to help uplift the race. And when she went to Mili Wong's social media page to check for comments there, she saw that it no longer existed. Philbert had obviously found out he'd been put on blast about his Asian persuasion.

As Fatima neared her building, she spied Melody sitting on the back of a green Kawasaki Ninja, holding a helmet. The sport bike was chromed-out, its rims and exhaust pipes glistened in the evening sunlight. Fatima almost didn't recognize Melody due to her new red day-glow weave.

"Melody?"

"Hi, Fatima."

"What you doing around my turf?"

"Waiting for my friend, Joe, to come downstairs. He stopped here to see one of his homeboys for a minute."

"He your boyfriend?" Fatima teased.

"No. We just kicking it."

Fatima lit a cigarette. Her eyes narrowed into slits as she exhaled the smoke.

"I've been hearing things in the streets about you, Melody. I'm concerned."

"Like what?"

"Stuff I'd rather not repeat."

"Chelsea talking about me again? Much as that bitch out here hoeing and—"

"I didn't hear it from Chelsea," Fatima interrupted.

A look of dismay appeared on Melody's face.

"Wasn't Nikki either," Fatima said quickly.

"Then who?"

"Answer this first. You plan on getting married one day?"

"Why wouldn't I?" Melody said defensively.

"That's gonna be hard, if you have a tarnished reputation."

Melody was silent.

"You ever think about that?" Fatima asked.

Melody's response was to look away.

"If not, I think you should," Fatima continued.

"*Yes*, Fatima."

Melody's tone of voice was patronizing. She was spared an impromptu sermon on being young and stupid because her so-called date returned.

The tall, rough-looking teenager didn't know who the woman standing near his bike, glaring at him was. Nor did he care. Joe Saab was focused on riding Melody over to his older brother's apartment and getting her butt naked. He glared back at Fatima as he straddled his bike. *If this woman interferes with my piece of ass, she's gonna get her feelings hurt!*

Fatima was silent as Joe fastened on his helmet and then cranked up his bike.

"See you tomorrow," Melody said and placed her helmet back on.

"We're starting the baby shower on time. Okay?"

"I won't be late," Melody replied as she leaned forward and hugged her date around his waist. Fatima sighed after the two sped off. She then went home to deal with her mother's madness.

.   .   .

The community center was decorated properly, given the short time Fatima had to set it up. A long table was positioned down the middle of the room. It was covered with a series of lavender tablecloths that depicted storks carrying bundles of joy to parts unknown. A lavender balloon was tied to each of the twenty-four chairs that encircled it. Against a near wall was a big arch made from more balloons, underneath it sat a rocking chair for Nikki to sit in when she opened her gifts.

There was a buffet table that held warmed trays of hot wings, meatballs, mac and cheese, and baked beans. Fatima had also sprung for a six-foot hero from a popular Jewish deli located in lower Manhattan. Her cupcake treats were placed on a small table along with ice cream, paper plates, and plastic flatware.

Fatima was mildly surprised when guests began to arrive on time. Chelsea was the first one there. Marisol was second. There were a dozen other teenage girls from The Dark Towers who attended and several adolescent girls from Greater Harlem Baptist were also there. Pamela escorted Nikki into the building at four o'clock sharp, looking extremely uncomfortable in her light blue cotton maternity dress.

When Melody arrived thirty minutes later, folks were still loading their plates with food. She greeted the people she knew and even traded a fake smile with Chelsea. Once the food and fun was over, it was time to open the presents.

Nikki racked up. She received a baby changing bag, a baby food blender, two car seats, blankets, a set of organic alphabet blocks, mountains of disposable diapers, and several stuffed toys. The only awkward moment of the event came when Nikki opened a small box that contained a baby bib, which read: *I love my Daddy*! It was common knowledge that Jamaal would never see his child use the thing. (The lady who committed the faux pas was a friend of Pamela's who didn't give a damn if the baby's daddy was locked up. The bib had been on sale for half price.)

The present that delighted Nikki the most was a fancy baby stroller with an adjustable sun canopy and Burberry pattern. The same one Nikki had admired when she and Fatima were shopping in East Harlem.

"Fatima!" Nikki gasped when the wrapping was ripped off.

"If this contraption gets stolen, me and you gonna fight, Nikki."

Everyone in the room burst out in laughter. With tears in her eyes, Nikki wobbled onto her feet and hugged her big sister.

"You need to thank Mama too, she's helping with the payments."

Everyone laughed again while Nikki hugged her mother.

.   .   .

As Fatima monitored people fixing plates of food to take home at the end of the event, Marisol eased near.

"You did such a great job. Nikki is very fortunate to have you for a sister."

"What is it, Marisol?"

"Excuse me?"

"I can read your ass like a dime novel. What are you buttering me up for?"

"I'm hurt by your allegation, Fatima."

"Come clean."

"I don't have anything to come clean about. But I do have a request."

"For what?" Fatima asked suspiciously.

"I received an invitation to a big campaign rally that's coming up."

"Good for you."

"And you've been invited as a special presenter."

"Marisol, don't you ever take a break?"

"From what?"

"Your anti-fucking crusade."

"You have a knack for turning a phrase, Fatima. That's why they want you to speak at this event."

"They?"

"The Mayor's public relations staff. They're having a big rally about fighting HIV and AIDS in the black community. It's going to be here in Harlem."

"Really?"

"Yes," Marisol answered. "With local politicians, prominent clergy, a few celebrities, television news crews, the works," she finished excitedly.

"Is that right?"

"This is going to be big."

"Marisol, I'm tired of speaking. You know this."

"Fatima, if this bozo gets re-elected, which is practically a given, we'll be set! You won't have to do much else for us."

"Repeat that last part?"

"You won't have to do anymore speaking. GASP will have enough publicity and political connections to start soliciting funds. Without your help."

"You're willing to submit that to me in writing?"

"Are you serious, Fatima?"

"Ya damn skippy."

"Okay," Marisol sighed. "I can do that."

"I'm also gonna need a few margaritas while I consider our deal."

"What's to consider? The Mayor's people want a short speech from you about the effects of HIV and AIDS in the black community that you've seen at your job. And what you suggest people do to combat it."

"It would be wiser to have a medical professional do that," Fatima said.

"Two doctors from Harlem Hospital will be on the program. I was told the Mayor's people want community activists to also participate."

"I'm not a community activist."

"Someone on the Mayor's staff saw your appearance on *Black Awareness*. She thinks you're a community activist and emailed our group about getting you to speak."

"I'm not a damn community activist, Marisol."

"Will it kill you to be one? Just this once? Shaconda and I'll write the speech. If you read what we write and stay on message, there's no way you can fuck this up."

"I appreciate your confidence in me, Marisol. Help me clean up so we can get to a bar."

TWENTY-SIX

PHILBERT STRIKES BLACK

Fatima promptly regretted agreeing to speak at the Mayor's function. Marisol had made the mistake of telling Pamela about the upcoming event as they cleaned the community center after Nikki's baby shower. The next day Fatima's mother made a surprise visit. Fatima was baking some peanut butter cookies from scratch and didn't appreciate the interruption.

"Have you picked out what you're going to wear?"

"Yes, clothes."

"Don't make me knock your smart ass out with that rolling pin you're using."

"Sorry, Mama. No, I haven't picked out what to wear yet."

"I saw a nice pantsuit in the window at Macy's the other day."

"I already own some nice pantsuits."

"Can you fit any of them?"

If Fatima wasn't afraid of catching a beat-down, she would've slapped her mother for being brutally honest. She was still gaining weight. The cheesecakes, ice cream, chocolates, and bags of chips that she snacked on regularly were good at helping her cope with her misery, but hell on her waistline.

"Thanks for the compliment, Mother," Fatima said sarcastically.

"I'm almost beginning to give up on you and Andre getting back together."

"Mama, please don't—"

"Let me finish," Pamela interrupted. "Even if you two don't make up, there's no excuse for letting yourself go, baby."

Fatima kept quiet as she finished rolling out the last of her cookies.

"And those cookies you making ain't exactly gonna help your figure, either."

"I'm starting back at the gym next week."

"Thank the Lord!" Pamela declared.

After putting her tray of cookies in the oven, Fatima fired up a cigarette. Pamela frowned.

"How's Nikki? Fatima asked as she wiped her counter with a dishcloth. She was desperate to change the subject.

"Nikki's fine. Since you want to change the subject, I'll ask something else."

"Thank the Lord!" Fatima said.

"What are you going to say at the Mayor's event?"

"I'm not sure. Marisol's writing my speech. I'm meeting with her later."

"Can you deliver it without cussing?"

"I can."

"You haven't been able to so far. There's gonna be news cameras there?"

"Most likely."

"Fatima, don't embarrass me again with that mouth of yours?"

Fatima held her right hand up, as if she was taking an oath of office.

"I promise not to embarrass my mother again in public, as long as I live."

Fatima noticed her mother observing her oddly when she finished with her pledge.

"What's wrong, Mama?"

"You really sounded sincere. You ever think about going into politics?"

"Do I look that damn stupid?" Fatima blurted out.

Pamela sighed in dismay at her daughter's filthy mouth.

•　　　　　•　　　　　•

Marisol was already in a booth at Harlem Heat when Fatima met with her later that day. The Lenox Avenue restaurant was reputed to serve the hottest buffalo wings around. Fatima approached unnoticed as Marisol was typing on her cell phone.

"What you doing? Trading stocks?"

"Hey, girl," Marisol said without looking up. Fatima sat across the table and picked up a menu. She scanned the back of it to see what desserts were on offer.

Marisol kept typing.

"Maybe I should come back later, Marisol?"

"Sorry," Marisol said and put her cell phone down. "I was setting up a second date."

"Second date? With who?"

"Kermit."

"Kermit? Does he live in a pond?"

"He's not a frog. We met online," Marisol said dryly.

"You still doing that?"

"I'm opening up my horizons."

"Open your horizons up to guys on the Internet if you want. But make sure to use a condom, so you don't download any viruses."

Marisol ignored the remark. "I trust you'll keep my Internet dating under your hat?"

"Like you kept news of this speech you want me to give from my mother?"

"You weren't going to tell her about it?"

"Hell no! She's plucking my nerves enough about me and Andre splitting up."

"You heard from him yet?"

Marisol observed the sadness that appeared on her friend's face.

"No," Fatima answered as she looked down at her menu.

"Look, Fatima, Andre put a ring on your finger. All Raphael gave me was lies. Quit being stupid and call him. I know you miss him."

Fatima held her head up as she stiffened her resolve.

"Andre knows how to reach me when he wants to apologize."

"I can't believe you!" Marisol sighed.

"Can we order food and start on this damn speech?" Fatima said. "I still have schoolwork to do."

After they went to the counter and placed their orders, they returned to their booth. Marisol reached in her bag and pulled out a pen and note pad.

"So," she began, "what I see this speech being about is the dispensing of info concerning our mission, and—"

"Mission?"

"Our goal to curtail teenage sexual activity?"

"Whoa! I thought this event was about fighting HIV and AIDS in Harlem?"

"We'll get to that. I want us to first mention our organization. Then, I want—"

"How about you give this speech, instead, Marisol?"

"Don't be funny."

"I'm serious. You know exactly what you want mentioned and whatnot."

"The Mayor's people asked for you. Fatima, if we get this right, you won't have to give another speech no time soon."

"We agreed to no more speeches, period."

"Did I say that?"

"Yep. That reminds me," Fatima said as she grabbed her purse and opened it. She pulled out a piece of paper, unfolded it, and handed it to Marisol.

"What is this?"

"Reading is fundamental," Fatima said.

Marisol read the paper and then looked up at Fatima in disbelief.

"You drafted an agreement to never have to speak for GASP again?"

"This will be my last speech, Marisol."

"Okay, I get it, Fatima."

"Good, now sign it."

Marisol mumbled to herself and scribbled her name at the bottom of the sheet of paper.

"Happy now?"

"No, but this helps."

Fatima folded the paper and returned it to her purse. Marisol's phone beeped at that moment. She picked it up and read her text.

"Confirmation to meet Kermit at his lily pad?" Fatima asked.

"No, Shaconda's a block away."

"How's she doing? I haven't talked to her in a minute."

"Fine. You know she designed and put up our website by herself?"

"Really?"

"Yeah," Marisol said. "I'm going to cry when she leaves for college next year."

Shaconda approached their table a minute later wearing a T-shirt with an image of the Egyptian Queen Nefertiti on it, blue jean shorts, and flip-flops.

"Sorry for being late," she said.

"Hello, Shaconda. Long time no see," Fatima said.

"Hi."

Fatima eyed the teen as she took a seat at their table.

"I see you showing off them legs, Shaconda. Be careful, you know how hard up these boys are around here now!"

"That pun was so lame," Marisol said.

"Marisol, don't have me check you like I did that idiot, Philbert."

"Yeah, right?" Marisol said. The two women shared a fist bump.

Shaconda looked at them in amazement.

"Didn't y'all see what he did?" she asked.

Fatima stopped smiling and sat up in her seat.

"What you talking about, Shaconda?" she asked warily.

Shaconda pulled her cell phone out her pocket and tapped on some keys. She then held the phone up for Fatima and Marisol to see.

"Look," she said uneasily.

A video launched that showed Fatima jumping off the stage in Marcus Garvey Park, rushing to get to the kid who threw his soda at her. She was seized and held by security. The video was looped, so every fifteen seconds the same sequence played over again. As the video played, The Young Turks hit rap song, "She's Too Ghetto" blasted noisily from the speaker in Shaconda's cell phone. A looping audio verse that accompanied the video clip sang:

She's all about drama… cause her life's a mess!

She can't keep a man cause she's too much stress!

Why she's jacked up? It's in her genes... I guess!

She's too ghetto, a little too ghetto for me!

Underneath the video in the left corner it read: *Posted by Philbert Phelps.*

The clip had been viewed over twenty thousand times in six days. Many viewers had liked it with a thumbs up icon. That fight video had flared up once again, like a bad case of herpes.

"Damn," Marisol mumbled.

Fatima was stunned. As much as she loathed Philbert's ass, even she had to give him props on his retribution. The idiot had punched back hard. Fatima had no choice but to step her game up too.

"Philbert also posted that clip on his Facebook page. It's going viral," Shaconda added.

"Damn," Marisol mumbled again.

Fatima shook her head in dismay.

"The gloves are off now," she said resolutely.

"What are you going to do?" Marisol asked.

"Not sure. But, I will get in that pipsqueak's ass."

When Fatima stepped into her cubicle early that following Wednesday she saw a flyer for the mayor's upcoming event in her chair. Her name was listed at the very bottom as one of the invited speakers.

That damn Inez!

Fatima picked up the flyer and found a printout of a news article underneath it that detailed the mayor's latest proposal of austerity, which included cutting staff at Human Resources. Fatima read it and then tossed both sheets of paper into her recycling basket. Before she could sit down and log into her computer, Inez was standing in front of her. A look of consternation was on her face.

"We sleeping with the enemy now?"

"Good morning to you too, Inez."

"Sorry, good morning. I found the article about that fool's budget while I was checking my lotto numbers online."

"I didn't know about the job cuts proposal, Inez."

"Yours could be one that gets eliminated, Fatima."

"I know. Last hired, first fired."

"What are you gonna do about it?"

"I only agreed to speak at this event a couple of days ago. I'll back out of it."

"Why would you do that?"

"I'm sorry?" Fatima said. A look of puzzlement was on her face as she stood.

"You're in the perfect situation to let the public know that we cannot do any 'more with less' around here."

"You asking me to put the mayor on blast? At his own event?"

"I'm asking you to help save jobs… maybe your own."

"Can I come stay with you after they fire my ass, Inez?"

Inez placed a hand on Fatima's shoulder. "Fatima, you have a gift. You inspired young girls around here to quit fucking! You had them sumbitches in that park riled up enough to fight outside in mid-July heat! Can't you say a few words at this rally and let the public know that Human Resources is already short-staffed? We can't afford more reductions."

Fatima was quiet as she searched for a bullshit answer.

"Okay… we'll see," she finally said.

"Don't give me that bullshit answer!"

"I said, *we'll see*," Fatima repeated. The edge in her voice was obvious. Inez opted not to respond and returned to her own desk.

Fatima was back-logged with paperwork. Mrs. Baker had advised her that management was pressuring supervisors to write up staff with unsatisfactory job performances. Her supervisor also told her not to hesitate asking for help getting caught up if she needed it. Fatima realized she was fortunate that Mrs. Baker was more concerned about helping her workers than gaining brownie points with management. Many supervisors were not like that.

The bad news about the possibility of layoffs deserved a cigarette, but Fatima was too far behind to take a break. When she checked her work email, she saw that she had an unscheduled client downstairs waiting.

"Shit!"

Fatima didn't recognize the person. She typed the name Chanita Garcia into her computer and pulled up her case information. The twenty-three-year-old undocumented alien from Ecuador was only receiving benefits for her two Brooklyn-born kids. She worked part time cleaning houses and the father of her children, Mario, was allegedly deported last year.

After a short wait for an interview booth to become available, Fatima went and called Ms. Garcia from reception. The infant the woman held in her arms flashed an angelic smile at Fatima. Fatima smiled back at the baby and prayed the little bastard stayed quiet.

"You speaka Spanish?" Ms. Garcia asked as soon as she was seated.

"*Nada.*"

Fatima recruited Consuela Lantigua, a young receptionist, to see what Ms. Garcia needed.

"She says that she needs to move."

"Why?"

Consuela redirected Fatima's question to her client.

"She says her place is infested with bedbugs. Her landlord won't pay to get rid of them."

Fatima recalled reading in her case notes that Ms. Garcia's rent was subsidized.

"Did she contact Section Eight?"

Consuela and Ms. Garcia conversed again in Spanish.

"Yes. They told her to talk to you."

Fatima slid a blank sheet of paper and a pen over the table to her client.

"Consuela, please tell her to write down what she needs, why, and to sign and date the letter. I'll see what I can do."

Consuela and Fatima's client exchanged a few words. The receptionist then laughed.

"What's up?" Fatima asked suspiciously.

"Ms. Garcia asked if you're the lady who was in the park fighting all those boys in that video. I said 'yes.'"

"What's so funny about that?"

"She asked me to please be her worker," the receptionist giggled.

"Tell her to write the damn letter, Consuela."

.   .   .

When Fatima made it back up to her floor, she noticed that two of her co-workers avoided eye contact when they passed her. Another one frowned as he walked by. The office grapevine was in action. People were identifying her as a sellout for speaking at the mayor's rally. Fatima ignored the foolishness and returned to her desk. Her phone rang a minute later.

"Human Resources, Ms. Richardson speaking—"

"Ya black bitch!" The caller hung up before Fatima realized she'd been cussed out again. She'd forgotten to screen the call.

Soon after Philbert's manifesto went viral she started receiving lots of crank calls from guys. Someone had disclosed her work number to the public. The harassment was so bad that she resorted to letting her calls go to voice mail. She returned the ones that were work related.

Fatima was hesitant to tell her supervisor about the problem and request a new line, because upper management would get involved. She didn't want those bozos questioning the cause behind the harassment and scrutinizing her. (If they weren't doing so already.) Fatima glared at her phone, praying that the prankster would call again. After five minutes elapsed, she grabbed her pack of menthols and headed for the exit.

Only one of the group of smokers already outside acknowledged her when she walked over and joined them. The others ignored her completely. Fatima opened her mouth to cuss their asses out, but thought better of it. In civil service employment, you never knew who might pass an exam and become your new supervisor. Fatima walked away from the group with an irritated expression on her face as she lit her cigarette. Marisol and the Mayor of New York were now both a pain in her rear end.

The majority of people living up in Harlem couldn't stand the mayor of New York City. The mayor knew this. The mayor's campaign manager knew this also. That was the reason she scheduled him to hold a massive event in front of Harlem Hospital. The mayor had to do something courageous to reignite his slumping poll numbers among people of color who voted. Hizzoner was slated to promise Harlemites that once re-elected, he would make the eradication of AIDS and HIV, and creating jobs for minorities in NYC, two of the top priorities of his next term.

The section of Lenox Avenue between 135th Street and 137th Street was cordoned off with metal barriers and lots of NYPD officers. A huge banner proclaiming Long Live Harlem! hung across the front of Harlem Hospital, above the renowned African American artist John Rhoden's bronze sculpture of a black family.

A temporary stage was erected to the left of the hospital's main entrance. On it sat some of City Hall's movers and shakers. The mayor was also reluctantly present. He was more concerned about the wind gusts that periodically blew through his hairpiece than the inspirational speech he had to give to get votes.

Over five hundred Harlemites had opted to spend their Saturday afternoon listening to whatever bullshit the mayor had to spew. Several news cameras were spread around the perimeter of the gathering to hopefully capture something on video worthy of reporting on that evening's broadcast.

. . .

Fatima sat in the very back row on the stage swearing under her breath. Never again would Marisol manipulate her. This was truly the last fucking time. Even though Marisol signed an agreement not to pester her about speaking in public again, Fatima didn't trust her any further than she could throw her.

The speech Marisol and Shaconda wrote for Fatima wasn't too bad, once it actually got down to discussing HIV and AIDS prevention. There was a tedious preamble about GASP's mission, and how it wanted to expand with the help of public donations and funding grants. Fatima planned to read directly from the pages Marisol had given her, so she didn't bother to memorize every word of the speech.

As she fretted over her looming oratory obligation, Fatima listened to the current speaker, the illustrious Dr. Che Hauser. The thirty-six-year-old HIV specialist was trained at New York Medical College and was one of the brightest physicians at Harlem Hospital. The Barbadian was physically fit, stood over six feet tall, and had a short military haircut, which gave her a striking appearance.

"Everyone within the sound of my voice who is sexually active needs to go and get tested," Dr. Hauser implored. "You can go and get tested for free! Know your status!"

Fatima looked down at her speech and mentally crossed that tidbit off. There was no need to be repetitive.

"And the stigma that's associated with HIV in the black community needs to be eradicated," Dr. Hauser continued, "because it keeps far too many people from being tested, and subsequently treated for the disease."

Fatima had that same message in her speech too. It was getting shorter by the minute.

"Are we all aware that roughly twenty percent of new HIV infections occur in youth aged thirteen to twenty-four? And to all of you young black women out there, I have a special message, because you're far more affected by HIV than young women of other races," Dr. Hauser said as she surveyed the crowd. "If you're sexually active, please use a condom on every conceivable occasion."

The pun generated a wave of laughter from the crowd. Fatima smiled too. If Dr. Hauser kept it up she wouldn't have to say shit to these people. Things were looking up.

"Before I return to my seat, I would like to spend a few minutes addressing the issues affecting our black gay and bisexual community. Because this segment of our community has especially been hit hard in terms of new HIV infections."

The butterflies in Fatima's stomach began their customary fluttering as Dr. Hauser wound down her speech. Fatima was scheduled on the program to speak after the doctor. She rubbed her sweaty palms on the sides of her black jeans and prayed that her heavy perspiration didn't show through her bright yellow blouse. Fatima tuned out the rest of the doctor's speech on how young gay and bisexual men made up the majority of new HIV infections among black males. Her thoughts were focused on the cigarette that she craved.

Fatima's eyes wandered along with her mind and she was surprised to spot Reverend Yizar standing in the crowd. Instead of looking up at the speaker onstage, the pastor had his eyes focused on the curvaceous rear end of the young woman standing before him. Fatima rolled her eyes in disgust. Seconds later she spied Shaconda standing near a news cameraman. Marisol stood next to her mentee, grinning like the Cheshire cat.

"Lastly, it has come to my attention that we have a couple of concerned sisters among us who have actually convinced some of our young women to abstain from sex altogether. I think that's amazing!"

Roughly half of the crowd applauded as Dr. Hauser turned and smiled at Fatima. Fatima smiled back weakly. She'd been praying nobody would bring that shit up.

"Our community needs more concerned adults. Our city needs more concerned adults. Thank you, Harlem! And don't forget to vote!"

.   .   .

A crescendo of applause and shouts of approval showered Dr. Hauser as she returned to her seat. Fatima was next. Her butterflies started to go bananas when she watched the host for the event, an elderly black radio personality named Chris Michaels, walk to the lectern.

"The next speaker to address us really needs no introduction, folks. And when I tell you that this sister is a soldier on the front lines, battling for change here in Harlem, I ain't lying."

The crowd caught the cryptic reference to the melee at Marcus Garvey Park and chuckled.

Asshole! Fatima thought as she frowned.

"Fatima Richardson is a mesmerizing young speaker who works for GASP. She is a powerful voice in our community. Her talent for motivating young people has led to the aforementioned sex strike around here that Dr. Hauser described as being amazing. I think it's miraculous."

Few laughed at the lame joke.

"She has appeared on the television program, *Black Awareness,* she's been written about in a few city tabloids, and she's currently starring in an action packed video that's circulating online."

Fatima groaned and balled up her fists. Chris Michaels had one more joke to make at her expense and his public ass whipping would be the next video to go viral. The emcee turned and flashed Fatima a smile. The acrimony in her eyes conveyed to him that he was fucking up.

"Ladies and gentlemen, without further ado, Ms. Fatima Richardson!"

The enthusiastic applause she received as she hesitantly got up and walked to the lectern surprised Fatima. Her stomach was in knots and the news cameras trained on her wasn't helping any. She placed her speech on the lectern and then grabbed it to steady her shaking hands. Even Fatima's knees were knocking.

She glanced to the left and out of the corner of her eye she saw the mayor looking at her with mild interest as he fought with his mussed hairpiece. He was short too, which was why Fatima could see over the lectern in front of her. Fatima was not a big fan of his at all. As far as she was concerned, he'd done little to help the poor in the city. All of his economic policies seemed geared to helping his Wall Street buddies increase their profits. Everyone else had to deal with the high costs of rent, food, and transportation the best they could.

To complicate matters, the leading candidate in the mayoral race claimed the city was already spending too much money on entitlement programs for the poor. She promised to slash spending as soon as she got in office. The future didn't bode well for the underprivileged in NYC either way.

Fatima saw Inez standing close to the stage eagerly waving. Drew was behind her. Fatima needed to see those two like she needed a hole in her head. Inez had remained adamant that Fatima put the mayor on blast. A day earlier she'd handed her a fact sheet with the number of jobs Human Resources had already shed under his tenure. Fatima had thanked Inez and then balled up the paper when she got back to her cubicle.

The one bright spot of the afternoon's event was that her mother would not be in attendance. Nikki's blood pressure was elevated, so Pamela had to stay home and monitor her. Fatima was so happy when she learned this news that she thanked Nikki via text. (She also wished her sister a rapid recovery.)

·   ·   ·

Fatima swallowed hard as she surveyed the gathering of humanity before her. There was a mutual look in a lot of the eyes that watched her. People wanted to hear something of substance. They wanted to hear something relevant. This made Fatima self-conscience about mechanically reading her speech to such an expecting crowd. That issue was quickly resolved when a wicked wind whipped the pages of her speech off the lectern and whooshed them in the direction of the 135th Street subway entrance.

Motherfucker!

To her credit, Fatima had the presence of mind to not cuss out loud with a bunch of microphones in her face. But she was pissed. And petrified. Now she had to wing the damn speech! If she weren't before a bunch of news cameras she probably would've walked off the stage and took her ass home. As she stood there a wave of murmurs spread through the crowd. Fatima nervously glanced over at Marisol and Shaconda. There were looks of horror on both their faces. Everyone was waiting for Fatima to speak… so she opened her mouth and spoke.

"Uh, even though it was my intention to have my speech blow you guys away, what just happened wasn't exactly what I had in mind."

The crowd politely laughed. Fatima was encouraged.

"Before I try to remember the thoughts I had written down, I'd like to take this time to clear up a couple of fallacies associated with that oft referenced video everyone has seen. One, I didn't start that fight in Marcus Garvey Park, and two, I am not against our young black men. I just want for them to do better."

"Me too, sugar!" an elderly woman yelled. Once the laughter subsided Fatima continued.

"The uh, the reason I stand before you today is because I was asked to give a short speech about the ills of AIDS and HIV in our community."

Fatima nervously ran a hand through her locks.

"But thanks to the stupendous job that Dr. Hauser just did, I feel it would be pointless for me to come behind her and try to add to the brilliant message she delivered."

Fatima raked through her hair again.

"But, but I will say that I hope you all listened to what she said. I really hope that the information and statistics Dr. Hauser gave us about how HIV and AIDS are devastating our community sink in. Especially with our young people here."

"Amen!" somebody in the audience hollered.

"See, I work for the Human Resources Administration, better known to some folks as, 'welfare.'"

A few in the crowd chuckled.

"And at my job, I get to see daily the results of bad decisions that our young people make. And the sad part is that most of these mistakes are avoidable."

"Tell it!" another member of the audience shouted.

Marisol nodded in agreement. A sly grin appeared on her lips.

"There's no need for anyone to be having unprotected sex. There's no need for HIV, or other sexually transmitted diseases to be spreading through this city."

"Put a hat on it!" a woman near the stage yelled. The crowd cracked up. Fatima politely paused for them to finish laughing.

"What that woman said might be funny, but she's right," she continued. "There are too many places around here to get condoms. And no excuse for a teenage girl becoming pregnant and jeopardizing her education."

Echoes of agreement circulated throughout the audience. Fatima recognized that she had the crowd's approval. No longer nervous, she pulled one of the microphones closer.

"Now, as Dr. Hauser mentioned earlier, there's a group of responsible young ladies here in Harlem who have successfully organized a sex strike."

"Really?" an unbelieving male yelled.

"Yes! Really!" Fatima answered. She waited for the laughter to subside. "And for one reason or the other, people are under the impression that I'm the person who started this strike," Fatima said as she turned and glared at Marisol.

"There is also a misconceived notion out there that I'm an angry, young black woman who hates men. Nothing could be further from the truth! I have nothing but love for our young men of color."

Shouts of approval came from the crowd.

"But, I do hate to see young men of color neglect to support the children they've fathered. I do hate to see young men of color dropping out of school, so they can get their hustle on in the streets."

Fatima had the crowd hyped. There were lots of yells of approval from the young women in the audience.

"Quitting school can severely limit one's potential to earn a livable wage. And that results in one of two things. You either do something unlawful, that could get your butt incarcerated, or you have to come to my agency and see me for financial assistance."

Even the mayor and his cronies chuckled with the rest of the crowd.

"I'd prefer if you young people did neither," Fatima said. "Our jails are already full, and our welfare offices are already understaffed with workers trying to do 'more with less'!"

The mayor and his colleagues stopped smiling. Inez and Drew clapped. Fatima lingered a few seconds to gather her thoughts...

"Another thing we need our young people to do to secure a decent future in this city, is to get them to vote!"

"YES!" the crowd yelled.

"If they don't vote, they don't count! Public officials today make long-term decisions that affect their futures tomorrow. As soon as your kid is old enough to cast a ballot, see to it that they do!"

The mayor began to feel uneasy. He fiddled with his hairpiece. His campaign manager glanced at her watch and then tried to get Chris Michaels' attention. The host didn't see her. He was busy listening to Fatima.

"I hope Hizzoner, our mayor, is going to stand up here shortly and tell us, not what we want to hear, but what he is actually going to do for us if we vote for him."

"Go head, sistah!" an elderly woman shouted.

"Preach!" an elderly man yelled.

Laughter floated through the crowd.

"You know, it's ironic that we're here in front of Harlem Hospital today, because we've grown sick and tired of politicians showing up in our community when they need our vote and disappearing after the election!"

The crowd roared its approval.

"Even Malcolm X, who preached on this very street we're assembled on today, pointed out the devious behavior of politicians toward the black community. He stated you never saw them until election time, and you can't find them until election time. Harlem, we need for that to change!"

The crowd roared its approval louder.

"Don't get it twisted, this is not a personal attack on the mayor. This goes out to anybody who's running for office and wants Harlem's vote!"

Fatima spun left and glanced in the mayor's direction.

"But while our mayor is here, I want to inform him personally that as an employee for NYC, trying to do more with less staff is a joke!"

Numerous people in the crowd doubled over in laughter. Inez among them.

"It never worked, and it never will, your honor."

Fatima was on a roll. She propped herself up on the lectern and leaned toward the crowd.

"Am I right about it?!"

"AMEN!" several people screamed.

•   •   •

Seeing a young black woman talk shit to the mayor of the largest city in America was uplifting for the older citizens of Harlem in attendance. It had been decades since they'd witnessed a gifted orator like Ms. Richardson in their community. The crowd cheered as Fatima went off on a tangent of problems the next mayor needed to fix. She had totally digressed from what she was asked to speak on. The mayor's campaign manager wildly tried to get Chris Michaels' attention, but he too, was caught up in the rapture of the exciting speaker before him.

Fatima listed a litany of issues: the high price of public transportation; the ridiculous rents people paid for housing, violent criminal activity in the city; and the exorbitant fees, taxes, and fines New York City charged people to fill its greedy coffers. As soon as she mentioned a mutual bone of contention, the crowd roared back its approval. The audience then started yelling their own problematic issues about Harlem to Fatima, and to the mayor.

"Liquor stores charging too much!"

"Too many white folks moving in!"

"Failing school systems!"

"Rats too big!"

Meanwhile, the mayor and his people were turning redder by the second. Fatima couldn't care less. She was on a tirade about the overaggressive policing of male minorities when she spotted a familiar face. Fatima stared at it a few seconds to be certain.

He had grown a beard. His mother Lois, was with him. They were both looking at Fatima in awe. Overjoyed at seeing Andre again, she lost her train of thought.

"And... another thing, to say that it's not unethical for the police stopping and frisking people of color, as a preventive crime measure, is asinine!"

A gasp rippled through the crowd.

"I didn't cuss," Fatima chuckled. "That word means stupid."

The crowd laughed. When Fatima saw Andre laughing her heart raced. Then she caught a glimpse of the mayor and his crew out of the corner of her eye. Their angry glares made her heart race even faster. It was time to sit her ass on down.

"There uh, seems to be a few folks here who'd love for me to shut up now. But I don't care, because this will be my last speech anyway!"

The crowd laughed harder. The mayor turned redder. Marisol frowned.

"I'll go sit down, but let me first say this. Politicians will come up to Harlem, and shake hands and slap folks on their backs, and they'll skin and they'll grin and pretend they're your friend, but I hope y'all know better than that!"

The crowd went bananas.

"Hallelujah!"

"Amen!"

Fatima ignored the loud applause and shouts of approval as she walked away from the lectern and stepped down from the stage. She had a nagging feeling that she'd soon be applying for unemployment benefits.

The number of people who patted her on the back, or grabbed and shook her hand convinced Fatima that she'd done a good job. Inez and Drew both gave her a thumbs up when she glanced in their direction. Fatima smiled cordially and continued on her path to Andre.

·   ·   ·

"I'm so proud of you!" Lois said as she intercepted Fatima and gave her a hug. She then nudged her toward her son and released her.

"Thanks," Fatima said once she was able to speak. She and Andre beheld each other. He cracked a smile first.

"Fatima… that speech… it was excellent."

"Glad you enjoyed it, Andre."

"Is this the best you two Negroes can do?" Lois asked in mock disbelief.

Humiliated by his mother, Andre took Fatima into his arms. They kissed.

"Your beard tickles," Fatima laughed.

"Want me to lose it?"

"Don't. It looks sexy."

"What are you doing here?" Fatima asked.

"This is my mom's doing. First, she begged me to drive up this weekend to help her look at some used cars in Queens. After that, she persuaded me to run her out here to visit the Schomburg Center, across the street from here. They had a new slavery exhibit that she wanted to see."

"They do," Lois interjected, smiling triumphantly.

"Once we got here, she just happened to have a flyer announcing the mayor's political event. Your name was circled, as one of the guest speakers."

Fatima looked at Lois and laughed.

"Thank you!"

"Don't mention it," Lois replied.

"Obviously, it was all a set up," Andre said.

"Damn right," Lois answered. She then disappeared into the crowd. Andre turned and faced Fatima again.

"You have no idea how bad I've missed you."

"Likewise, Andre. How long are you in town?"

"Depends."

"On what?"

"Whether I can spend time with you."

"Right now I have to go check on Nikki. She's not feeling well."

"Maybe later?" Andre asked.

At that moment Inez appeared. She embraced Fatima jubilantly.

"You castigated that clown!"

Fatima was too breathless to reply. Inez released her and turned to Andre.

"Andre, I presume?"

"That's me."

"I'm Inez. I work with Fatima. I'm so proud of her!"

"I am too," Andre replied. He glanced lovingly at Fatima.

"I'd love to stay and chat, but I have to go put my numbers in now," Inez said. "See you at the wedding, Andre."

Fatima and Andre stood silent as they watched Inez rush off. Andre then turned back to Fatima.

"About later on?" he repeated.

"After I check on Nikki we can meet."

Marisol arrived next with Shaconda in tow.

"Andre! Nice to see you again!" Marisol said as she hugged him.

"Hello, Marisol," Andre replied.

After introducing Shaconda to Andre, Marisol turned to Fatima. A troubled look was on her face.

"That was some speech."

"You saw what happened to the one you guys wrote for me. I did the best I could."

"I see," Marisol replied evenly.

"I think the mayor's annoyed at you, Fatima," Shaconda said.

"I can live with that."

Fatima gave Marisol a stare that conveyed she and Andre had unfinished business.

"Come on, Shaconda, let's go hear the other speeches," Marisol said and gave Fatima a hard look as she walked off. "We'll talk later, Fatima."

"I'm sure we will," Fatima answered.

Andre wasted no time picking up where he'd left off.

"So, you'll let me know what time we're meeting up?"

"I'll call you, Andre. I promise."

"Thanks, Fatima."

They kissed again.

.　　　　　.　　　　　.

When Fatima reached home she heated up leftover lasagna, poured a tall glass of red wine and sat on her couch to eat before she checked on Nikki. She was anxious about her possible loss of employment so she drained her glass and poured another round to help calm her nerves.

As she sipped more vino, Fatima made a mental note to update her resume. She also reminded herself not to forget about getting even with that runt Philbert Phelps. She wasn't sure how she'd retaliate against that bastard, she just knew that it had to be something wicked.

TWENTY-EIGHT
GIRL INTERRUPTED

She woke up three hours later.

"Shit!" Fatima exclaimed as she sat up on the couch. She picked up her cell phone and saw it was after seven. She also saw she had missed eleven calls. Three from her mother, one from Nikki, one from Andre, and one from Quinn. Five of them were from Marisol. Fatima freshened up in the bathroom and then hurried out the front door.

As she headed to The Dark Towers, Fatima noticed the Harlemites who stopped and stared at her as she walked by. A few even smiled and gave tacit nods. Fatima's first thought was that some new illicit drug had been introduced to the community. Something Harlem didn't need any more of.

She reached her destination and spied Birdman sitting on a bench opposite a young kid. A chessboard lay between them. Fatima was low on smokes, so she changed course and cut across the grass in the opposite direction. Her attempt at stealth was unsuccessful.

"Yo! Fatima!"

Damn.

"Hey, Birdman! I didn't see you."

"You stirred up some real shit with the mayor today," Birdman chuckled.

"You were there?" Fatima asked as she approached.

"Heck naw. Saw that shit on my phone," Birdman said as he took one of his opponent's pieces off the board. "Think before you move, son. That's the only way to win at this game."

"Okay," the poor boy sighed.

"Fatima, can I get a couple smokes off you?"

Fatima hesitantly opened her bag. She handed him two cigarettes.

"Thanks, I'll get you back."

"Don't smoke in front of the kid while you're teaching him chess. It nullifies the good deed you're doing."

"Damn, you sound like you gonna be the new mayor, now."

Fatima ignored Birdman's comment and walked to her mother's building.

.   .   .

Nikki was spread out on the living room sofa watching television when Fatima opened the front door and walked in. She looked like she was ready to give birth any minute now.

"How you feeling?"

"Better. Thanks."

"What you watching?" Fatima asked as she locked the door behind her.

"Your ass on the news," Nikki said. "It'll be a minute before the mayor asks you to speak at another event with him."

Fatima turned and saw a rebroadcast of her speech. She was in the middle of harping on the mayor's "More with Less" policy. As the clip of Fatima's criticism played, the camera zoomed in on the mayor... his face was beet red and his hairpiece askew.

A young white female reporter then appeared on the television screen.

"The mayor's unruly hair turned out to be the least of his problems today."

The newscast then showed a clip of the mayor standing at the lectern trying to calm a disorderly crowd while being mercilessly booed. Finally, in disgust, he threw up his arms in defeat and walked off the stage.

"Shit!" Fatima said.

The news reporter reappeared on the screen.

"Sources in City Hall tell us that the mayor's team is very displeased by Ms. Richardson's remarks and the ensuing uproar it caused. Sources also tell us that a major shakeup of his campaign staff is imminent."

Fatima picked up the remote, and changed the channel.

"Hey!" Nikki shouted.

She ignored Nikki's protest and sat down on the sofa next to her.

"Damn! I am so fired."

"What? You didn't know what went down?"

"I left after I finished speaking."

"Fatima!" Pamela yelled from the kitchen.

"I meant to tell you, Mama's been looking for you," Nikki whispered.

Fatima sighed deeply and then trudged into the kitchen. Her mother was standing at the sink peeling a bunch of sweet potatoes.

"More pies for Reverend Yizar?"

"Sit down!" Pamela said sternly. She didn't bother to turn around.

Fatima obeyed.

"You trying to get your black ass fired on purpose?"

"No, Mama."

"You turned that crowd against that man for no reason at all?"

"I didn't plan that. I just said what was on my mind... it was the truth."

"Damn the truth! You know how hard it is to find a decent-paying job in this city?"

"Yes, I do."

Pamela swore under her breath as she grabbed another sweet potato. Fatima noticed the gray hairs sprouting on her mother's nape.

"And you decided to embarrass the mayor anyway. What in the hell were you thinking? I called your ass three times after I saw that mess on the news. Why didn't you call me back?"

"Sorry, but after I spoke to Andre at the rally I went home and fell asleep."

"You saw Andre?"

"He was there."

Pamela spun around.

"Andre was at the rally?"

Fatima knew better than to get smart with her mother for asking the same dumb question twice, especially while she held a knife. She simply nodded in the affirmative.

Pamela dropped her knife and the sweet potato in the sink, and joined Fatima at the table.

"What did he say? I hope you didn't argue with him again?"

Fatima bit her tongue and waited a few seconds before she answered.

"We talked."

"About what? Did he mention the wedding?" Pamela asked eagerly.

"We admitted how much we missed each other. He wants to see me later."

"Thank the Lord!"

"Thank his mother, too. She tricked him into coming to Harlem where I was speaking."

Before Pamela could respond, Fatima's cell phone rang. She walked to the living room and grabbed it out of her bag. It was Marisol. Fatima put the phone back in her bag.

"Was that Andre?" her mother asked when she returned.

"No."

"Fatima, all I want in this world is for Nikki to have a healthy baby, and for you and Andre to get back together."

"I understand, Mama."

"I also want you to stay employed. You need to contact the mayor's office on Monday and tell them folks you're sorry about what happened today."

Fatima stood up from the table and forced a smile.

"May I be dismissed now?"

"Go. And give Andre my regards."

·   ·   ·

Fatima and Andre met for dinner at Harlem Hibachi. The eatery was located on 116th Street and Madison Avenue. It was part of the tide of gentrification that was inundating Harlem. Marisol had gone there on one of her blind dates and had raved about it. However, she had refused to give Fatima details on how the rest of the date turned out.

Fatima had returned home from her mother's and changed into an enticing red sundress to remind Andre of what he'd missed. (The garment fit a lot tighter than it used to, but she still felt sexy in it.) She wore a pair of black leather sandals that poor Nikki could no longer slip her swollen feet into and she sported her new pair of reading glasses to look extra chic.

She admired the image of the giant Kabuki on the restaurant's glass door as she walked inside. Andre was sitting at a nearby grill, along with eight other customers. Fatima thought she saw an elderly couple exchange whispers as they watched her.

"May I help you?"

She turned and saw a young black waiter staring curiously at her.

"I'm here to meet someone. I see him over at that grill."

"Okay, follow me."

The young man led Fatima over to the grill and pulled out her seat when she stopped next to Andre. He politely waited as they kissed.

"Would you folks like to order anything to drink?"

"Bring me your best scotch, and bring her a margarita, please?" Andre said.

Fatima was mesmerized by the way his beard moved when he talked. The waiter glanced at Fatima for a few seconds after he wrote down their order. She picked up on it.

"Is something wrong?" she asked and then gave the waiter a hard stare.

"No."

When the waiter left to get their drinks, Andre leaned in close to Fatima.

"I forgot how sexy you look in a sundress." (He ignored the snug fit.)

"Thanks."

"This place is nice," Andre said. "Good call."

Fatima was busy looking at the two middle-aged black women seated across the grill from them chatting as they looked in her direction.

"You okay?" Andre asked.

"Yeah," Fatima lied. "What were you saying?"

"I said coming here was a good idea."

"Marisol suggested it."

A second later Fatima's cell rang. She knew who it was without checking the caller ID.

"Yes, Marisol?"

"Where the hell you been? I've been calling all evening!"

"I went home after I left the rally. I'm with Andre now."

"I'm sure you've heard what happened to the mayor?"

"Unfortunately, yes."

"Two local news networks, a journalist from the *Daily Sun*, and the campaign manager of the mayor's opponent have contacted me about interviewing you."

"I am so fired," Fatima sighed.

"Look, you have a lot of brand potential right now."

"I got what?"

"We need to explore how to take advantage of this publicity, so you can increase your media presence."

"Marisol, all I'm interested in taking advantage of is my dinner with Andre."

"That's all good, Fatima, but what you need to realize is—"

"Goodbye, Marisol."

Fatima ended the call. A second later she received a text message: *Call me later!* Fatima chuckled to herself and put her phone away.

"What did Marisol want?"

"For me to increase my 'brand awareness.'"

"You really did give a great speech, baby."

"Et tu, Brute?"

"I had no idea you're that good at inspiring people."

"Think I motivated myself into the unemployment line."

"They did boo the mayor's ass pretty badly."

"You saw it?"

"Lead story on the six o'clock news."

Fatima looked glum as she picked up a menu and studied it.

"Don't fret," Andre continued. "I can easily take care of both of us. With my promotion."

"Already?" Fatima asked in awe. She put the menu down.

"My old boss, Mrs. Trapp, took an executive position at our main office in Harrisburg. Don't think we have to worry about her coming to our wedding."

"You took her job?" Fatima asked, ignoring the good news about Mrs. Trapp.

"I wish. A senior person at my office got that spot. They bumped me up to his old title."

"That's great, baby."

Andre held Fatima's hand.

"I tried to prove to myself that I'd be all right without you. I couldn't do it."

Fatima swallowed hard. She'd been waiting for what seemed like an eternity to hear that confession.

"I've been miserable, too, Andre. I'm sorry for everything."

Their waiter returned. "Here we go," he said setting down their drinks. He smiled and again looked at Fatima.

"What's this?" Andre asked him.

"Your rum and coke. And her mojito."

"I ordered a scotch. And a margarita for my lady."

The waiter's smile disappeared.

"Sorry. I mixed up your order."

"You might wanna focus more on your job, instead of me," Fatima said.

The waiter grabbed the drinks and hurried off. When he returned a few minutes later his eyes avoided Fatima.

"Got it right this time," he said as he set their drinks down.

"What's your name?" Andre asked.

"Marvin."

"You new here?"

"My second week, sir."

"Here," Andre said as he placed a twenty-dollar bill in Marvin's hand. "Keep up the good work."

"Thank you!"

"What was that?" Fatima asked once Marvin walked away. "He fucked our order up."

"I'd rather him be in here fucking up my order, than outside fucking up my car, trying to break into it. He's trying to do the right thing."

"Valid point."

Fatima realized why Marisol gave the restaurant high approval after a master chef rolled a cart loaded with utensils and ingredients over to their grill. The aged Japanese woman graciously introduced herself and then confirmed everyone's order. Once that was done, she fired up the grill, pulled items off her cart and executed a culinary spectacle.

Fatima and Andre applauded with the other customers as the chef playfully created huge balls of smoke and flames, sliced and diced food, and cracked bad jokes as she cooked. It was the happiest Fatima had been in a long time. Being with Andre again had her feeling euphoric. The second and third margaritas she drank added to her bliss.

It took her awhile to notice that the chef was hooking her up. Fatima's rice volcano was higher than the others and her share of hibachi shrimp and broccoli was more than the rest. She looked at the chef questioningly. The woman winked at her and continued cooking. Apparently, she was not a big fan of the mayor's either. Fatima let out a sigh as reality hit home. The odds of her continuing to be employed by the City of New York seemed slim to none.

She put her fears on hold and enjoyed dinner with Andre. They talked and laughed as they shared food. His hibachi filet mignon was off the hook. Fatima made a note to order it the next time they visited the joint. She was certain there would be a next time. The more alcohol they consumed, the swifter the memory of their quarrel evaporated. Fatima playfully fed Andre a piece of shrimp from her fork and then kissed his nose.

"So, have we officially made up?" she asked.

"Looks that way," Andre said after munching his food.

"How about some dessert at my place then?"

"I was thinking the same thing, baby."

Andre stood up and looked around the restaurant.

"Where's that slow-ass Marvin?" he grumbled. Fatima laughed while she drained the rest of her margarita.

•　　　　　　•　　　　　　•

They couldn't wait to peel each other's clothes off when they reached Fatima's apartment. She surprised Andre with the black camisole she'd worn under her sundress. She'd ordered it from Paris months ago. It used to fit back then. Now it barely stretched across her midsection. Fatima made a mental note not to sneeze.

"Baby, you look sexy," Andre said as he slipped on a condom. "Now, do me a favor?"

"What's that?" Fatima asked.

"Give me some pudding."

Before Fatima could respond her cell phone rang.

"Ignore it?" Andre asked.

"It might be Nikki."

Fatima pulled her phone out her purse. She saw who the caller was and frowned as she answered.

"*Manana*, Marisol! We'll talk tomorrow!"

Fatima ended the call and Andre walked her to the bed. He then spun her around and bent her over. He carefully forged a crevice between her thighs and entered familiar territory. Andre held Fatima's ass in a death grip as he pounded away inside her like a piston from Detroit.

In no time at all Fatima's insides were soft and wet. Andre had forgotten how good she felt. Both of their faces were moist, his from sweat, and hers from ecstasy. The sweet sensation Fatima endured from the steady slamming made her tremble. She soon reached her point of no return.

"Girl, I missed you!" Andre mumbled as he worked her over.

"We shoulda made up sooner!" Fatima grunted.

Twenty minutes later Andre released his pressure and they collapsed on the bed in a harmonious heap.

"Fatima?"

"Yes?"

"We still getting married?"

"I have my wedding dress from Mrs. DeLuca. Shame to waste good money."

"Same date?"

"No need to waste our deposit," Fatima answered.

"Works for me."

The two were quiet as they listened to Toni Braxton sing "Breathe Again" on the radio.

"I need to move to Philly as soon as I graduate, Andre. My unemployment checks will stretch a lot further there."

"Fine by me," Andre said. He gave Fatima a kiss and sat up in the bed. He then picked up her bible from off the nightstand. "What's this?" he asked.

"The Bible."

"I get that part. What's it doing here?"

"I've been reading through it," Fatima said.

"That's good. I found a nice church in West Philly I think you'll like."

Fatima got up from the bed naked, grabbed her purse, and rummaged through it.

"What you looking for?" Andre asked.

"I need a smoke after that workout."

Fatima put the purse down, grabbed a washcloth from a dresser drawer, and left the room. She returned minutes later and put on a T-shirt, jeans, and a Yankees cap. She then sat on her bed and began putting on sneakers.

"Where are you going at this hour?"

"For cigarettes."

"Now?" Andre asked. He suppressed the irritation in his voice as best he could. Fatima still recognized it.

"If you wait until morning, I'll treat you to Annabelle's."

(Annabelle's was the small coffee shop on 110th Street that served the best omelets in Manhattan as far as Fatima was concerned. She credited Andre for knowing the right carrot to bribe her with. However, she was dying for a puff.)

"Be back in twenty minutes, Andre."

She saw the dismay on his face.

"Besides," Fatima said as she stood up and winked at him. "I'm sure we'll have another workout before morning. What am I supposed to do until then?"

Andre grinned a tacit consent.

·   ·   ·

Harlem was crammed with diverse sounds traveling through the night air as Fatima stepped outside. A nocturnal creature was scavenging through the trashcans by her steps. The alarm on someone's car up the block was finally dying out. (Those devices were triggered accidentally so often, most people ignored them.) Salsa music echoed out the window of the tenant on the top floor of her building, while in an apartment across the street, a cranky baby was bawling its head off. The infant's crying reminded Fatima that she had forgotten to check up on Nikki. She'd do it in the morning.

There was no place like Harlem. Fatima would miss it. But Andre was back and they were going to be wedded; she would leave her beloved community to be with her man. Fatima was grateful he was back, and she was most likely going to need financial assistance from him. Her rainy day fund was washed-out pursuing her Masters Degree.

Fatima was certain her ass would be fired when she went to work Monday because of political fallout from City Hall. Moving to Philly was looking better and better. And the new church Andre mentioned also sounded promising.

On instinct Fatima kept her head down and watched out for dog poo as she walked. This left her unaware of the white Audi SUV that trailed behind her. When Fatima did turn and see the vehicle it was too late. She noticed a black hand pointing an object out of the window in her direction. Then three sharp explosions, sounding like the illegal fireworks New Yorkers played with during the summertime, rang out. Then blood and brain matter sprayed everywhere.

TWENTY-NINE
PEACEFUL JOURNEY

The sky was muted gray from the mist that fell when the funeral limousine carrying the Richardson family pulled in front of Greater Harlem Baptist. Throngs of curious onlookers were gathered, as were several news vans with their antennae raised toward the wet heavens. All the news media outlets in New York City speculated that Fatima had been slain as a result of her incendiary speech at the mayor's event. It made a sensational headline. So much so, that international media outlets picked up the story. News teams from BBC and Al Jazeera flew to New York and reported on the murder. They showed the world clips of Fatima's last speech.

City Hall went into crisis mode when they found out about her murder. The mayor's spokesperson offered his condolences to the Richardson family and then issued a series of statements condemning the senseless act of violence. It did nothing to quell rumors of a political hit. The mayor's team then hastily arranged a visit to The Dark Towers so Hizzoner could personally express sympathy to Fatima's mother. It was a public relations disaster.

Tenants became alarmed when the five-car police convoy pulled up with the mayor's black SUV sandwiched between them, trailed by a local television news van. NYPD's sudden arrival had the looks of another drug raid. Blunts were flushed down toilets, illegal street number slips were swallowed, and various weapons were tossed down trash chutes.

Adjusting his hairpiece, the mayor cautiously stepped out of his SUV. Many of the tenants in the housing project had known Fatima personally. And almost everyone had heard of her death and City Hall's possible role in it. The fact that the mayor had the gall to bring his monkey ass uptown again was too much for them. And the fact that he had caused a massive alarm by visiting The Dark Towers with a bunch of police was unforgivable. They cussed that man out severely. Some tenants even threw objects at him from their windows. The poor man had no choice but to retreat back inside his SUV and haul ass. Twice Harlem had shown the mayor no love. And twice it had been caught on news cameras.

.   .   .

Pamela had to be helped out of the limo by her older brother and guided into the church. Her legs were too rubbery to walk on her own to her daughter's burial service. She wore a long black pleated dress and a matching felt funeral hat with a veil. A pair of dark shades covered Pamela's bloodshot eyes. She had not stopped crying since she received that horrific phone call from Andre.

She was still in the kitchen putting the finishing touches on her sweet potato pies when Andre had called. It was fortunate that she was sitting at the table when she heard the bad news instead of standing. Pamela had screamed and collapsed into a sobbing heap on her kitchen table.

As she sat in a front pew, Pamela was numbed by the sudden death of her daughter. She'd felt guilty about coming down on Fatima so hard about her speech at the mayor's event and had planned to take her out for cheesecake to make amends. That would never happen. Her first child was gone. The wedding she had so looked forward to would never be. The wet handkerchief Pamela held to her eyes was useless; it could absorb no more tears.

Nikki was a basket case. She had been resting uncomfortably in her bed when her mother's scream roused her. Sensing something amiss she rushed as fast as she could into the kitchen where she got the news. An EMS crew arrived shortly thereafter. They treated Nikki for hyperventilation and made sure her vitals were okay. Nikki's doctor suggested she not attend the funeral due to the complications with her pregnancy. Nikki cussed his ass out.

At the funeral Nikki leaned against her mother and sobbed despondently, wetting the only dark dress she could still fit in. As she grieved, Nikki avoided looking at her sister lying in a coffin twenty feet away.

The morticians had performed a remarkable job reconstructing the section of Fatima's head destroyed by the bullet that killed her. She was reposed in a black satin dress. A look of tranquility forever fixed on her face. Her locks were styled and splayed across her shoulders. Her arms were folded over her breasts and clothed in elbow length, white, fingerless gloves that Mrs. DeLuca had donated from her dress shop. A diamond wedding ring was on her left hand.

Andre was seated a row behind the Richardson family in a state of shock. He held his mother's hand tightly as he wept. Lois was irreconcilably grieved over Fatima's death and her son's pain. Andre initially thought the pops he heard outside Fatima's apartment were some assholes shooting fireworks late at night. People did ignorant shit in New York all the time. Then Andre heard a horrific scream. Someone had witnessed Fatima's shooting. The girl's shriek would remain etched in his mind forever.

When Andre looked out of the window and saw the woman he loved collapsed on the sidewalk below, his heart stopped. The grisly image of Fatima soaked in her own blood was also something he'd never forget. Andre had franticly thrown on his pants and shoes and dashed outside. He cried when he reached Fatima because he already knew that she was gone.

The night before Fatima's home going service Andre had vowed to keep his composure. He intentionally left his mother's house without a handkerchief. For the first twenty minutes of the funeral he did hold it together. It was the choir that had fucked him up. They started to sing "I Stood On the Banks of Jordan" and the organist, Sister Denise Greene, skillfully began to make her instrument moan.

An emotional wave of grief crashed over Andre's soul as he realized all of the things that would never happen. He would never see Fatima again. He would never hold Fatima again. He would never love Fatima again. They would never be one in matrimony. Those wretched facts overwhelmed Andre and he began to sob. His world as he knew it was over. Lois instinctively pulled her son's head into her breast to console him.

•   •   •

Marisol was seated on the opposite side of the church, still in disbelief. It was Nikki who called her. Marisol had remained silent at first, trying to decipher the horrific news of Fatima's murder between breaks in Nikki's heavy sobbing. Then Marisol lost it. The two women bawling over the phone together was a gut-wrenching experience.

As she sat in Greater Harlem Baptist listening to the choir, Marisol could not escape the guilt that ate away at her. It was her aspirations that caused Fatima's death. Her best friend was not supposed to be killed for trying to help young people better their lives. The remorse Marisol felt over Fatima's demise had yet to allow her a full night's rest and the sleep deprivation showed. Her once attractive face now appeared drawn and pale from exhaustion. Her once mesmerizing eyes were bloodshot, and her disheveled hair gave the mayor's hairdo some serious competition.

Shaconda sat at Marisol's side. She too, held her head down and wept. She had admired Fatima and considered her a big sister who was making all the right moves. Fatima was socially conscience, had a college education, a good paying job, and a man who wanted to wed her. Now, she was dead. It was a lot for a teenage girl to absorb.

A group of Fatima's coworkers, including Inez, Drew, Ella Watkins, and Mrs. Baker sat several rows behind Marisol and Shaconda. Everyone's eyes were red from crying. Inez was dumbfounded at how her young friend's life had been so suddenly snuffed out… over bullshit. It occurred to her after hearing of Fatima's death that she'd never told her how proud she was of her. Many times Inez had wanted to tell Fatima, "If I had your hand, I'd throw mine back." Instead, she found it easier to tease her. She volunteered for the heart-rending task of packing Fatima's personal belongings at work and delivering the boxes to her mother.

Quinn sat in one of the last pews of Greater Harlem Baptist. He'd received word of Fatima's death the next day while he was driving his cab. It had come via a text from his sister. Quinn had refused to believe the message was accurate and blew up Fatima's cell phone. To no avail. When he drove down her block and saw the police crime scene tape and candles burning in front of her building, his worst fears were confirmed.

There was a hole in his heart that Quinn knew would never heal. If only he'd pressed Fatima more to give him another chance. There was no way he would've allowed someone to gun her down like a criminal. Quinn looked around the church congregation and saw Andre. He was surprised to find himself feeling sympathy for the pretentious motherfucker. Why Fatima had remained loyal to that fool he'd never understand. But Quinn did know he would never forget the only women he actually had real love for.

•   •   •

The last time Greater Harlem Baptist had standing room only at a home going was back in 1979 when Sister Mozelle Ridley was eulogized after eighty-seven years of hell-raising. A renowned drinker, Sister Ridley began her public service career as a numbers runner and gradually worked her way up to overseeing one of the most lucrative betting parlors east of the Hudson River. Sister Ridley made a difference in her community by extending credit to anyone who asked… and also agreed to her exorbitant interest rates. The woman had a photographic memory for recalling who owed her what, and a mean left hook for collecting accounts receivable. It was rumored most of the people who attended Sister Ridley's service that day were there to verify her demise and their ensuing debt relief.

Greater Harlem Baptist was packed for Fatima's funeral too. Many of her relatives from the south made the trip to support the family. There were dozens of people Fatima had grown up with in The Dark Towers who came out to pay their respect. There was an exceptional number of female teenagers at her service too, there to pay homage to the cause Fatima had initiated.

Faced with the biggest audience he'd ever had to preach in front of, and a large media presence, Reverend Yizar knew he had to pull out all the stops. As soon as his choir finished their soul-stirring hymn, he stood and went to work.

"Let the church say, amen," he began.

Most of the congregation faintly obeyed.

"Let the church say, *amen!*" Reverend Yizar repeated.

"Amen!" the congregation responded.

"That's better," the pastor said as he lowered his head and leafed through the pages of his bible. He then looked back up at the congregation. "You know, one day, we're all going to have to cross that River Jordan, and go home."

Members of the congregation shook their heads in agreement.

"But sadly, this morning, we're here to say goodbye to a loved one who has made her journey on to Glory Land."

"Well..." an elderly woman moaned.

"We're here today to say goodbye to dynamic young lady who... stood in this pulpit not too long ago, and graced this congregation with an amazing message."

"It sure was..." another member concurred.

"Church, I am sure no one here this morning will disagree with me when I say that, Sister Fatima Richardson will truly be missed."

"Yes!" a young woman in the choir said.

"Church, it is hard to come to grips with the senseless act of violence that has brought us here. It's hard to comprehend this tragedy, because before us lies a young sister who tried to do good in the community."

A succession of people in the congregation yelled "amen!"

"Sister Richardson wasn't out here ripping and running, partying, wasting her life, like we see so many of our young folk do. She was out here trying to get other young people to do the right thing."

"Yes, she was!" a deacon who sat near the pulpit, added.

"Sister Richardson was going into our neighborhoods, into our schools, urging young folk to think before they act, not after, when sometimes it's too late..."

Reverend Yizar walked to the edge of the pulpit and peered at Fatima's casket.

"And now, she lies here before us. Slain by some... twisted individual."

Reverend Yizar looked up at his audience with a grim expression.

"We have a lot of sick people, church, who don't know the Lord."

"Amen!" the crowd yelled.

"We have way too much crime in our community. This madness must cease."

Reverend Yizar paused for dramatic effect.

"Part of the reason this madness is prevalent is the idiotic notion that people shouldn't snitch to the police. Otherwise known as... the po-po."

A few members of the congregation chuckled.

"Excuse my French, church, but I pray somebody drops dime on the bastard who killed this young lady, so the police can lock that ass up!"

The congregation showed its agreement with a round of applause. Reverend Yizar held his hands up to quiet everyone.

"To the Richardson Family," he said softly, "let me offer you our deepest condolences during this time of sorrow. We know you're grieving with heavy hearts."

The congregation mumbled its consent with the pastor once again.

"But let us remember," Reverend Yizar said, "that if we believe, we shall see her again!"

This reminder stirred up the congregation like a hornet's nest poked by a stupid kid. A current of joy ran through the church. The hope of living eternally was a powerful stimulant. People nodded in agreement; shouts of consensus were declared.

Feeding off the church's energy, Reverend Yizar utilized gentle metaphors for death as he preached. He stated that Fatima had entered into her eternal rest. Fatima had taken her peaceful journey. Fatima had gone up yonder to be with her Lord.

The congregation ate it up. People began to get the spirit. Especially the senior members of Greater Harlem Baptist, folks who had dealt with more than their fair share of crap living in NYC. They were delighted to hear of some better days ahead. They clapped and yelled at Reverend Yizar's every word. This further inspired him. The pastor began to strut back and forth across the pulpit as he preached.

"Sister Richardson, is in no more pain now! Sister Richardson, knows no more sorrow now! Sister Richardson, will not shed any more tears!"

Sister Greene then began to add emphasis to her lover's remarks by banging preacher chords on her organ after each statement.

"I came by here this morning to tell you church! If we live right, we too, can receive these heavenly rewards!"

The congregation went bananas. Sister Greene let loose with a nasty riff to further the frenzy. Even Fatima's mother briefly forgot her grief and shouted out praise.

"There'll be no more trouble! No more death! No more taxes!" Reverend Yizar yelled.

His last declaration almost caused a riot. Half the church stood up on their feet and applauded. The pastor was keenly aware of the news cameras watching his every action. Thus, he postured and gesticulated for them every moment he could. The man did his damned best to preach

Fatima into heaven. After thirty minutes however, the pastor had to wrap it up when he felt lightheaded.

"As I close church, I want us to keep in mind that, though Fatima's candle may have been put out, her glow will forever remain with us. I also want us to keep the Richardson Family in our thoughts and prayers as they struggle to get through this great loss. Amen?"

"Amen," the congregation responded.

The choir hummed "Soon and Very Soon We Are Going to See the King" as Fatima's casket was then rolled down the aisle of Greater Harlem Baptist toward the exit. Family and friends trailed reluctantly behind it.

.   .   .

Hundreds of Harlem's denizens stopped their hustle and bustle to watch the large funeral procession drive to Ferncliff Cemetery, in nearby Westchester County. Most had no clue whom it was taking to their final journey and figured it was an old politician, or wealthy businessperson, based on the length of the motorcade. At the gravesite Nikki collapsed. Melody and Chelsea escorted her back to the family limousine.

The ceremony to commit Fatima to the ground was brief. Reverend Yizar led a moving prayer after reading a few verses from the bible, and then the casket was gently lowered into its grave. Onlookers solemnly dropped roses on it and then walked away.

Quinn remained at the plot while others gradually dispersed. He wept silently as gravediggers covered Fatima. He almost didn't notice Birdman standing across from him. When Quinn lit a cigarette to calm his nerves, Birdman walked over to strike up a conversation... and to bum a smoke.

THIRTY

AFTERMATH

The high spirits that Christmastime brought permeated every apartment in The Dark Towers. Except the Richardson's. The veil of sorrow that hung in that unit had yet to dissipate. The holidays brought ambiguous feelings to Nikki. It was hard for her to enjoy her first Christmas with her son when she'd never enjoy another with her sister.

Nelson Jordan Richardson was born a week ahead of schedule, but he arrived as healthy as a horse. And as hungry as one. Nikki had honored her late sister by not calling him Tyrique, the name she'd initially chosen for a boy. She knew Fatima would have been thrilled over Nelson because the baby had the same big head as his late aunt.

It didn't take long for Nikki to recognize the daunting responsibilities that accompanied her newborn. The baby seemed to cry, eat, and shit nonstop. And his sleeping schedule was crazy. Finishing high school was not going to be easy. Completing a college degree would be even more difficult.

Fatima's absence was increasingly felt as Nikki struggled with her new motherhood. She would've loved to have Fatima around to make emergency runs to the store for infant formula, baby wipes, or diapers. Nikki missed her sister's visits. She yearned now for another of Fatima's unsolicited sermons on making good grades in school, or ignoring peer pressure. As annoying as they always were, Nikki missed the inquisitions Fatima would conduct concerning her personal business. Nikki missed

Fatima period. She was wiping tears from her eyes when the doorbell buzzed. Nikki walked into the living room and opened the door.

"Hey Chelsea."

"Hey girl, Chelsea said as she walked into the apartment. "Where's Nelson?"

"His little ass is sleeping. He was up all night crying."

"It's Saturday. Wake him up and tell him his godmother's here."

"Godmother gonna take him home with her if he starts crying again?"

"Hell no."

"Okay then."

They laughed.

"I came to give him this," Chelsea said as she held out a bag.

"What is it?"

"Open it."

Nikki opened it and pulled out a pair of tiny, black leather sandals.

"These are nice! Thanks!"

"I don't want Nelson crawling around here, looking like no bum," Chelsea said. "I got em for free in the Bronx."

"That Muslim dude with the sneaker store? Saladin?"

"Bingo," Chelsea answered. She was in the midst of laughing when she began to cough violently.

"You alright?" Nikki asked.

"Think I'm coming down with the flu," Chelsea said and began hacking again.

"You might wanna go to the doctor," Nikki said as she backed away from Chelsea.

"I'm good," Chelsea said nonchalantly. "Just gotta shake this shit off."

"Okay," Nikki said warily.

"How's your mother doing?" Chelsea asked, ready to change the subject.

"The same," Nikki said softly. "She tries to keep busy with work and helping me with the baby, but I still hear her crying every night."

"Wow," Chelsea sighed. "I said hello to her the other day in the lobby and she walked right past me, like she was spaced out."

"She was really bad the day we put up the Christmas tree for Nelson."

"Memories of past Christmases with Fatima?"

"Exactly," Nikki said. "Please continue to pray for us?"

"No doubt," Chelsea replied. "Any leads on her murder case yet?"

"Still nothing," Nikki sighed. "All we know from the cops is that it wasn't a robbery, since Fatima still had her cell phone and money on her."

"Somebody has to know something, Nikki."

"I hope the detectives solve her case soon. This shit is eating away at us."

"You think this sex strike had something to do with it?"

"Anything's possible, Chelsea."

Before she could reply, Chelsea started coughing once more. When she finally stopped Nikki was staring at her with concern.

"Yo, I saw your girl climb out some dude's Jeep around three o'clock this morning, in front of the Chinese take-out spot," Chelsea said with a sly grin.

"Melody?"

"Hobbling like an old woman."

"Damn."

"Heard that slut's getting banged around Harlem like a cheap set of bongos now. She's real popular these days."

"And what were you doing out at three in the morning?"

"Me?" Chelsea asked.

"Did I stutter?"

"I was outside for a few minutes, to get some fresh air."

"Yeah, I bet."

"Nikki, I know you ain't questioning my virtue?"

"You lost your virtue years ago."

"I don't have to stay here and take this," Chelsea said in mock indignation.

"Then leave, heifer," Nikki said as they chuckled.

"I do need to go if Nelson's not up. Got errands to run," Chelsea said as she headed for the door. "Kiss him for me? And tell your girl to slow her roll."

"And you get that cough checked out."

"I'm good, Nikki!" Chelsea said as she left the apartment.

"Thanks again for Nelson's gift," Nikki said closing the door.

Chelsea frowned as soon as she stepped into the hallway. She was sick of people nagging her about her coughing. First her moms and her cousin, now Nikki. It was flu season! People coughed all the time in the winter!

·   ·   ·

Andre woke every morning with the mission of finding out who killed his woman. He called the detectives in charge of investigating Fatima's murder daily and quizzed them about their progress solving her case. He received the same answer each time. "When they had a break, he'd be one of the first to know."

Andre blamed himself for letting Fatima go out that night for a pack of damn cigarettes. He should've insisted she stay home. Now his life was shattered. The sympathy he received from family and friends had done little to dispel the aching numbness that engulfed him. His pain was showing on him physically as well. If people at the office didn't know that his fiancée had been recently murdered they would have sworn he was doing drugs because Andre's eyes stayed bloodshot.

He took a break from his desktop and looked out his office window at downtown Philly. The Schuylkill River and its boardwalk were blanketed with fresh snow, yet there was a young couple, wearing parkas for the harsh cold, holding hands as they walked the river trail. Andre's heart burned when he remembered the snide comment Fatima had made the day he showed her the view of the river from his office. He missed her droll sense of humor.

That was one of the traits he noticed about her when they started courting. Their first date was at The Funky Buddha in the East Village. The legendary nightspot was one of the coolest places to hear jazz in New York City. Cramped seating in the venue gave Andre and Fatima no choice but to get acquainted with each other. That night he learned that Fatima had finished college, had a job, her own place, no kids, and loved cigarettes.

At the end of the date, when their tab was placed on the table, Fatima had opened her purse and fished out her debit card. Andre was impressed. He offered to pay the check but Fatima told him he could pay the next time. Andre didn't argue. And another Negro love affair began.

The ringing of his cell phone interrupted Andre's thoughts. He knew who was calling.

"Good morning, mother."

"How you coming along?" Lois asked.

"I'm okay," Andre said softly.

Lois called her son every morning to gauge how he was coping. It pained her to hear him lie to her daily. The misery in Andre's voice always gave him away.

"What are you doing?"

"Working on a project at the office."

"On a Saturday?"

"Making sure my team completes the assignment on time."

"Andre, why won't you go to grief counseling? I'll come down and go with you."

"I don't need counseling."

"You can't fool your mother."

"Mom, I'm fine. I need to get back to work."

"We're going to discuss this more when you come home for Christmas."

"Okay, Mom, thanks for calling."

"Take care son. I love you."

"I love you, too."

Andre ended the call and sighed. He hated lying to his mother but there was no need to give her something extra to be stressed about. Lois was also grieving over Fatima's death. Andre was thrilled at the way the two women he loved most had become fast friends. He'd heard his share of horror stories where oil and water mixed together better than a mother and her daughter-in-law, and the poor son was stuck in the middle as the peacemaker.

Andre had anticipated years of them doing fun activities with Lois. What he hadn't anticipated was the cruel irony of having to go from planning a wedding with Fatima to helping out with her funeral. (The deposit the two had put down for their reception venue had been sympathetically refunded and used to defray some of the burial cost.)

There was no cure for his pain. Nothing but time. And all Andre could do over time was endlessly reminisce about the girl he had planned to wed. A few friends had advised him that eventually he'd heal and be able to start over, looking for a new mate. But Andre didn't want to start over. He didn't know how. And as far as he was concerned, Fatima could never be replaced. He'd miss her smell, he would miss her taste, and most of all he'd miss her smile.

•   •   •

Remarks from worried family, friends and coworkers to Marisol about her weight went ignored. Even Shaconda expressed concern over her physical decline. As far as Marisol was concerned she couldn't eat enough comfort food to help her cope with her misery. The grilled cheese sandwiches, chocolate bars, and pints of ice cream that she steadily ate gave her the short-lived relief she needed to deal with her remorse… and guilt. She'd worry later about taking off the extra weight.

The guilt over her friend's murder suffocated her. At night Marisol still lay in bed wondering if Fatima had felt any pain when the end came. She regularly dreamt about Fatima's shooting when she dozed off long enough to dream. The situation was affecting her livelihood. She often started crying while instructing students in her physical education classes. Twice Marisol had to go and meet with administrators about her slumping job performance.

There was small comfort in knowing GASP would be around for some time to come. The media sensation the murder produced had generated a ridiculous influx of donations to the cause. Legions of socially conscious females who heard or read about Fatima's murder sent money. This was why she and Shaconda were meeting at Harlem Heat, to plot out the future of their organization. Marisol was already in a rear booth when Shaconda arrived.

"I see you beat me here again."

"Sit down, Shaconda. I already ordered us some hot wings, fries, cheesecake bites, and a fudge sundae we can share."

Shaconda looked at her mentor with concern as she sat down.

"What?" Marisol asked innocently.

Shaconda lowered her gaze to Marisol's midsection.

"I can lose this anytime," Marisol said as she patted her protruding stomach.

"If you say so," Shaconda said. "Did you deposit those checks we received last week?"

"Thanks for reminding me. I'll do that on Monday."

"By the way, we got emails from girls in Oakland, Houston, and Des Moines who want to start their own chapters of our organization."

"Really," Marisol said.

"This sex strike is spreading like crazy."

"Tell me about it," Marisol said. "We already got girls in Baltimore, Philly, and New Haven who want to start chapters of GASP."

"We need help, Ms. Aquino."

"I'm thinking about hiring two or three people. Lord knows we have the funds to pay them with."

When their food arrived they temporarily put all business on pause and dug in.

"Ready for your first big speech?" Shaconda asked after she ate a few wings.

"Please, don't remind me."

There was an upcoming teen summit at a school in the Bronx that Shaconda had badgered Marisol into agreeing to speak at... and she got nauseous every time she thought about the impending event. Marisol now understood why Fatima had bitched and moaned about speaking in public. The anxiety could be paralyzing.

The barrage of cameras and microphones that news reporters had shoved in Marisol's face following Fatima's death had given her a crash course on public speaking... and public scrutiny. She failed it badly. She had frozen up often in mid speech when the right words escaped her. At other times Marisol had rushed her reply then forgot her train of thought and wound up sounding mentally unstable. Karma was indeed a bitch.

"I can come over and help you practice it?" Shaconda offered.

"That sounds like a plan," Marisol sighed. "If I could speak as half as well as Fatima did in public, I'd be happy."

"No one could speak like she did," Shaconda said wistfully.

"Yeah, right? She was something else."

Their eyes filled with tears. At that moment Marisol's cell phone rang. She looked at the caller ID, frowned and set the phone back down on the table. The call went to voice mail.

"Was that Rupert, the news reporter again?" Shaconda asked.

(Ever since Fatima was killed Rupert had been blowing up Marisol's cell phone, trying to get an inside scoop on the story. The fact that many political pundits blamed the mayor's upset loss for re-election on Fatima's murder also had Rupert and other reporters calling her ass like crazy for comments.)

"No, that was my ex, Raphael."

(Ever since Raphael saw Marisol at Fatima's funeral he'd also been blowing up her phone, trying to reignite their romance. She was contemplating putting a block on his number.)

"Any plans for tonight?" Shaconda asked as she grabbed some fries and ate them.

"Going home after this, probably just watch some television."

"But it's Saturday. You need to go somewhere and do something."

"I'm not up to it, Shaconda."

"You can't stay in your house and grieve forever, Ms. Aquino. Even I know that. I'm sure Fatima wouldn't want you doing that either."

"How old are you, Shaconda?"

"Seventeen, why?"

"You are too advanced for your age, young lady," Marisol said as she forked a cheesecake bite and swallowed it.

"I'm just trying to keep it real, like Fatima did," Shaconda said nonchalantly.

They looked at each other and shared a much needed smile.

CODA

Quinn went to the roof of The Dark Towers to clear his head. His thoughts were clouded by indecision. The occasional blasts of arctic air from the Harlem River did little to dissipate the fog in his mind. He hadn't seen Basketmouth Jones in a minute. (Quinn had forgotten the dude's real name.) They'd been cellmates at Riker's Island for a few months before heading upstate to different penitentiaries.

Luckily for Quinn, Basketmouth turned out to be an affable brother. Scuffling with his giant ass in their tiny prison cell would have been problematic if they had not gotten along. But while chatting in their bunks, they discovered they were both from Harlem, that they shared a love for Yankees Blue, and that they loved smoking good weed.

Quinn was driving cab along Frederick Douglass Boulevard when he saw Basketmouth walk out of a bank, one he wasn't robbing this time. Quinn honked and pulled over to the curb. As they caught up, Quinn mentioned Fatima's murder. That was when Basketmouth told him about an inmate named Jamaal Jackson who had bragged to fellow convicts in their prison block about a hit he'd ordered on a bitch in Harlem. No one paid much attention to him because people in prison lied frequently to each other to help pass the time. Basketmouth said the incident occurred two months ago, right before he was released on parole.

This information corroborated with the rumor Birdman had shared with Quinn at Fatima's burial. Word in the street was that Jamaal was behind her murder. Quinn knew Jamaal was Nikki's baby daddy and that

Fatima had hated the motherfucker. Fatima had also shared with Quinn how she helped get Jamaal's ass locked up on a weapons charge. Now Quinn had to make a tough decision. Street Justice dictated he seek revenge. Street Logic dictated that he avoided a return to prison. Jamaal's flunky, Po Dawg was said to be the alleged shooter. No one had seen hide nor hair of him, or his white Audi Q7 since the murder happened. There was no reason for Po Dawg not to be on the block slinging drugs as usual. Unless he was guilty. Quinn lit up a cigarette as he calculated his options. Jamaal could easily be touched. There were countless inmates upstate ready and willing to beat a motherfucker down, or worse, for the right price.

Quinn already had a few good leads on Po Dawg's current whereabouts. The strongest one coming from information Birdman had obtained for him last week. As soon as he verified Po Dawg's location, Quinn would surprise his ass with a piece of lead pipe and get answers. If the rumor turned out to be true, Quinn would then tip the NYPD off to the identities of Fatima's killers, after he whipped Po Dawg within an inch of his life. But everything would have to be done without him being recognized. That would be the hard part.

After taking a few last pulls on his cigarette, Quinn stamped it out. It was Christmastime. Plenty of Saturday shoppers in Harlem needed a ride back home with all the shit they'd purchased for the holidays. Quinn had to go to work. For passengers… and more information.

AND NOW... A SNEAK PEEK AT THE NEXT
BOOK IN THE URBAN STRIKE SERIES...

BUSTED

The place did not look inviting at all. It was sandwiched between Mt. Moriah Fire-Baptizing Holiness Church, a storefront sanctuary that advertised bingo every Tuesday, and a rundown laundromat that had a long crack along its front window. Duct tape covered the glass fissure.

There was no need to check the address that Google indicated on her cell phone. The black, tattered awning above the business confirmed that she was standing in front of the Harlem Community Center for Health. With a sigh, she adjusted the dark shades on her nose, pushed open the front door, and entered.

At least twenty adults and children were already sitting inside waiting to be seen. She wanted to turn around and leave, but she'd come this far. She walked over to where a Latino receptionist sat behind a small counter, typing on a computer. After a few seconds passed, the receptionist looked up at her and smiled.

"Good morning, how may I help you?"

"I need to see a doctor," Chelsea said.

"For?"

"I think I have… the flu. I'd like to get checked out."

"Have you been here before?"

"No. Do my mother have to sign a consent form?"

The receptionist detected the desperation in her voice. She'd heard it from countless other young women visiting the clinic without a parent.

"You can get checked out for 'the flu' without your parent's consent. Do you have ID?"

Chelsea handed over her student ID card. The receptionist copied the card and gave the item back, along with some forms attached to a clipboard.

"I need you to fill these out. Come back when you're done."

Chelsea grabbed a pen off the counter and found a seat in the back corner of the waiting area. There were a lot of mundane health questions she had to answer after jotting down her personal information. Being in perfect health, most of her responses were no. As she finished up the last form, the front door opened. A squat, mocha complexioned woman wearing a bad weave dragged a sobbing, seven-year-old girl behind her through the door.

It was nosy ass Shirley Jackson! She was good friends with Chelsea's mother and lived two floors below them in The Dark Towers. Chelsea deftly angled her chair toward the wall and then slumped forward in an effort to be incognito. As soon as she had a chance she would slip out and return another time. Maybe.

Shirley Jackson went straight to the receptionist. Chelsea unclasped the forms she had filled out on the clipboard and folded them. She then stood up, ready to slink out of the clinic.

"Chelsea, is that you?"

Damn!

Chelsea turned around, slipped off her shades and gave her a weak smile.

"Hey, Ms. Jackson."

Busted now, Chelsea sat back down. Ms. Jackson grabbed her clipboard with forms to complete, and dragged her crying kid over to Chelsea. They sat next to her.

"What you in here for?" Ms. Jackson asked.

"The flu."

Chelsea threw in a nasty coughing fit for good measure, hoping the bitch would get up and move away. Ms. Jackson didn't flinch.

"Rachel's been crying because of an earache all last night. Gotta get her examined."

"Oh."

The aforementioned kid sat in her chair with her head down, sobbing softly.

"This is your last year of high school, right?"

"Yes, Ma'am."

"You going to college?"

"Yes, Ma'am."

"Good."

It amazed Chelsea how Ms. Jackson didn't look away once as she completed the forms on the clipboard she held and pried into Chelsea's business at the same time.

"Your mom's doing okay? I haven't seen her in a minute."

"She's fine. Working all the time."

"I'm missing work now, 'cause I had to come here."

Chelsea didn't reply. She unfolded her own forms and started again to complete the last page. It would look too suspicious if she left out now without seeing the doctor.

"You still keep in touch with Nikki Richardson?"

"I'm her son's godmother."

"Damn shame they still don't know who killed Fatima."

"Yeah, right?" Chelsea mumbled.

"That family's suffering. Pamela looks like a hot mess."

"They miss her badly," Chelsea said.

"That sex strike Fatima started is something, most of these boys walking around Harlem so hard up, look like they about to pop any damn minute."

"Isn't that something," Chelsea chuckled as she finished her paperwork.

(She had heard that Shirley's eighteen-year-old daughter, Felicia, was giving Melody a run for her money in the strike-busting category. Both of those scabs were popular with the local boys now.)

Chelsea stood up from her chair.

"I'll be back," she said. "Gotta turn these forms in."

"Okay, dear," Ms. Jackson said.

Chelsea headed to the receptionist's counter. Shirley Jackson frowned as soon as she walked away. If she remembered correctly, Chelsea Rivers had been fucking before she could crawl straight. And who wears dark shades inside a clinic? The woman smelled a lie. Whatever that girl was here to see the doctor for, it wasn't no damn flu…

ABOUT THE AUTHOR

J.T. Smith is a proud alumni of the University of South Carolina Fighting Gamecocks. He enjoys watching college football, writing, and sampling fine beers. He lives in Harlem USA, where he is at work on the next book in the *Urban Strike* series.

URBAN STRIKE is available on Amazon.com and B&N.com
Email the author at jayteesmith@yahoo.com

Connect with J.T. Smith
Find me on Facebook: J.T. Smith
Follow me on Twitter: @realjayteesmith
Visit my website: www.jayteesmith.com